THE SIGHT ON THE VIEWSCREEN BROUGHT COMMANDER SISKO TO HIS FEET . . .

His pulse was racing in his ears. He'd seen other destroyed ships before. This was just another one.

But it wasn't. This was the *Nibix,* the lost ship that had held the leader of an empire that now spanned eighty worlds.

The *Nibix* had been thought a myth. And people didn't just beam into a myth.

But he was about to.

Look for STAR TREK Fiction from Pocket Books

Star Trek: The Original Series

Star Trek: The Next Generation

Star Trek: Deep Space Nine

Star Trek: Voyager

STAR TREK
DEEP SPACE NINE®

THE LONG NIGHT

Dean Wesley Smith
and
Kristine Kathryn Rusch

POCKET BOOKS

New York   London   Toronto   Sydney   Tokyo   Singapore

This book is a work of fiction. Names, characters, places and incidents
are products of the author's imagination or are used fictitiously. Any
resemblance to actual events or locales or persons, living or dead, is
entirely coincidental.

An *Original* Publication of POCKET BOOKS

POCKET BOOKS, a division of Simon & Schuster Inc.
1230 Avenue of the Americas, New York, NY 10020

A VIACOM COMPANY

STAR TREK is a Registered Trademark of
Paramount Pictures.

This book is published by Pocket Books, a division of
Simon & Schuster Inc., under exclusive license from
Paramount Pictures

ISBN: 0-671-55165-5

First Pocket Books printing February 1996

10 9 8 7 6 5 4 3 2 1

POCKET and colophon are registered trademarks of
Simon & Schuster Inc.

Printed in the U.S.A.

For Jim and Paul

THE LONG NIGHT

PROLOGUE

THE DEEP-SPACE SHIP *Nibix* felt cold, as if it had already turned into a burial chamber. The Supreme Ruler pulled his long black robes around him. His cold-sleep chamber stood on a platform, like a raised bed. The spotlight above would be one of the last lights off when the ship entered deep space and one of the first lights on. It would highlight his still face even though there would be no followers to watch him awaken.

He shuddered.

The sleeping cocoon looked like the glass coffin that kept his father's body lifelike for nearly two generations. The faithful had trooped through the Rubis daily during those years, so that they could gaze on the face of the former Supreme Ruler of Jibet, a man, his mother reminded Jibim Kiba Siber, who was well loved.

Her implication was that the current Supreme Ruler was not.

The Supreme Ruler clasped his hands behind his back. Always present a semblance of calm, he had learned, even when he didn't feel it. That axiom had allowed him to get this far, to the *Nibix,* his salvation and his only hope.

Around the platform, five technicians bent over the vast machinery that would keep him alive. His assistant, Bikon, had chosen the best, most loyal subjects to make certain the equipment worked, and still the Supreme Ruler worried.

He had thought all his subjects were loyal once.

More technicians worked in the chambers beyond. The *Nibix* had a thousand passengers already in cold sleep, family and loyal followers all, their belongings —a good half of the wealth of Jibet—stored in chambers even deeper in the bowels of the ship. The technicians were putting the final touches on all of the equipment now. Then they would sleep in the beds in the room just ouside of his.

Their beds would rouse them at the same moment his spotlight came on—seventy years from now. At the dawn of the new beginning, or so he had whispered to his wife as he held her hand a few moments ago. In the new beginning, he would wake her with a kiss.

She had laughed and called him a romantic. It had been the first laugh he had heard from her on the *Nibix,* and it warmed him. She had fallen into cold sleep with the smile still on her lips.

But she looked like his dead father had, her cheeks artificially flushed behind the glass door of a glass coffin.

He had turned away then and come here, to his own

spectacular resting place. His cocoon was the same as hers on the inside. Only the outer trappings showed it belonged to the Supreme Ruler. Not the man who had gentled his wife to sleep, but the all-powerful being who held the future of Jibet in his hands.

"We are ready." The voice was deep and steady.

The Supreme Ruler turned slowly, even though the voice had startled him. His chief of science, Bikon, stood the requisite half step behind him, head bowed as he awaited the Supreme Ruler's response. Bikon's shaved head had black stubble along the top, a sign that he had been concentrating on preparation of the *Nibix*, not on the rituals of everyday life. His black uniform had a tear along the elbow and creases along his back. Additional lines had formed on his face these last few months, adding to its severity. Those lines were the only evidence that the revolt had disturbed him as deeply as it had disturbed all the rest.

Bikon slowly raised his head. His black eyes held no hint of emotion, only the levelness the Supreme Ruler had come to depend on over the years. There was no turning back. He would have to trust Bikon now with his life and the future of Jibet and all its people.

The Supreme Ruler nodded. He took the Staff of Life from the wall where he had let it rest. The staff glowed green. It was slightly warm to the touch, as it always was, a small reassurance in a world suddenly empty of them. He gripped the staff firmly in his right hand. "We will make this last inspection short."

Bikon glanced at the raised platform. The glass door to the Supreme Ruler's cocoon was open and waiting. To his credit, Bikon did not shudder as many of the technicians had.

With a nod, Bikon led the Supreme Ruler out of the

chamber and into the wide corridor. Behind the walls, behind the paneling, some of Jibet's most precious treasures were stored. Beyond them, the equipment that would guard a people for a long and dangerous journey hummed.

The corridors were dark except for the traveling lights, as Bikon called them. The Supreme Ruler thought of them as night lights, even though the darkness of space knew no day or night.

Bikon and the Supreme Ruler moved slowly from his chamber in the very center of the huge ship and toward the smaller chambers where his family had already been put into cold sleep. The Supreme Ruler wondered how many ghosts would roam these halls in the next seventy years. Ghosts of those lost in the fighting. Ghosts of followers left behind because there was no more room. The Supreme Ruler forced the bad memories from his mind. He had done the best he could. The *Nibix* could only carry one thousand souls. It was not enough, but it would do.

At the door of the royal chamber, the two men stopped. The Supreme Ruler had half hoped he would not come here again. His wife lay in state, her much-loved face almost hidden by the opaque air created in the first stage of deep cold. At least she no longer looked like his long-dead father. Now his wife looked like a woman drowning in fog. He turned away, forcing himself to examine the sleep cocoons of his two sons, the future of the Jibetian people. Their young faces lacked the serenity of his wife's. His younger son had asked Bikon if men dreamed in cold sleep, and Bikon had not been able to answer. The Supreme Ruler knew that the boy had had nightmares ever since the attack outside the Supreme Palace that had signaled the start of the revolution.

His older son had laughed at the question, but the Supreme Ruler had seen fear in his eyes as well. The older boy knew that this sleep process was experimental, that for each question Bikon could not answer, a dozen more lurked.

The Supreme Ruler ran his fingers along the glass top of his older son's cocoon. The material was cool against his fingers, not cold as he had expected. His good-byes to his sons had been emotional, yet dignified. They knew there was a chance that many of the sleepers would not awaken in seventy years when the *Nibix* found its new world, the New Jibet. This technology was still young, and only the revolution had forced its speedy development.

Jibim glanced at Bikon. It had been his suggestion to build the huge deep-space ship, *Nibix*, just in case the revolution won. Bikon had argued that finding a new world for the royal family and all the followers to live in peace was preferable to dying in a revolution. Jibim had agreed, never thinking that the ship would actually be put to use. Never thinking that the revolution would succeed.

But four months ago the *Nibix*, high in orbit over the planet had been his family's only lifeboat away from certain death. And he had been glad it was there.

Too glad, for a man who prided himself on calm.

The inspection of the rest of the sleep chambers went quickly. The chambers looked the same. Cool, dark places with oval-shaped cocoons on the floor and the monitoring equipment gleaming on the walls and ceiling. Sleeping body after sleeping body of friend after friend, follower after follower. If he tried, the Supreme Ruler could identify them all and cite their importance to him, his family, and his government.

Bikon claimed their importance now lay in their

distinct and different genetic heritage. He said what they had done in the past no longer mattered.

But it did matter. What they had done in the past had allowed them to come on this ship, had allowed them an extra four months of life. It would allow them a peaceful death instead of a state-ordered execution. Even if that peaceful death occurred inside a sleep cocoon instead of on a mysterious planet seventy years away.

Maybe he and all his followers really had been killed in the revolution that overthrew the seven-thousand-year reign of his family. It was just taking them all some time to die.

The Supreme Ruler left the last chamber, Bikon trailing him. The difficult part of the inspection was through. He could think about the real future now, the future the *Nibix* would take them to. They inspected the bridge and ship's control centers. No live person interrupted their path as only machines hummed in faint life. Here and there a light shown. The ship was on fully automatic. It would remain that way for seventy years.

The Supreme Ruler turned to Bikon. "I have seen enough."

Bikon nodded and at an unhurried pace lead the way back to the Supreme Ruler's chamber. The Supreme Ruler wondered if his steady advisor was feeling the same fear he felt. Or if he even felt anything at all. The Supreme Ruler shook his head. Far too late to ask now. Maybe in seventy years, when they reached their new home.

Around the center chamber the few remaining technicians were helping each other into sleep cocoons. The Supreme Ruler stopped and watched, nodding to a few worried faces but not speaking. Finally, the last cocoon lid dropped down over the last technician and the Supreme Ruler turned to his advisor.

Bikon moved quickly to his sleep cocoon, just outside the door of the Supreme Ruler's chamber. Without emotion he crawled in and then with one hand on the lid glanced up at the Supreme Ruler. "It will seem like only a few moments before you awake on a new future."

Jibim nodded. "I know."

The Supreme Ruler prided himself on a calm exterior, but Bikon truly had one. Climbing into what could be his coffin, the instrument of either life or death, seemed as routine to Bikon as climbing into bed. The Supreme Ruler was pleased that he would climb into his cocoon alone. He would allow himself to feel the fear that he had been hiding all these months.

Bikon lay back and pulled the lid closed over him. The automatic machinery kicked in with a soft hum, and after a moment the clear lid of the sleep chamber fogged slightly.

The Supreme Ruler glanced around the ship at the sleep chambers in sight and then back at his own through the open door. He was the only one still awake, the last to sleep, as was his wish on this flight to freedom. He shuddered at the weight of the trust these thousand followers and family had put on him. They believed him when he told them a new world existed out there, where their beliefs could be followed without fear. All they had to do was find it. And if they followed him, they would.

He just hoped he'd been right.

With a wave of his hand over a panel, the Supreme Ruler dimmed the last of the lights. Only the panel lights remained. A cool silvery glow emanated from within his sleep chamber. The spotlight remained on, would remain on, until his cocoon was closed and on.

No time to turn back now. With a last glance down the dark corridors, he whirled and entered his sleep chamber. The cocoon on the platform glowed like the throne had glowed the day he received the Staff of Life, the day his father had died.

He gripped the staff tightly, leaning on it as he walked the remaining distance. His mouth was dry, his shoulders tight. No one would say good-bye to him. No one would gentle him into sleep.

No one could.

His mistakes had brought him there. The revolution had happened on his watch, not his father's. The Staff of Life, once the center of the Jibetian government and the Jibetian religion, was now in exile with the family of Jibim Kiba Siber. The Supreme Ruler glanced at the glowing rod and wondered if seventy years would dim its light. He hoped not.

He mounted the platform with as much ceremony as he had when he walked to the throne the day of his coronation. Then he gathered his black robes around him, crawled into the cocoon, and adjusted his shoulders and back until he was comfortable. It did not feel like a bed. It felt as if he were lying in a box. A cold, dark, empty box that he would have to trust with his life. Then he touched the green staff again. In a loud voice he said to the dark and silent ship, "May the power of belief and the strength of the true followers lead us all to a new home."

He lifted his hand from the green rod and touched

the button to lower the cocoon lid. It slid down into position silently and then with a slight hiss, the chamber filled with a sleeping gas. The Supreme Ruler of Jibet slid into the first level of cold sleep.

And into the pages of history and folk tales throughout the galaxy.

CHAPTER
1

JADZIA DAX STOPPED outside Quark's Bar. She tossed her ponytail over her shoulder and tugged on the sleeves of her uniform. She wasn't officially on duty—but she would be doing enough legitimate work that she would have felt uncomfortable in a loose blouse and silk pants.

Besides, Julian seemed to be over his crush on her, but she had learned in her various lifetimes that what seemed to be true often wasn't.

Quark's was full. Several freighters had arrived in the last few days, all with crews who hadn't had shore leave in much too long. They crowded into the bar as if it were the only place of interest on the station. Brightly hued uniforms, from gold to purple, mixed with the most hideous lime green she had ever seen, added spots of color throughout the dimly lit rooms. Some of the crews had come directly to Quark's—the smell of deep space, grit, and interspecies sweat hung over the familiar smells of Bajoran ceremonial wine and Tirellian stout.

She wished Quark had taken her advice and put up a sign, ALL CUSTOMERS MUST BATHE BEFORE ENTRANCE. He had refused, as she had expected him to, his first reason being the one she expected ("Come now, Lieutenant, you don't want to interfere with fair trade, do you?") and the second a bit more of a reasoned surprise ("And besides, bathing would kill half my customers—literally"). Just as the stench might kill her.

Still she had promised to meet Julian here.

She squared her shoulders and entered, knowing that without the Curzon part of her Dax self, she would have lost her lunch long ago. Curzon had frequented places that smelled worse than this. Curzon himself had smelled worse than this on many occasions, and he always thought it part of the joyous ritual of living.

Jadzia had been raised to believe that cleanliness was a courtesy, and deep in her heart of hearts, she still believed it.

The crowd around the Dabo table shouted with disappointment. Quark glanced over his shoulder and grinned as the house raked in the profits. He was scurrying among all the customers, shouting at his brother to hurry. Rom was carrying a tray laden with too many drinks. His thin arm bowed under its weight, and Dax held her breath (gladly) as she watched him swerve around the customers.

Nog was nowhere to be seen. If she saw the boy before he returned to the bar, she would warn him of his uncle's temper. Quark hated paying help, but when the bar was full, he expected everyone to work.

She pushed her way past two freighter engineers whose light blue uniforms were almost black with grease and dirt. One of them grabbed at her, and she kicked him in the shin, more as a warning to the other lonely pilots around than as a deterrent. She had seen one of these boys mess with Kira once, and the offender had ended up in Julian's infirmary.

The voices were loud, the conversations drunk and disorderly, but no fights had broken out—yet. She couldn't see Julian anywhere, and she hoped she hadn't shoved her way into this crowd because she had misunderstood their meeting time.

Then she saw him in the far back corner where Quark had placed the dart board, back when he didn't understand how much profit a free game could bring him. Julian rolled a dart between his long, narrow fingers, balancing it perfectly before raising it and, with the flick of his wrist, tossing it at the board. The dart flew through the air, narrowly missing a tiny winged Ardwanian, who had drifted down from the ceiling from the weight of too much nectar. The dart hit the bulls-eye, and over the crowd, Jadzia could hear Miles O'Brien shouting, "Foul."

Miles was standing beside Julian—she hadn't seen him at first—his arms waving as he shouted and pointed at the winged Ardwanian. Julian took a step closer to Miles and shouted back.

And Jadzia sighed. Her meeting with Julian to work on a paper on Trill immune systems just got postponed until the game—and the fight—was over.

But still, she had to let him know she was there. Maybe he would want to escape.

"Julian!" she shouted over the din.

He turned, saw her, waved, and then lurched forward as Miles poked his chest, still shouting. Julian took a step backward, made a motion that looked like fluttering wings, and then called to the winged Ardwanian, who got a frightened look on her frail face, shook her head, and flew away.

Dax turned her back on the disagreement. Obviously Julian was enjoying himself. And she couldn't fault him that. He worked too hard, even though he admonished the rest of the crew not to, and he took his responsibilities—and his reputation—far too seriously. Because she had often requested that he take time off, she really couldn't be the one to drag him away from his fun.

Besides, she wanted a drink.

She shoved her way to the bar. Quark was behind it, his small hands working furiously as he piled drinks on another tray for Rom.

"You seen my nephew?" he asked Dax.

She shook her head.

"You here on business."

She shook her head again.

"Ah, a paying customer." Quark reached across the bar and shoved Morn's shoulder, dislodging the hulking barfly from his favorite stool. "Give your seat to the lady, Morn."

"I'm not a lady," Dax said, smiling.

"Close enough," Quark said. He set a coaster with the bar's logo in front of her—one of Rom's innovations that Quark had complained about until Rom explained that some customers would keep the coasters, thus advertising the bar all over the galaxy. "I've got some lovely Trill amber shot."

Dax suppressed a shudder. Curzon had gone on a

two-day drunk on amber shot and the memory of that hangover was still fresh. "How about synthale?"

"Working?" Quark asked, since synthale had none of the morning-after punishment that the expensive —and real—liquors had.

"I might be," she said.

"I have Ardwanian sweet nectar." The sweet nectar was like sugar to humanoids—and it was more costly than the Trill amber shot would have been.

She nodded. "And a squadron of winged Ardwanians losing loft because of it."

Quark piled the last drink on the tray and shoved it at Rom, who staggered beneath its weight. He tottered off through the crowd. Quark grabbed the synthale and placed it in front of Jadzia.

"I expect you to drink at least five of those to make up for the cost of taking Morn's place."

"I thought he wasn't a paying customer."

"He is. He's just not regular about it. And he drinks whatever I place before him." Quark reached under the bar for more glasses.

"You're not usually this grumpy when you have a full bar, Quark."

"I can't get the drinks to them fast enough," Quark said. "The last time this happened, a group of Cordwellians smashed every chair in the place. If this goes on too much longer, I might have to make you a barmaid, Lieutenant." Then he smiled. "In fact, I have the most perfect little dress. If you help out for just an hour or two—"

"Just how little is the dress?" Dax sipped the synthale. She would have preferred the sweet nectar.

Suddenly Quark took a step backward and brought a hand up to his nose. The odor of rotted steak wafted over Dax, and she blinked back tears. Only a Caxtonian would have body odor bad enough to overpower the other stenches in the room. Caxtonians were big, hairy humanoids who made excellent pilots but knew few social skills. And bathing—something they could benefit from—was one that seemed to always be left out of the lessons.

A huge Caxtonian, his shoulders bulging against a shirt that hadn't been washed since Dax was first joined *ever,* leaned between Jadzia and the ensign beside her.

Quark, obviously holding his breath, set a coaster in front of the Caxtonian and started to back away.

The Caxtonian reached across the bar and grabbed Quark by the lapels. The Caxtonian pulled Quark forward and spoke directly into his face. "I have something to sell you."

Quark leaned his head back as far as it would go. The Caxtonian's breath was twice as bad as his body odor. Dax was glad she was upwind.

"I—ah—I'm too busy to look at goods right now," Quark said. "Perhaps if you come back after you've taken a room and—ah—had a chance to freshen up—"

"I won't wait," the Caxtonian said. "But if you're not interested, I'm sure someone else would be."

Dax hid her nose in her synthale glass and watched Quark wrestle with the dilemma. If he asked to see whatever the Caxtonian had to sell, he would have to put up with the stench a few moments longer. But if he didn't, then he might miss an opportunity for profit.

"All right," Quark said, pulling his lapels free and stepping away from the Caxtonian's breath. "But make it quick."

The Caxtonian pulled a pouch from the inside of his filthy shirt. The pouch was made of stained leather, and it too had seen better days. Dax sipped her synthale but kept the glass protectively over her nose. The young ensign on the other side of the Caxtonian did the same.

Quark took the cork off a bottle of Ardwanian sweet nectar and wafted the bottle around as if it held perfume. The Caxtonian didn't seem to notice. He carefully pulled a small statue out of the pouch.

"If you think . . . ." Quark started and then he stopped. He set down the sweet nectar and leaned forward, right into the stench.

Dax frowned. Only one thing could grab Quark's attention like that. Something rare. Something expensive. Something that might make him a profit.

She took one more sip before replacing her glass on its coaster. Then she leaned in as well.

The statue stood about a hand high and seemed to glow a faint green all by itself, even in the bright light emanating from behind the bar. The statue was of a delicate woman humanoid. She twisted upward in a spiral toward some unseen light above. Her delicate hands formed a point at the top, and the woman's dress flowed out onto a simple base at the bottom.

Dax's stomach seemed to float as well, and she was glad now she had ordered the synthale. She studied the woman's skirt, looking for a tiny oval design she half hoped she wouldn't find.

As if picking up the daintiest of flowers, Quark reached out and touched the statue. "Where did you find this?"

"Never you mind that, little man," the Caxtonian said. "Do you want to buy it?"

Quark nodded, never taking his eyes from the statue. He didn't even quote a price. He had to be in as deep a shock as Dax was.

"How much?" the Caxtonian pilot demanded.

Quark looked up at the pilot as if suddenly remembering his place. "I'm sure we can come to an agreement," he said, half choking. "But first, my friend, a drink."

On the flare of the woman's skirt, just above the base, was the tiny oval. Dax pushed away from the bar and moved into the crowd. Her hands were shaking. She wanted to be wrong—and she wanted to be right.

Either way she had to move quickly. She quietly tapped her comm badge. "Dax to Sisko."

"Sisko here," the commander's deep reassuring voice answered almost immediately.

"Benjamin," Dax said. "You need to come to Quark's right now."

"Problem?" Sisko's voice softened with concern.

"I think that depends on your point of view," Dax said.

"Dax—" Sisko's voice held a warning. He hated mysterious comm messages. She knew that, but she was reluctant to state her hypothesis out loud.

She moved out of the crowd into the hallway, the action taking less than a second. "Benjamin," she said as softly as she could, "I think someone has found the *Nibix.*"

There was a very long moment of silence on the other end as the news sank in, then Commander Benjamin Sisko said with an urgency she had never heard before, "On my way."

Nog and Jake Sisko were as far away from Quark's as they could safely be and still be on the Promenade.

Several stores in this out-of-the-way sector had closed, probably due to lack of customers. A lot of people came this way but only on station business. The guests at *Deep Space Nine*—the freighter pilots, the Federation representatives, the starship crews—never seemed to make it back this far.

And that served them just fine.

"Fastball this time," Jake said. He was in a crouch, mimicking as best he could the poses of the great pitchers in his father's favorite holoprogram. "Be ready."

Before Nog could complain, Jake wound up and hurled the baseball as hard as he could at the outstretched mitt.

Nog gave a little shriek and ducked as the ball barely missed him and banged into the bulkhead. The bang reverberated, and the metal rang hollowly.

"You could have killed me," Nog said as he scrambled after the ball. He grabbed it and tossed it against his mitt. "Then I would never have gone to Starfleet Academy, and it would have all been your fault."

Jake still wasn't sure how he felt about Nog attending the Academy. Sometimes he was proud that his father and the other members of Starfleet had inspired Nog. And sometimes Jake was lonely in advance. He wasn't sure what he would do around *Deep Space Nine* with his best friend gone.

"You've been complaining since we started this game," Jake said. He rubbed his shoulder. The movement had pulled something. That's what he got for not warming up properly.

"This is a hu-man game," Nog said. "It's not fair for a Ferengi to play a game designed for tall humans."

"I can't help it that I've grown."

"You didn't have to grow so tall." Nog tossed and caught the ball with one hand.

"I may not be done growing yet," Jake said. Nog scowled at him. Nog had reached his full growth.

"You make fun of me," Nog said. He whirled.

Jake hurried toward him. Nog had a habit of throwing the ball at anything when he was annoyed. "Nog!"

But Nog didn't pause. With a perfect imitation of Jake's form, Nog slammed the ball against the bulkhead, right in the same spot it had hit before.

The bang sounded like an explosion. The sound reverberated again, and the metal pinged. Jake frowned, then caught the ball absently as it bounced toward him.

"I don't care if I ever learn to play stupid games," Nog said.

Jake walked toward the bulkhead. Chief O'Brien had said to pay attention to sounds. Sounds held the key to almost everything in engineering. Machines, metals, even lights, had their own voices. And this bulkhead spoke with a tone different from all the others.

"If you keep getting taller, you can—you can—"

Jake passed Nog without giving him a second glance.

"You can play catch alone!" Nog said, triumph in his tone, as if he had thought of the perfect revenge.

Jake crouched in front of the bulkhead. The metal was slightly dented from the impact of the ball. Other than that, it looked like any other bulkhead in the ship. Gray metal with Cardassian bolts holding the panel in place.

"I said—," Nog started, his voice even louder.

"I know what you said." Jake pulled off his glove,

put it on the floor, and placed the ball in it. "Come here."

Nog sighed loudly. He hated to have his tantrums interrupted. "I suppose you broke something," Nog said.

"You're the one who threw a fastball against the metal," Jake said.

"You made me!"

Jake shook his head. Then he tapped on the panel. The sound had a wobbly edge to it. "Hear that?"

"I hear you going crazy is all I hear," Nog said, but he crouched beside Jake and ran a stubby finger over the dent.

"It's hollow." Jake said. To prove his point, he banged his fist on it again. The wobbly sound reverberated, then faded.

"So?" Nog said.

"So what's behind this? There should be equipment here."

Nog shrugged. "Probably a maintenance tube. Let's go. I don't want to play any more."

"You want to go work for your uncle?" Jake asked.

"It beats staring at dented metal." Nog stood. Jake understood now. Nog was still afraid he would get in trouble for throwing that ball against the bulkhead.

"Go ahead," Jake said. "I'll meet you in the rec area in two hours."

"And don't be late," Nog said, even though he was the one who was always late these days.

"I won't," Jake said. He waited until Nog had disappeared down the Promenade before rapping a final time on the bulkhead, listening as the chief had taught him to do. The wobbles and pings meant the echo was inside the bulkhead, not outside.

Jake frowned, trying to remember the schematic of

the station. He still didn't have as much memorized as the chief. And Jake was glad that Nog had left. Nog had told him once that this kind of interest in machines was unbecoming. But Jake loved the engineering tasks he had learned with the chief, and he loved learning. Jake felt that each experience was going to be important, whether he became a writer, an engineer, or a Starfleet officer like his father.

Nog's view of the world was a lot more utilitarian. If he didn't have an immediate use for the information, it was worthless. Sometimes he used that as a cover for his spotty knowledge of hu-man things. But sometimes Jake believed that Nog meant it.

Jake picked up his mitt and ball and hurried back to the cabin he shared with his father. He tossed the equipment on the couch and pulled up a station schematic. It took a moment to isolate that particular bulkhead.

Then he stared at the diagram. The area behind the panel was blank, according to the diagram. Not hollow. The bulkhead should have thudded when the ball hit it.

Jake grinned. At last, something the chief hadn't found. A little mystery all Jake's own.

CHAPTER
2

DAX HAD WORKED her way back into the crowded bar. She stood on the stairs leading into the holosuites. From there, she could face the dart game still going on between Julian and Chief O'Brien and still see the Caxtonian and Quark discuss the statue at the bar.

The Caxtonian had forced most of the other patrons away from the bar. He and Quark leaned together as close as possible given the Caxtonian's stench and were discussing things heatedly.

The dart game was equally heated. Julian had agreed to forfeit his bull's-eye in exchange for one of O'Brien's bull's-eyes. The chief had declined that offer, saying his bull's-eye was untainted by the wing speed of an Ardwanian. Then a heated discussion of the physics of movement followed, ended by Dax herself when she said that if the wings of an Ardwanian could affect dart trajectory, so could the breath of

23

all the nearby observers. Knowing that Quark would not let darts in his bar without the wagers placed on the games, O'Brien had begrudgingly agreed to Dax's interpretation.

The fighting ceased, and she was able to stare at the darts while actually watching Quark and the Caxtonian. For once, the stench worked in her favor. None of the other patrons, traders all, had noticed the detail work on that statue. She hoped none of them would.

That statue sent shivers down her spine. Its existence meant that someone had found the *Nibix,* the legendary lost ship of the Jibetian Confederacy. Eight hundred standard years ago a revolution on Jibet had sent the ruling family, most of the crown jewels and wealth of the planet, and about a thousand of the ruling family's loyal followers into a cold-sleep ship, fleeing into space in search of a new world. The ship was never seen again.

But the revolution failed shortly after the ship left. Jibetian belief said that the royal family descended directly from Jibet's gods. Suddenly the Jibetian culture found itself with a missing god and royal family. It set up a provisional council to rule until the Supreme Ruler was found, and that council had ruled now for eight hundred years.

Within a hundred years of the revolution the Jibetians had developed their own form of warp drive and began expanding into the systems around them in search of the world where the *Nibix* had landed. Jibetian space was an area much farther from the galaxy center than the Federation. The neighboring systems around Jibet are spread extremely far apart. But the Jibetians over the centuries still managed to hold together a rough confederation of eighty planets.

Finally, one hundred standard years ago a Jibetian warp ship met a far-reaching Federation starship.

A cheer from Julian's supporters made Dax focus on the dart game. Another bull's-eye. O'Brien's face was red and not from the growing heat in the bar. If Dax were still going to have her meeting with Julian, she would call the game, but she couldn't. She had to wait for Benjamin.

He knew almost as much about the Jibetians as she did. Maybe more when it came to Jibetian and Federation relations. If the Jibetian Confederacy did join, they would add a large area of space and eighty worlds. The economic impact of such a joining would be felt throughout the sector, because many of the Jibetian worlds were very rich indeed.

Since the first meeting of the Federation and Jibetian ships, the legend of the lost ship *Nibix* and all its treasures had spread through space. Rumors of its discovery always sent both Federation starships and Jibetian Confederation ships speeding to the area. Recently, the Federation Council, in an effort to improve relations with the Jibetians and slow the treasure hunting, passed an edict that the *Nibix,* if found, would be protected under Federation law and returned in its entirety to the Jibetians.

Curzon Dax had mixed feelings about the ruling, although Jadzia Dax saw the sense of it. Curzon Dax had been on two *Nibix* salvage missions in the early years after the first meeting of the Jibetians. Both missions had found ghost ships but not the *Nibix.* Dax had studied the listed contents of the ship, all the royal family wealth packed on that one cold-sleep ship. Dax knew the type of art and wealth on that ship. She knew what to look for and how to identify it and how to spot fakes.

The tiny oval design was difficult to duplicate. The faint green glow was impossible to make without Jibetian gemstones—gemstones that had been protected for centuries. Dax would have to do tests, but they would be redundant, for Starfleet records only.

She knew the statue that Quark was poking with his greedy little hands was from the *Nibix*.

Another cheer went up, this one from the Dabo table. Quark didn't even look up. So he recognized the statue, too. That might make things more difficult.

"Come on, Benjamin," Dax whispered.

As she spoke, Commander Benjamin Sisko strode into Quark's. His chin was up, his broad shoulders back, and his uniform was smartly pressed. His hands were loose at his sides, and his eyes had a ferocious look, even from Dax's distant perspective. He was prepared for battle.

She climbed down the stairs, keeping her gaze on Sisko. His attitude surprised her. She expected him to slip into Quark's as he usually did, manipulate things slowly, and then get what he wanted. But he was going full bore, like the commander a rumor said he would become.

Odo was the one who slipped around to the side. His ability to blend in, even when he hadn't shapeshifted, amazed Dax. He should have been so noticeable with his not-quite-distinct features, his brown uniform, his always somber expression. And yet those things somehow made him fade into the background more than most would.

Sisko sought her out. She nodded her head toward the bar. He turned in that direction, and she pushed through the crowd, hurrying to Sisko's side. She arrived at the same moment Sisko did. He stopped behind the Caxtonian, and Odo stopped alongside.

Dax made her way around the bar. Caxtonians were known for having a temper when cornered, and it made no sense to take any chances. She'd be in position if he came this way.

"Gentlemen," Sisko said, his mellifluous voice rising and falling within that one word. Benjamin could have been a better con artist than either man who actually worked the trade, with that mobile face and that expressive voice. He leaned around the Caxtonian and picked up the statue with reverence. "I understand you're trying to sell this beautiful item."

His fingers rested lightly on the statue, as if he were afraid of shattering it by holding it too hard. Dax held her breath. She, who had held a thousand treasures in half a dozen lifetimes, found Sisko's delicate grip terrifying. She almost felt that if he dropped the statue, the fate of eighty worlds would change.

Quark reached for the statue, then brought his hands back. Dax moved closer to him, wincing at the Caxtonian's stench. Quark had a stronger stomach than she did, to be able to put up with that smell as long as he had.

"Well, Quark?" Odo asked in his most threatening rasp.

Quark swallowed hard, glancing first at Dax and then at Odo. "We were just talking."

The Caxtonian turned his solid smelly body away from the bar and faced Sisko. "That statue belongs to me." His voice was loud enough to carry. Conversations nearby stopped.

Quark's eyes widened with panic. He waved his hands. "It's under control. Go back to your games."

But no one went back. They were all staring at the commander and the Caxtonian, waiting for violence to erupt.

27

"Do something," Dax whispered to Quark.

"I can't. Caxtonians hate being crossed."

"About the audience."

Quark shrugged and wrung his hands together. He hadn't taken his gaze off the statue. Neither had the Caxtonian. Or Sisko.

If anyone else identified it, they would have a riot on their hands. So Dax decided to create one of her own.

"Drinks on the house!" she shouted. "Rom will take orders."

A huge cheer went up and extended to the farthest reaches of the bar. Immediately Rom, who had paused to watch O'Brien's shot in the dart game, was mobbed.

"You can't do that," Quark said. "I can't afford it."

"You can't afford it if they start breaking chairs to get to that statue." Dax kept her voice as low as possible and still be heard above the din.

"Good point," Quark said. But he frowned as the crowd pushed against Rom, five deep.

"You're holding my statue," the Caxtonian said again.

Sisko nodded, a small smile playing across his features. A dangerous smile. One that did not meet his eyes. Dax put a hand on her phaser.

"Your statue?" Sisko said. "Do you have a bill of sale?"

"It was in my family for generations."

"Really?" Sisko's voice was as smooth as honey. "And you've decided to sell the heirloom in Quark's?"

"I can sell wherever I want," the Caxtonian said.

"Of course you can," Sisko said.

The Caxtonian peered at Sisko, obviously mollified by Sisko's reasonable tone. "Are you interested?"

"Very," Sisko said. "I've never seen anything like this."

The crowd around Rom had grown eight deep. Rom was shouting drink orders from the center. Quark was ignoring them. The crowd was interrupting the dart game. Dax's good idea might actually start a riot if things didn't change quickly.

"It is a beauty," the Caxtonian said.

"Do you have more like it on your ship?"

The Caxtonian shook his head. "It's a one-of-a-kind."

Sisko smiled. "Then I'm sure it will show up on your cargo report, the one you gave to our security people before you docked."

"Give me that," the Caxtonian growled and reached for the statue. Sisko moved it away, and then Dax realized that his grip wasn't as delicate as it had seemed.

"I think I'll hold onto it for a while," Sisko said.

"It's mine," the Caxtonian said, and moved closer to Sisko.

"That seems to be a matter for debate," Odo said. He took the Caxtonian by the arm. "Both sides can present their arguments in my office."

"I haven't done anything wrong," the Caxtonian said loudly, trying to pull away from Odo's firm grasp.

"Oh, I think you have," Sisko said.

"The statue's on my cargo report!" The Caxtonian was shouting now, but no one seemed to notice. The group around Rom had started shoving.

"I don't care what's on your report," Sisko said. "You've violated Federation law. This item is obviously contraband. I'd say you may be in our custody for some time unless you decide to talk to us."

"I have nothing to say." The Caxtonian wrenched his arm but couldn't get free. He shoved Odo, and Odo shoved him back.

"I think you'll want to talk with us," Sisko said. "I'm sure it would be in your best interest to tell us how that *heirloom* managed to come into your possession."

The Caxtonian started shouting, but Sisko grabbed him by the collar.

"You'll cooperate," Sisko said. "You'll do everything I tell you or I will trace each and every item in your cargo hold back to its original owners. The Federation deals with the sale of contraband by imprisoning offenders. The Klingons punish such behavior with death. But the Cardassians have reserved a slow form of torture for such offenses, and we all know that the Cardassians have made torture into an art form."

The Caxtonian's jaw worked. He glanced at the surging crowd, then at Quark. "I don't want to talk here."

"I didn't think you did," Sisko said. "The constable will take you to his office. Dax and I will join you shortly." He nodded at Odo. "Constable."

Odo led the Caxtonian out of Quark's, keeping a firm grip on the trader the entire time. As they went out the door, the Caxtonian glanced over his shoulder at the statue, a look of longing on his filthy face.

Sisko ran his other hand over the statue. Dax knew that Sisko was also an expert on the *Nibix* and its contents. After a lecture at the Academy on the *Nibix,* the lost ship had become one of his hobbies. He and Curzon used to discuss it at length.

Sisko's fingers trembled slightly when he found the tiny oval at the base of the skirt. He swallowed, then glanced at Dax. She nodded. Once. Quark didn't see it. He was watching the growing riot.

"I think we'll have to search his ship," Sisko said to Dax. "Let's impound it until we get him to talk with us."

"He'll talk," Dax said.

"I don't think you should assume that just because a Caxtonian trader automatically has contraband," Quark said. "You're discriminating against my patrons. And," he added, waving at the shoving match going on near the dart game, "disturbing the peace in my bar. I should—"

"Do you want me to arrest you as well?"

Quark looked shocked. "I was only talking to him."

"No, you were negotiating for this." Sisko's soft voice had a firmness. He clutched the statue to his chest. "If one word of this interchange gets past your lips, I will personally close this bar down and have you imprisoned for trying to sell contraband items. Am I making myself clear?"

Dax was shocked at the threat from Benjamin. Threatening anyone was not usually his style. But in this case she agreed completely. If word that the *Nibix* had been found leaked out, this station would be overrun.

Quark took a deep gulping breath, staring at Sisko almost in shock.

Sisko did nothing but stare back. Dax could tell he was very, very serious.

Finally, with a quick glance at Dax, Quark nodded. "Not one word. Not one. But if you find the ship, I want to see it."

"No deals," Sisko said.

"But—"

"No deals." He held the statue carefully and threaded his way through to the door.

Rom broke free of the crowd and was running toward the bar. Quark glanced at the growing mob, then at Dax. "I—"

"You have customers," she said.

"I want to see that ship," Quark said.

She sighed. "If you say nothing, I will see what I can do."

Rom skidded into the bar and began reciting drink orders like a Bajoran ceremonial rite. Quark grabbed glasses. Dax put her hand on his arm. "One thing, Quark. I've known Benjamin a long time. He never makes idle threats. I would believe him when he says he'll arrest you."

Quark shuddered. "Oh, I do, Lieutenant. Believe me. I do."

CHAPTER
3

THE DIN FROM QUARK'S was deafening. Jake heard the shouting before he entered the Promenade. At first the yells were a jumbled mess. Then he could pick out phrases in the half-dozen languages he sort of understood: "Where's my drink?" *"You promised a free drink."* "I'm thirsty. Give me my drink."

Fights had spilled out into the corridor. Rom sat on the stairs in the Promenade, his shirt torn and a scratch running down the side of his face. Two Caxtonians shoved each other to get into Quark's. A Klingon was shouting orders and being ignored. Three Vulcans were leaving, speaking calmly about the ill-mannered clientele, their voices at odds with their ripped and stained clothing.

"What happened?" Jake asked Rom.

Rom put a finger to his lips. "I barely escaped with my life."

Over the roar of the crowd came Quark's voice. "Sit down! Sit down! If you don't sit down, you don't get anything!" A crash followed his words. "And if you break chairs, you have to pay for them! Now sit down!"

Rom gazed at the bar, twisting his hands together. "He'll know I'm gone. If he catches me out here, he'll make me pay for all the drinks."

"Then we'll have to get you back inside." Jake helped Rom up. Rom was limping and missing one shoe. The back of his pants were shredded from the waist as if someone tried to grab the nonexistent belt and pull Rom. "What happened in there?"

"It was a nightmare. A nightmare. And Quark will think it was all my fault. But I couldn't take those orders. I couldn't—and then all those bodies pressing down on me . . ." Rom shook his head as if to clear it. The Caxtonians' fight had moved farther away from the bar. Two Bajorans tumbled out the door and then shoved their way back in, but the sound was dying down. Inside, patrons were scrambling for seats. In a moment, Quark would see Rom reenter.

"Hurry," Jake said. "Stay behind me."

He grabbed Rom's arm and pulled him toward the bar. When they got to the door, the line in front of the bar was still three patrons deep.

"I've got your Enutian pint," Quark snarled at a customer. "And yours." He was moving quickly behind the bar, handing out drinks without even tallying the totals. "Where's Odo when you need him? He's always here when I don't need him, but he's never here when I do." He turned his back and continued muttering. The patrons around him were waving their hands and calling orders.

Jake shoved Rom inside. Rom scuttled against the

windows. Jake pointed at the bar. Rom winced, then made his way around the group. People at tables clutched for Rom and began shouting orders at him.

". . . an absolute madhouse."

Jake recognized Chief O'Brien's voice above the roar. O'Brien and Dr. Bashir were pushing their way through the crowd. Bashir said something to O'Brien, and O'Brien shook his head.

"We'd be better off replicating something ourselves."

Jake got out of the doorway and went into the corridor. The Caxtonians were still fighting, but they were near the door of Garak's boutique now. Jake couldn't hear the sounds of the fight over the cacophony in the bar. They appeared to be punching each other in utter silence.

O'Brien came out of the bar, moved around two more Bajorans who were hurrying in, and wiped the sweat off his face. Dr. Bashir followed, his uniform scuffed. With one hand, he combed his hair into place. With the other, he brushed the dirt off his uniform.

"Even without the riot, that was quite a match, Chief."

"It would have been if you hadn't cheated."

Bashir laughed. "I didn't cheat. It would have been cheating if I had paid the winged Ardwanian to interrupt the game, but I didn't. She descended on her own."

"Her timing was bloody convenient," O'Brien said.

"I'll say." Bashir adjusted his cuffs. "If she hadn't arrived, I would have lost one bull's-eye sooner. You really shouldn't complain when you win, Chief."

"I'm not complaining," O'Brien said. "I would just like a peaceful game of darts. Once is all I ask."

"At Quark's? You'd have better luck wishing for all the wealth in the known galaxy."

They had stopped a few feet away from Jake. Their conversation was nearly over. And even though Jake was leery about Chief O'Brien's sour mood, Dr. Bashir seemed to be leavening it.

"Excuse me, Chief?" Jake approached them. Dr. Bashir smiled at him. Jake nodded back.

Bashir clapped O'Brien on the shoulder. "Can I interest you in a rematch when the crowd is gone?"

O'Brien nodded, his attention now on Jake.

"Good. I'm off to see if I can salvage my paper on Trill immune systems. Make sure he gets something to drink, would you, Jake?" And without waiting for an answer, Dr. Bashir headed down the hall toward the infirmary.

"I suppose I should find the nearest replicator," O'Brien said. "I certainly don't want to go back into that fracas. Come with me, Jake, and you can tell me what you need."

The chief was getting to know him well. Jake's dad always asked questions about the questions: What do you need that for? Is it really important? Can't it wait? But Chief O'Brien always made time for Jake and only answered the questions asked, although he sometimes added warnings to his answers. The warnings had always proven valuable.

They headed toward the family quarters. The Cardassians had designed the station wisely, placing no replicators near the restaurants and bars, except those in the replimat. Judging by the crowd in Quark's, the place must have been hot. The chief was clearly thirsty. His pace was about as rapid as a man's got.

Jake had to match the chief's stride to keep up with

him. He didn't mind the scramble; it gave him a moment to consider how to ask his question. He wanted to do so in a way that allowed him the greatest opportunity to work on his own.

"Chief, are all the station's areas mapped on the computer schematic?"

The chief shot him a look that said, *You came all the way for this?* but he didn't speak the thought to Jake's great relief. "If they were, I wouldn't have as much trouble as I do with all the systems. Those Cardassian devils had more secrets in this place than Quark does. And that doesn't count all the areas they neglected to map."

Jake nodded, uncertain whether to leave his questioning at that or to continue.

The chief took the dilemma from him. "If you tell me what you found, I'll be able to say whether it's on my revised schematic."

No harm in telling him, Jake supposed. He'd learned a long time ago that being honest was a lot better than trying to keep things secret. "I found a panel near the far end of the Promenade, where all the closed shops are. It rang hollow, but nothing shows up on the schematic."

"I haven't mapped that area. To be honest, I've been putting it off." The chief stopped outside the door to his quarters. "If you look at the schematic closely, you'll see that the spaces and corridors don't entirely add up."

"What do you mean?" Jake asked.

"Meaning I'd invite an entire week's worth of extra work by officially discovering the true layout of that sector. I've been waiting for something to go wrong in that area. Then at least the work would be justified."

Jake bit his lower lip. "Would you mind if I take that panel off to see what's back there?"

"I don't think you're wanting to do this to exercise your mapping skills. Are you planning some treasure hunting?" O'Brien did not smile. If he had, he would have been patronizing Jake, and that had no part in their relationship. But O'Brien actually meant the question, so Jake decided to give it a serious answer.

A flush warmed Jake's cheeks. He was glad for the darkness in the corridor. "I thought, since the panel was so close to those shops, and Quark once said those shops were a hotbed for smuggling on *Deep Space Nine,* back when the Cardassians were here—"

"That you'd see if they left a few goodies behind."

Jake nodded.

"Well, you can take the panel off if you measure the space behind it and record it for me. You'll need Nog's help on this one. The Cardassians often had some unpleasant warnings built into their storage areas. I've encountered more than a few electric charges built into the bolts themselves that weren't serious enough to injure me but that left my hands sore for days."

Jake grinned. "Thanks, Chief."

O'Brien opened the door to his quarters. "Just be careful," he said. "If you find any old Cardassian equipment, come and get me before you touch it. Okay?"

"Okay, Chief." Jake could barely repress his excitement. He turned and walked down the corridor until he heard the hiss of O'Brien's door closing. Then Jake jumped, tagged the ceiling, and ran for Quark's. He had to find Nog. They had some work to do.

* * *

Commander Sisko arrived in Odo's office in time to see, through the monitors, Odo checking the force field around the Caxtonian's cell. So the man hadn't cooperated quite as much as Sisko had hoped.

Traces of the Caxtonian's body odor still filled the constable's small office. The ventilation system functioned well but couldn't work with an odor that overpowering. At least the stench would clear soon. Sisko doubted that after this he would ever forget that smell.

A door hissed as Odo emerged into his office.

"Trouble, Constable?" Sisko asked.

Odo shook his head. "Nothing we haven't seen before."

Sisko was about to ask more when Dax entered. She glanced at both men, sniffed, then looked at the monitor. The Caxtonian sat on his bunk, arms crossed over his thick chest.

"Nothing is ever easy, is it, Benjamin?" she asked.

"I learned that from you, old man," he said. And he had, over many years and many adventures.

Major Kira Nerys strode in. Her shoulders were back, her face determined. She had been in the middle of something and clearly wasn't pleased about being interrupted.

"This had better be good," she snapped. "And what is that smell?"

"Caxtonian." Quark spoke from behind her. "I would like to make this quick, too, Commander. Your friend started a riot in my bar. I have a mess to clean up and a brother's pay to dock."

"Your bar can wait," Odo said. He pulled back his chair and sat in it, still commanding the room even though he was the only one sitting down. Sisko always admired the way he managed to do that.

"I take it you got nothing from the Caxtonian," Sisko said.

"On the contrary," Odo said, "he proved to be very talkative when I reminded him of your threat and added a few of my own."

"Then what's he doing in the brig?" Dax asked.

"Let's just say I didn't believe he would stay in his assigned quarters without help." Odo folded his hands on his desk. "I'd offer you all chairs, but I'm afraid I don't have enough."

"It doesn't matter, Constable," Sisko said. "Let's have some answers and then we can move on." The sudden appearance of that statue had tied his stomach into a tight ball, and that ball was making him want to hurry.

"Do you think Quark should be here?" Dax asked.

Quark shot her a nasty look. "I'm the one who found the Caxtonian—"

"Actually, he found you," Dax said. "I was there, remember."

"I don't care who was there!" Kira said. "I have fifteen log sheets to process from those arrivals, two dead docking clamps, and five more ships due in the next hour. I would like to know what this is about."

"It's about a statue, Major. A priceless one," Sisko said. "It's from the *Nibix.*"

"We have no proof of that," Quark said. His tone carried worry.

Sisko pinned him with a look. He wasn't going to let Quark have the upper hand here. "I recognized it. Dax verified it. Are you saying that you have more expertise than we do?"

"I'm not saying anything," Quark said. He looked down.

"Good," Sisko said. "We'll keep it that way."

"I don't see any statue," Kira said.

"And you won't," Sisko said. "It's in safekeeping." His safekeeping. He'd placed it under a protective force field in his quarters, with two makeshift alarms around it. Quark knew the access codes to most of the station's safes. Besides, there were a lot of strangers on the station at the moment. Sisko didn't want to take any chances, so he hadn't told anyone where it was at.

"If that's all then," Quark said, "I have a bar to clean up."

"That's not all," Sisko said. "The constable is going to tell us what he learned from the Caxtonian, and so will you."

"He didn't tell me anything," Quark said.

"You were talking a long time," Dax said.

"About value," Quark said.

"Haggling?" Kira asked.

"No!" The force of Quark's denial made Kira raise her eyebrows, and Sisko made sure he didn't even let a hint of a smile on his face. Dax put a hand over her mouth to hide her smile.

"But he did imply," Quark said, "that there was more where this came from."

"He said as much to me," Odo said. "The statue is not an heirloom as he originally claimed. He found it in an old wreck crashed on an asteroid."

"What asteroid?" Quark asked.

Sisko could almost see the drool of greed dripping from Quark's mouth. "I thought you weren't interested in the *Nibix*," Sisko said softly.

"Don't be silly," Quark said. "Everyone's interested in the *Nibix*."

"I'm not," Kira said. "I don't even know what it is."

The conversation stopped. Everyone stared at her.

This time Sisko let himself chuckle. The *Nibix* had been such a passion for him for so many years, he couldn't comprehend anyone not knowing about the most famous lost ship. But since Kira had spent her years fighting the Cardassians, she would never have had the chance to learn or even hear about it.

"What's so funny?" Kira demanded as Sisko's chuckle spread lightly through the others in the room, easing the tension that had started to build.

Sisko took a deep breath, forced himself to get control, and held up his hand for the others to stop laughing. "Major," he said, "the *Nibix* is one of the most famous lost ships in the history of the galaxy."

"So you're laughing at my ignorance?" She raised her chin, clearly angered at the thought. "I don't find this at all amusing. What's so important about a wrecked ship?"

"A great deal, I'm afraid," Sisko said. The least of which were the thousand bodies that had to be scattered among the wreckage. Except for one body. One body that might or might not be recognizable. But if something as delicate as the statue survived, then perhaps the wreck wasn't as bad as it sounded. "I'll download some information on the *Nibix* for you after this meeting. You will need to read it at once."

Kira started to object, but Sisko stopped her with a sharp look. He had to have her up to speed on this. He had to have all his people working on it. It might turn out to be the most important thing they did with their careers.

"We really should know what asteroid it's on," Quark said again.

"That information is privileged," Odo said. "It's against Federation law to touch the *Nibix*. That statue alone could cause an intergalactic incident. And I won't let you make things worse, Quark."

"I didn't ask him to bring the statue to me!" Quark said.

"Maybe not," Odo said, "but you're not going to make any profit off of anything to do with the *Nibix*, do you understand?"

Quark opened his mouth, but Sisko interrupted before the situation got out of hand. "You're here, Quark, because I want you to have the information we give you instead of starting rumors by trying to discover what we know. You promised you would say nothing about the *Nibix*, and I expect you to say nothing, to do nothing, and to pretend everything is normal until I tell you otherwise. Am I clear?"

"You were clear earlier," Quark said sullenly.

"Good." Sisko crossed his arms. "Because I will not hesitate to shut the bar down and to place you in the brig with the Caxtonian."

"Now wait a minute—"

Sisko made sure his gaze never left Quark. He wasn't kidding, and he needed to make sure everyone knew it.

"Quark," Odo said in his most menacing voice.

"He can't shut me down," Quark said. "It will hurt the station. Do you know how many people stop here just for Quark's?"

"Too many," Odo said.

"I can and I will," Sisko said. With one final hard look at Quark, he turned toward Dax. "We have a trip to take, old man."

Dax grinned. That grin didn't belong to Jadzia. It was pure Curzon, and Sisko ached for the friend he used to know. "I've been waiting for this for a long time."

"I know," Sisko said. He hadn't been waiting quite as long, but he felt a rumble of excitement all the way to his toes. "Have Chief O'Brien make sure the *Defiant* is ready. I want her shipshape and fully armed."

He didn't want to tell them why he wanted the *Defiant* fully armed. He'd let that worry stay with him for the moment. Dax nodded her understanding. She, of all of them, knew why the weapons might be important.

Sisko turned to Kira. "Major, you and Odo will take charge of the station. I want all communications monitored, all public conversations noted, and all suspicious personnel watched. If anyone mentions the *Nibix* outside of this room, I want to know about it. Anyone who sends communications about the *Nibix* will be sent to the brig until I return." He glanced at Quark as he said that. "If this wrecked ship actually is the *Nibix,* I want to be the one to release the information through Starfleet channels. And I want us all to be ready when I do. Understood?"

"Your orders are clear, sir," Kira said. "But I don't understand how a lost ship can cause so many problems."

"You will after you read the files," Sisko said.

Sisko knew his answer wasn't enough, but he just didn't have time at the moment. Dax put her hand on Kira's arm. "The *Nibix* is full of priceless art. That would be enough to cause problems. But the main problem comes from the ship's most famous passenger."

"Who's dead, right?" Kira asked.

"I'm not sure if alive or dead matters," Dax said. "What does matter is that the *Nibix* carried the religious leader of eighty worlds. Worlds that are now about to enter the Federation."

Kira shook her head. "I don't get it. Won't they be happy that we've found the guy?"

Odo stood. "Major, for the past hundred years there have been thousands of books discussing that question. Starfleet has issued nearly that many communiqués about the ship ever since they outlawed scavenging for it. The issues are these: What will happen to the Jibetian culture if the *Nibix* is found? Will it bring on a civil war? Will the discovery finally settle the eight-hundred-year-old conflicts? Or simply refuel them? These questions are not idle speculation."

"At least, not any more," Sisko said. He ignored Major Kira's wide eyes and turned to Dax. "We leave in two hours."

CHAPTER
4

THE END OF the Promenade was deserted. The noise
from Quark's had died down long ago, and Nog had
sneaked out while his father was dealing with the last
of the disgruntled customers. Jake had watched that
from the stairs, hoping to catch Nog before he went to
their rendezvous point.

But Nog's reaction to the proposed plan was not
what Jake had hoped for.

"I don't care about some dumb panel," Nog had
said, and Jake experienced a half second of déjà vu
until he realized that Nog had just said the sentence
for the hundredth time.

Jake's hands were covered with dirt. He had the
tiny all-purpose tool that the chief had given him long
ago and was removing the ancient bolts. It was mind-
numbing, sweaty work—for Jake. Nog had to hold

the bolts so that they wouldn't get lost, not exactly the toughest task he'd ever had.

"An Academy cadet should not be sitting in the dark, playing with the wall," Nog said.

"You're not a cadet yet," Jake said.

"I am, too."

"No." Jake untwisted another bolt and dropped it into Nog's full hand. "You're a candidate. You don't become a cadet until you actually arrive."

"Cadet. Candidate. What's the difference?"

Plenty, Jake wanted to say but didn't. He had made a point of supporting Nog's attendance at the Academy since his uncle was so opposed to it. "Four letters," Jake said.

"I thought jokes were supposed to be funny," Nog said.

"I thought friends were supposed to be helpful," Jake said, removing another bolt.

Nog sighed. "It's just that it's been a long day."

"The afternoon started out fun."

"Yeah, and then I went back to my uncle's bar just in time to watch the customers go nuts." Nog's voice was soft. "I wish he wouldn't blame my dad for everything."

So did Jake, but Jake also believed that Nog's dad could learn to stand up for himself better. Rom did stand up once in a while, like when he supported Nog's decision to attend the Academy. But those occasions were too rare to keep Quark's bluster from affecting Nog's day-to-day existence. And Jake's.

Once Jake complained to his father. His father had remained silent for a long moment afterward, something Jake learned meant that his father actually agreed with the things Jake said but couldn't express that agreement because of his leadership role. Finally, he had said, "The Ferengi are different from us, Jake. Their customs may seem wrong to us, but they have worked for the Ferengi for a long time." His dad's way of saying that he hated the way Nog was treated, too, but he could do nothing about it.

Maybe that was the hardest part of being a space brat and traveling from port to port with his dad. Jake saw a lot of things he didn't like and would never have the power to change. At least, not directly.

"What do you think we'll find back there?" Nog asked.

"Probably nothing," Jake said.

"Then why are we doing this?"

"Because." Jake grimaced as he worked the last bolt. "This is really close to the Promenade. And all kinds of stuff used to be for sale here. Some stuff was smuggled in. Some stuff was lost. Maybe this is one of those secret safes that the Cardassians made to hide things from each other."

"You mean we could be rich?"

"I doubt it," Jake said. "My father would probably make us try to find the original owners if we found something."

"But what if we couldn't find them?"

Jake shrugged. "Then maybe we'd get to keep it." He braced the panel with his shoulder, then dropped the last bolt into Nog's hand. "This is the part that the chief warned me about. We have to take this off carefully because they might have a charge around the opening."

"Oh, great," Nog said. "How do you propose to do that?"

"We need to let the panel fall toward us, then stick that wooden rod in before we go in."

Nog scowled at him.

Jake grinned. "You don't expect to find treasure without doing some work, do you?"

"A Ferengi always expects to find treasure without doing any work," Nog said. He carefully set the bolts down and heaped them into a pile so that they wouldn't scatter.

"What Rule of Acquisition is that one?" The panel was getting heavy against Jake's shoulder. He wished Nog would hurry.

"It's not a rule," Nog said, bracing his hands against the metal. "It's too obvious to be a rule. It's common sense."

Jake laughed as he moved away from the panel. He put his hands out, too, and the panel fell against them. It was heavier than he expected. Thicker, too, than most of the panels he had worked on around the station. That surprised him, given the hollow sound it made when the ball had hit it. There had to be an empty space behind it. There was no question in his mind now.

Together the boys eased the panel back and then leaned against the opposite side of the wall, away from the bolts. Jake shined a flashlight inside. Behind the plate was a dark, empty square area, barely big enough for Nog to stand upright and not much wider than Jake's shoulders. And it only went back in about two meters. It was just an empty space in the wall.

"Nothing," Nog said. "What a waste of time."

"You don't know it's nothing," Jake said. "The space has to be here for a reason."

"Yeah. A reason no one remembers any more." Nog reached toward the darkness, but Jake blocked him, remembering the chief's warning.

"Use the stick."

49

"Or what?"

"Just do it," Jake said.

Nog picked up the stick and waved it through the hole as if he were stirring a bowl of punch in his uncle's bar. "See? Nothing."

He reached for the panel, but Jake grabbed his arm. "Not yet. I promised the chief we'd measure this."

"Great. All I need is more work."

Jake bit back his irritation. Clearly Nog wasn't as excited about this adventure as Jake was. "All right," Jake said. "I'll measure it."

He bent over and went inside the small opening. About a half meter of the ceiling was missing. Jake had to duck to reach the inside wall, but when he got there, he could stand, his head and shoulders up inside the opening in the ceiling.

"Hurry up," Nog said, but his words sounded hollow and seemed to echo off into a distance.

"Hand me a light," Jake said. He could hardly contain his excitement. So far they had found nothing, but he had a feeling there was more. Much more.

"The tricorder can measure in the dark," Nog said.

"I don't want to measure. There's a passage in here." Jake's voice echoed upward, reverberating around him, throwing his words back at him until they faded.

"A passage?" Nog finally sounded interested. Jake could hear the rustle of fabric against metal as Nog climbed inside. Then a flashlight appeared beside Jake, the beam pointing upward. A shaft about a meter high led into a much larger area that disappeared deeper into the wall. Jake could barely reach the edge above with his outstretched arm.

Nog was under him, looking up. "Is there treasure?"

"There's just dirt," Jake said. On a starship the lack of dust would be normal, even in a closed-off tunnel like this. But here, Jake always expected things to be dirty. His first image of DS9 always stuck in his mind: the mess of fallen ceiling beams and debris left in the Cardassian evacuation. Cleanliness on DS9, while the norm, still felt odd to him two and a half years later.

"Do you think there's treasure?" Nog asked.

"Look, Nog," Jake said, finally letting his irritation show. "If you don't want to come, just say so. I'm going to go exploring whether you come or not."

"I didn't say I wouldn't come," Nog said in his I'm-about-to-pick-a-fight voice. He often got into this mood after he'd had a bad day.

"Good," Jake said. He handed Nog the flashlight. "If you change your mind, just tell me."

Then Jake used both hands to reach up, grab onto the edge, and pull himself up the metal chute into the dark area above. Once there, he turned around and looked back down into the beam of the light Nog was shining upward into his face.

"Hand me the light before you blind me," Jake said, and Nog did as he was told.

"You're not going to leave me here in the dark, are you?" Nog asked. He wouldn't be able to lever himself up as easily as Jake did.

But Jake didn't want to dwell on that problem at the moment. He shined the light at the area around him. It felt like a hall of some sort. By stretching out his arms in both directions he could almost touch the walls. The ceiling was an arm's length above his head. The passage went off into the distance before it turned.

"It's huge!" Jake said, and his voice played back to him.

Huge . . . huge . . . huge . . . huge . . .

"Is there any treasure?" Nog asked, but this time his voice had a smile in it, as if he knew that the question was dumb.

"Piles of it. Gold press latinum as far as the eye can see!"

"Really?" Nog asked.

Jake got down on his hands and knees, set the flashlight to one side, and peered over the edge. Nog was looking up at him with a mixture of greed and disbelief on his face.

"Really," Jake said. "And a big fat dragon to guard it all."

"You're making fun of me," Nog said.

Jake nodded. "There isn't any treasure, but there's a lot more passage than the station schematics have room for. Want to go on an adventure?"

"Sure beats working in my uncle's bar," Nog said and raised his hands like a child wanting to be picked up.

It took less than two hours at warp five for the *Defiant* to reach the red-star system in which the Caxtonian said he had found the wreck. Sisko spent most of that time in the commander's chair, issuing terse orders, and staring through the viewscreen at the vastness of space.

He had taken a small maintenance crew with some of his best people, most trusted people. If there was any hint that this crashed ship was the *Nibix*—and Sisko believed in a small corner of his heart that it was—then only those he trusted could know. The six ensigns he picked were all known for their attention to duty and their closed-mouthedness. They had few close friends and were not known as gossips. He rounded out the rest of the *Defiant*'s crew with Dax because she knew more about the *Nibix* than he did, O'Brien because he was a whiz with not only Federation technology, but any other technology Sisko had seen, and Dr. Bashir because . . well, Sisko didn't want to examine that because.

The red-star system they were heading to was nothing but a number on the star charts. The system had been lightly surveyed eighty years earlier and was noted only for its large concentration of asteroids in four wide belts around the star. There were no known habitable planets. The system was near the Cardassian border but still clearly in Federation space, a fact for which Sisko was greatly relieved. If this ship really was the *Nibix*, he would have more than enough on his hands with the Jibetians and the Federation. He didn't need to be dealing with the Cardassians at the same time.

Throughout the voyage, Sisko kept his right hand clenched. It was the only physical sign of his tension. Occasionally Dax would glance at him. Her normal unshakable calm had a giddy edge beneath it. For most of the ensigns, this was their first official mission on the *Defiant*. They concentrated on their stations, pretending that Sisko's presence didn't make them nervous.

Only O'Brien and Dr. Bashir were acting normal. They were standing to one side on the bridge, watching the viewscreen and arguing over a game of darts they had played earlier in the afternoon. They had no idea what they were about to walk into.

Sisko did. And he was having trouble thinking about it. Every commander he had ever met and certainly every starship captain knew the space legends about lost ships. Most captains also knew the legends about lost seagoing vessels on various worlds, from the disappointing treasure vaults on Earth's *Titanic* to the immense wealth discovered on Seleda Five's *G. Menst.* Sisko's favorite seagoing legend showed his Earth roots. The *Marie Celeste* haunted his dreams and his nightmares in more ways than he imagined: a ship that was found with its stoves still on, a meal half eaten, and a missing crew in the middle of the ocean.

He half imagined he would find that here.

But his favorite spacefaring legend, his favorite what-if, had always been the *Nibix.* From the moment he had heard about the ship at the Academy, he had studied every book about it, every article ever written, listened to every theory. He still had a capture file in his personal computer on DS9, so that any time a new theory was discussed on the *Nibix,* his file would download it, translate it if necessary, and notify him it had arrived. He had several other capture files for several other interests, including baseball, and he had been so busy with the station in recent months that he let material accumulate.

Now he wished he hadn't.

As they neared the system, Sisko stood. He couldn't contain his excitement or his nervousness any longer.

"Dropping out of warp," said Ensign Dodds. She was a soft-spoken human woman whose small stature belied her physical strength. Sisko had sent her on two other missions, one to Bajor, and her competence had impressed him.

"Chief, I need you in position now," Sisko said.

O'Brien nodded and moved to one of the empty stations. Dax sat before the science station, her long fingers playing on the panel. Sisko resisted the urge to do the same. He would not give in to his romantic fantasies. He would command this mission like any other.

"I want full scans of the entire system," he said. "Ensigns Kathé and Coleman, you will help Lieutenant Dax and Chief O'Brien in their search."

"Aye-aye, Commander," the ensigns said in unison. Ensign Kathé bent her head over the board. She was a long, slender Yominan whose most arresting feature was her long mane of rainbow hair.

Ensign Coleman, who had been on DS9 less than six months along with his wife and two children, glanced at Kathé before beginning his own scan. Sisko both liked and disliked the boy's caution. In a situation that required quick thinking, it would get him killed. In a situation like this, his thoroughness might help them all.

"Start with the bigger asteroids first," Sisko said. He had spoken to the Caxtonian before the *Defiant* left, asking for more details than Odo had received. The Caxtonian said the ship was on a large asteroid in the outer band. He said he had discovered it while doing repairs on a broken warp drive. He had only gone into the ship a short distance, grabbed two items that looked like they had value, and then got out. He had no idea the name of the ship. He just said it frightened him because of the bodies.

The Caxtonian's cargo bay showed that he lied about how many items he took. But the fifteen tiny pieces that Sisko found there did show that the pilot had been spooked. If he had found the *Nibix*, fifteen pieces were less than a handful.

Bodies.

Sisko had seen a lot of bodies in his day, but space

death was never pretty. He knew, deep down, that the bodies alone would probably remove the last traces of romance about the *Nibix* from his memory forever.

But for the moment, he would hang on to the excitement. Trapped in his clenched fist was the feeling he was trying to reign in, the feeling he wouldn't admit to anyone but Dax, and then he would do so only after several drinks many months from now.

He felt like a kid. A kid on an adventure. A kid about to discover all the secrets of the universe.

Nothing like the commander of a space station on the Cardassian border or the commander of a ship on a mission, however short, that might change the future of the Federation.

"Commander," Dax said, startling him.

He focused on her, ignoring the jump of excitement in his stomach.

"I have a reading. It appears to be the hull of a ship on the largest asteroid this side of the red star." She paused and met his gaze. "There are no life signs."

Something inside him relaxed. He had been afraid, very afraid, that the tales of the Jibetian religion were true, that their religious leader was indestructible.

"The coordinates?" Sisko reminded her.

"Seventy-eight mark two," she said.

"Take us there," Sisko said to Ensign T'plak, the quiet Vulcan in the navigator's chair. T'plak nodded and plotted their course. Ensigns Kathé and Coleman were still scanning, as was O'Brien. Sisko was relieved he didn't have to tell them the drill. In an asteroid field this big, several ships could have crashed. Dax might not have found the correct spot right away.

"I'm finding nothing else, sir," O'Brien said.

"Keep scanning," Sisko said.

"Benjamin." Dax's voice was soft, showing the depth of her shock. She always followed protocol in a professional situation—except when she was rattled. "My preliminary scan shows the ship matches the reported size and configuration of the *Nibix*."

Sisko's heartbeat increased. He tightened his fist, holding his excitement back as best he could. "Let's get a closer look, Ensign."

"One moment, Commander," T'Plak said. Then, in what seemed like seconds, the *Defiant* was in a stationary orbit over the asteroid.

Sisko took a deep breath. Protocol demanded that he remain on the *Defiant*.

Protocol be damned. He didn't want the ensigns down there, playing in the dark. He would take Dax for her knowledge and O'Brien for his trustworthiness.

"Doctor," Sisko said, "you have the comm. Dax, Chief, let's see what we've got down there."

Dax stood before Sisko finished speaking. Dr. Bashir looked flustered, and O'Brien frowned. The ensigns huddled over the stations, trying not to be noticed.

Sisko was standing, too, although he didn't remember getting out of his chair. His stomach felt like it had tied itself into a knot. He'd been on other destroyed ships before. This was just another.

But he couldn't convince himself of that. The ship on that asteroid held the body of the religious leader for an entire culture. Not to mention the priceless artwork from generations of Jibetian culture.

Or the future relationship between the Jibetian Confederacy and the Federation.

The *Nibix* was a myth. People didn't just beam into a myth. Yet he was about to.

CHAPTER
5

THE AIR WAS STICKY and filled with dust. Jake's hands were filthy, and he didn't want to look at his clothes. But he couldn't contain his excitement. He felt like one of those explorers in the stories his father used to read to him. Even though Jake was still in the station, he felt as if he were touching a forbidden world, one forgotten a long, long time ago. He felt as if he were conquering new territory.

He felt like he was on the verge of something big.

"I wonder if my father finished cleaning up the bar yet," Nog said, his voice echoing.

Jake whirled, raising dust. "That's all you can think about? Cleaning the bar?"

"There isn't much more to think about," Nog said. "This place is as exciting as a Vulcan wrestling match."

"I don't know," Jake said. "I think it's kinda cool."

And he did. They'd moved through twenty small linked rooms in the last ten minutes. The floors were covered with a fine gray dust, and the dust had caked in ventilation patterns on the walls. Jake had no idea where they were at the moment, but he had no worry about finding their way out. The rooms just lead one into another. All he and Nog had to do was follow their own footprints in the dust.

Nog sneezed. It sounded like an explosion in the enclosed area. "Sure was a good idea," he said. "Crawling around in the dust to find nothing."

They stopped in the middle of a room the size of a holosuite. Jake flashed his light around the walls and ceilings. Only gray metal. No sign of old furniture or equipment. Nothing had disturbed the dust in here in years.

The entrance to the next room was about a meter above the floor and looked more like a maintenance tunnel. They'd have to crawl on their hands and knees to get through it if it lead anywhere.

"We really should be mapping this out," Jake said.

"*You* should be mapping this out," Nog said, pointing his flashlight at his clothes and trying to pat off some of the dust. All he managed to do was fill the air around them, making the lights look like they were being shown through a thick fog "I only came along because you asked."

Jake frowned at him. "Why are you being so difficult about this?"

Nog stopped patting. "I'm tired of people making me do things I don't want to do."

"You didn't have to come."

"You wanted me to."

"But I told you that you could leave if you wanted."

"You *said* that, but you *mean* I should stay."

Jake looked away. He had made it clear that he wanted Nog to stay. "You don't always have to do everything everyone else wants you to do."

"I'm not like you!" Nog had raised his voice. The room shook with the force of his words. "I'm not the commander's son. No one on the station gives me special permission to map stupid maintenance tunnels. No one tells me that I can spend all day watching the chief engineer. No one gets me three days away from the station so I can fly in some special ship with my father. I have to stay here and work for my uncle. And when I get back tonight, I'll get yelled at for not helping clean up and for being so dirty."

"Is that what's bugging you?" Jake asked.

"Isn't that enough?"

"I thought you didn't care that I was the commander's son."

Nog sighed in his impatient way. "It's just things are easy for you, and they're never easy for me. It's like these tunnels. You think it's cool to walk through them and map them, and Chief O'Brien will pat you on the head and tell you how good you were, and no one will thank me."

"Sure they will," Jake said.

"No, they won't," Nog said.

"They will if I tell them you did all the work."

"You'd do that?" Nog asked, his mood clearly brightening. Jake was always amazed at how surprised Nog was whenever anyone offered to do something nice for him.

"Sure. Because I don't want to do this by myself." Jake turned the flashlight toward the tunnel. "Come on. Let's see where this goes."

About three meters ahead, the tunnel ended in what

appeared to be just another empty room. Jake pulled himself up and into the tunnel.

"Wait," Nog said.

Jake could see Nog's light from behind him as they crawled through the dust. The dust coated Jake's face. He was sweating. The air was close in here and smelled dry and ancient, as if it hadn't been used in a long time. But that couldn't be. All of the station's systems were hooked together, or at least, that was what the chief once told him.

Nog coughed at the dust Jake was kicking up into his face. "On the way back, I lead," Nog said. "Hurry up before I choke."

Jake crawled quicker, kicking up more dust. The tunnel opened up into the new room at floor level. Jake shined his light around the dust and gray walls until the beam stopped on a metal door. A moment later, Nog joined him.

Then he saw where Jake's flashlight beam was pointing and stopped. "Don't you wonder what all these rooms were used for?" Jake asked.

"Something secret," Nog said, "Or else they would be on the schematic."

That was what Jake had thought. Nog's voice finally held the same excitement that Jake had felt from the moment he discovered the panel.

"Yeah, real secret," Jake said. "But what?"

The two crossed the dust-covered floor and stopped in front of the metal door. It was the first door they had seen in nearly an hour of climbing and crawling through room after room of dust.

"I wonder where this goes to?" Jake said, noting that the door handle had the standard Cardassian latching and didn't seem to be locked, at least from this side.

"Let's find out," Nog said. He reached for the handle and pulled it down.

Suddenly Jake wanted to stop him. Maybe the door was a trap. Maybe it was wired to explode. Chief O'Brien had warned him about such things. But it was too late. Nog had already opened the door.

And nothing happened.

Except for the blinding light. After all that darkness any light seemed bright. Jake blinked, waiting for his eyes to adjust.

There was no dust on this floor. The room was the size of his bedroom, yet seemed bigger because three more tunnels led off in different directions.

The light came from small ventilation grates spaced near the ceiling around the room. Only it was clear from this side of the grates they had never been designed for ventilation. Small steps lead up to each so that someone could stand on the top step and look out through the grate.

Three chairs, Cardassian design with metal backs, were spaced around the otherwise empty room.

"What is—"

"A spy hole," Nog whispered. "I've heard about rooms like this. Keep your voice down." He climbed the nearest stairs, but even standing on his tiptoes he couldn't see through the grate.

"Why is everything on this station built for tall people?" Nog whispered.

"Maybe because it was designed by Cardassians," Jake whispered back. He climbed the same set of steps and looked through the grate. And choked.

He could see into the back room of a shop on the Promenade. He couldn't tell which one, because he hadn't been in the backs of too many of them.

"What do you see?" Nog hissed.

Jake stepped down and moved to another grate. This one looked out into the main area of the Promenade. Laughter filtered through as two ensigns walked past arm in arm.

"Who's laughing?" Nog whispered.

"No one," Jake whispered back. He frowned. The cleanliness of this space bothered him.

"Well, someone was laughing." Nog whispered.

"No one important," Jake clarified. He glanced down at Nog. "We're on the Promenade. I can see the shops. How many of these spy holes do you think there are?"

"A bunch," Nog said. "I wonder if we can see into my uncle's bar."

Jake grinned. "That would be great if we could. Then we'd know if all the work was done."

"And I wouldn't ever have to go back in the middle of a riot." Nog turned around.

So did Jake. Three more tunnels. Even though he had been smiling, this whole thing left him disquieted. Of all the things he had expected, this was the last. Part of him wanted to go back, but turning around meant turning his back on adventure.

Nog was already down the stairs. "Let's figure out which passage leads to my uncle's bar."

"All right," Jake said. He was committed. For the first time since he had entered the panel, he wondered if this was the right thing to do.

CHAPTER
6

As HE GAVE the command to energize, Sisko closed his eyes. He didn't want the transition from the bright transporter room on the *Defiant* into the darkness of the crashed ship to be abrupt. He wanted a moment to feel the place before he saw it.

Dax's readings had shown that much of the ship was still intact. Only a few sections had been damaged by the crash. The news wasn't a complete surprise: for something as fragile as that statue to survive, the crash couldn't have been devastating. Sisko had Dax prepare the coordinates for beam down into the main section of the ship that still had rudimentary life-support systems. That alone had surprised Sisko, but O'Brien had assured him that ships from the beginning of space travel on were always designed so that the life-support systems had double and triple backups. On a ship the size of the *Nibix*, most of the outer shell would have to be destroyed before the life-support systems would quit entirely.

Still, Sisko thought it damned unusual on a ship this old. If, indeed, it was as old as he hoped.

As the beaming process ended, the first thing he noted was the cold. It went through the protective layers of his uniform. He had expected a chill—the asteroid had no atmosphere—but nothing as penetrating as this. He took a tentative breath—the air was cold but real—and sighed.

The life support did work.

He could also feel the antigravity units they were all wearing adjusting them to eight-tenths of Earth normal. The asteroid's gravity was actually less than half.

Then he opened his eyes, cringing slightly, expecting to be surrounded by bodies. Instead, he was in a dark, wide hallway. He tugged on his gloves, slipped the end of them beneath the wrists of his uniform so that the only skin he exposed was on his face. Dax already had her light on and was examining the wall panels. O'Brien switched his on after a moment and looked at the paneling as well.

"I thought we'd see more than this," O'Brien said.

"This ship is huge," Dax said. "This is just a corridor. A small one, judging from the readings I took on the *Defiant*."

Sisko switched on his light and glanced at the panels as well. The diagrams were clear, using an old spacer's code that had been outdated in this sector for centuries, but the words were in a language that looked only vaguely familiar. And he wasn't sure if the familiarity was because he hoped he would see something he recognized.

"Can you make out anything, Chief?"

"Nothing of use to us," O'Brien said. "We studied

this type of system at the Academy. It could belong to any one of a hundred star systems that developed similar technology, long before humans had space flight."

"But it's familiar?" Sisko asked.

"Yes, of course. Familiar enough anyway." O'Brien's breath floated like a ghost in the darkness. Dax had her tricorder out, and its hum echoed in the silence.

"No life signs," she said. "But behind these walls are all sorts of storage areas."

"And there's equipment behind those," O'Brien said.

Sisko pulled out his tricorder as well but didn't use it. Not yet. He wanted to take this slow, not to come to any more conclusions than he already had. "Come on," he said. "Let's see what else we can find."

He led the way down the silent passage to a doorway that had jammed open. The door was tall—he could get through it without much effort—and it was wide enough for two people to pass. His light caught coffinlike shapes scattered throughout the room. He glanced at Dax. She was staring intently ahead, her own light playing on the surface of the coffins.

Cold-sleep chambers. Ancient ones that looked like long narrow bullets. The kind that, when jettisoned into space, provided enough protection for the being inside to survive a short trip through a planet's atmosphere.

No one in the Federation had used this type of technology in a long, long time.

"I count fifteen of them," O'Brien said.

"I get no readings," Dax said. "If they were working, something would show on the tricorder."

The cold bit into Sisko's cheeks and nose. He

climbed over a pile of rubble near the door and crouched near the closest cold-sleep bed. Through the opaque lid and the slight fog of his own breath, Sisko could see the body of a man, somewhat well preserved, yet obviously dead. The skin on his face had sunken in and his eyelids seemed flat. He had been a middle-aged man. He wore robes that had no markings on them. Through the lid, Sisko couldn't even make out the robes' fabric.

"A few of them smashed open," O'Brien said. He had gone deeper into the room. His voice had a quiet power in the silence. "Nothing left except skulls, a bit of bone, and some metal jewelry. This ship has been here a long time."

The Caxtonian hadn't come into the aired section of the ship; he'd only been to the small outer area exposed to the vacuum of the asteroid. There the bodies hadn't decomposed at all.

Dax crouched beside an intact cold-sleep bed. She ran her tricorder over it. "I can't tell how long this man's been dead," she said. "The cold, the lack of oxygen in the unit, and the drugs they used to ease into cold sleep have messed up any reading I can understand. Julian did some work on cold sleep. He might be able to get a better idea than I have."

"If this turns out to be the *Nibix*," Sisko said, "I'll bring him down."

So far they had seen nothing that indicated they were on the *Nibix*. Of course, nothing had shown that they *weren't* on the *Nibix* either. Sisko would hate for this mission to prove inconclusive.

O'Brien stood, following his tricorder as if it were a native guide. "Do you hear that?" he asked.

Sisko looked up. He heard the hum of the tricorders, the rasp of their own breath, and something else, very faint. A quiet *thrum* he wouldn't have noticed if O'Brien hadn't mentioned it.

"Equipment," Dax said. "Something's still working."

"It's probably the life-support systems," O'Brien said. "Or what's left of them. There's a chamber just beyond this one. I'm going to investigate."

Sisko stood. He'd learned all he could from the dead man. He pulled out his tricorder. It slid in his gloved hands. He adjusted a few settings and then found the same unusual reading that seemed to be leading O'Brien forward. A low level of power, running on its own system, separate from the systems behind the panels in the corridor.

"Would that be life support?" Dax asked. "It's an independent system."

"If I were designing a ship for deep space with this primitive technology," O'Brien said, "I'd make damn sure that life support, at least to the important areas, had its own system or at least its own backup."

"Was that usual, Chief?"

"It depends on the culture," O'Brien said. "Some early space travelers from this section had no life support going into the cargo bays. If a worker got trapped back there, he died. It wasn't practical, but it was cheap."

"A waste of life," Sisko said, and he was referring not just to the practice O'Brien mentioned, but to the bodies around him.

"In some cultures, life wasn't valued very much," O'Brien said.

Neither Dax nor Sisko responded. They had both seen places where life wasn't much valued. After those experiences, the Federation's rules about accepting advanced cultures made much more sense.

Sisko's hand was shaking, and he hoped it was from the cold. The readings on his tricorder remained constant. His heart was pounding hard. Dax had an intent look on her face. She maneuvered through the coffins toward the chamber.

O'Brien reached it first. "The readings are definitely coming from here," he said.

Dax reached it second and gasped. "Benjamin."

His mouth was dry. He crossed the distance in half the time it took the others. Dax was wiping the side of the door, as if to clean something off. O'Brien was running his tricorder over the wall.

"All the systems from this wall inward are active and working," he said. "Life support, environmental controls, power bays, everything."

His voice held a kind of awe. He punched the tricorder two and three times, obviously checking his readings, but they apparently remained the same.

Sisko was watching Dax. She continued to wipe, glancing over her shoulder at him, the excitement on her face so reminiscent of Curzon when he found a toy that Sisko saw not Jadzia, but an old Trill man, his white hair thinning over his markings.

"There are redundant systems like I've never seen before," he said. "They wanted to keep whatever is in there alive and running. There must be ten backup systems in this wall alone."

Sisko had to swallow before he could speak. "This ship's been here a long time. No system can run forever."

"The power needed here is low," O'Brien said. "And at least half these systems are linked. If one shuts down, another takes over. I'd say this part of the ship could live a good long time yet."

"That's not all," Dax said. "Benjamin, take a look

at this." She moved away from the part of the door she was polishing. The paint on the door had long since faded to gray, but the outline of the design was still visible.

Sisko looked at the pattern for a moment before the shape sprang out at him. An oval with a green staff in the middle. Or at least the staff was supposed to be green. In some areas on Jibet, the staff even glowed. The design was all over anything that had to do with the House of Jibim Kiba Siber, including the *Nibix.*

To have the symbol on or near a door meant only one thing.

"The royal chamber," he said softly to himself.

Dax nodded. "We found it."

Sisko let the thought sink into his cold mind. Now, more than at any other time in his career, he had to be very careful. He glanced at Dax.

"We should confirm," she said.

He knew it. And he also knew that he wanted to be the first to look on the Supreme Ruler's face. If the man still had a face. What a disaster it would be if the Supreme Ruler's cold-sleep bed had broken open.

Sisko switched his tricorder onto record. He would need a record for the Federation and for the Jibetians. "Dax, O'Brien, I'm using my tricorder to record all of this. State your name and rank and the time we've already spent on this mission."

They did, and he followed suit. O'Brien shot him a concerned glance. Even though they had briefed him, no one apparently had told him all the things of import that he needed to know.

"Chief, can you open this door without harming anything?"

O'Brien frowned at Sisko's tricorder. "Judging from the way this equipment works, I can."

"Nothing appears to be blocking the door from either side," Dax said, using her own tricorder. Her hands were shaking, too. Her breath left a small bit of condensation on the wall.

"All right then," Sisko said. He watched as O'Brien reached forward and touched a small square area beside the door. With a scraping of metal that sent shivers down Sisko's back, the door slid back.

A light went on inside, startling all of them. Dax put a hand on Sisko's arm. "If this is the chamber of the Supreme Ruler," she said, "there might be protections."

"I don't read anything," O'Brien said.

"But that doesn't mean they aren't there," Dax said.

Sisko nodded. He didn't care if a green glow from the Jibetian god struck him dead. He was going to be the first person in that room in over eight hundred years.

He slipped inside the door and found himself in a chamber filled with art and more designs. The equipment on the wall glowed. The light was a single spot over a cold-sleep bed on top of a raised platform.

Sisko let his tricorder scan the room so that he could show it undisturbed. Then he walked carefully toward the platform. The light was eerie, a recognition of life where there was none.

Dax followed as did O'Brien.

"I don't like this," O'Brien said.

But Sisko would wait to get O'Brien's opinion after they had looked at that cold-sleep bed. Sisko climbed the stairs. Beside the bed, a long staff still glowed green. It was the symbol of the Supreme Ruler. It never left his side.

"Benjamin," Dax said softly.

71

"I see it, old man," he said.

He ran his gloved hand over the top of the staff, careful not to touch it. Then he peered down into the opaque lid.

The soft light made the Supreme Ruler's skin look faintly gray. The ruler was a young man, maybe in his late twenties, his features still perfectly formed. His face hadn't sunken in like the other dead man's had. The Supreme Ruler had the ridged cheekbones that marked a Jibetian, and Sisko knew that his eyes, if open, would have flecks of green in the whites.

The man's age surprised Sisko, even though he knew the history of Jibet. He figured that the Supreme Ruler would be a broken old man with a long white beard and features filled with age and wisdom. Not a man who, in real time, hadn't lived as long as Sisko had.

"We found it," Dax said, her voice barely containing the excitement. "We found him." She, too, reached down and reverently touched the green symbol.

"That we did, old man," Sisko said. "That we did."

"You may have found a little more than you were expecting." O'Brien's voice held none of the reverence that Dax's did. Sisko recognized the tone. It was O'Brien at his most cautious. He didn't know how Sisko would react to his find.

Sisko turned to him. O'Brien was kneeling beside the cold-sleep chamber, his tricorder in his hand. After a moment he looked up at Dax and Sisko. "This is still working."

Sisko, for what seemed like an eternity, couldn't get his mind to wrap around O'Brien's words. He couldn't let the thought in. And then when it did

Sisko broke into a cold sweat, and his stomach clamped down hard.

He hit his comm badge with so much force that it felt like he slapped himself in the chest. "Doctor Bashir! We need you on the surface immediately."

The doctor shot back a quick response that Sisko ignored. He crouched over the opaque glass and looked into the young face of Jibim Kiba Siber. The young and very much alive face of the Supreme Ruler of a peaceful empire that might soon be peaceful no longer.

And Sisko shuddered.

CHAPTER
7

IT TOOK KIRA an hour after the *Defiant*'s departure to settle the issues of docking clamps, cargo logs, and incoming freighters. Then she retreated to the commander's office to examine the files he left for her.

She sat in his chair and read as quickly as she could. The chair always felt awkward to her—Gul Dukat had sat in it so much that it had molded to his shape. Try as she might, she could never get comfortable in it. Nor, if she were completely honest, could she ever be comfortable in an officer's room of Cardassian design. It had gotten so that she could ignore most of the Cardassian designs in her normal haunts around the station, but places like this—and Odo's brig— made her extremely uncomfortable. Try as she might, she could never leave the past completely behind.

Nor, it seemed, could the Jibetians. When their Supreme Ruler left, eight hundred years before, Jibetian culture continued to follow him as spiritual leader of their world. In search of their leader they spread out over outlying planets, eighty in all, forming the Jibetian Confederacy. The same confederacy was now in the middle stations of applying for membership to the Federation.

Centuries of research and speculation discussed the whereabouts of the ship and the consequences of finding the Supreme Ruler or his descendants on some distant outpost. Even more documents dealt with the wealth of the ship itself, which had to be Quark's interest in all of this.

She had just finished reading the first three files on the *Nibix* and now couldn't shake the fear of impending doom. She was starting to understand why Dax and Sisko had acted so harshly. If they actually did find the lost ship, the station would be overwhelmed with curiosity seekers, treasure hunters, and a thousand Federation and Jibetian officials. At the moment the calm around the station felt like the calm before the storm.

A very powerful storm if her guess was right.

At least she could use the time to become more informed. She pulled Commander Sisko's chair up closer to his desk and punched in the request for information on the current status of Jibetian and Federation treaties and the Jibetian's request to join the Federation. After a moment the screen brought up the file, and she settled in for a long afternoon of technical reading when her comm badge chirped.

"Kira here."

"Major," said Ensign Stafa, whom she had left in charge of communications in Ops, "there's an incoming message for you from the Jibetian High Council."

Kira couldn't have heard that right. She had been

reading about Jibet, so she must have inserted that word in for something else. "From whom?"

"The Jibetian High Council. Do you want me to pass this along to someone else? They're saying it's rather urgent."

And odd. She squared her shoulders and put on her best military poker face. There was no way the Jibetians would know about the discovery of the *Nibix,* or what could be the *Nibix.* She and Odo had been monitoring all outgoing communication and nothing had been leaked. Nothing. This had to be about some other matter unrelated to the *Nibix* and the timing was just bad.

She forced herself to take a deep breath. "I'll take it here."

The screen on Commander Sisko's desk cleared to show a middle-aged man with an almost albino complexion and thinning blond hair. His cheekbones were ridged, and his deep blue eyes had green dots in the whites.

Kira smiled as if greeting any dignitary. "I am Major Kira Nerys, first officer of Federation Station *Deep Space Nine.* How may I be of service?"

"Forgive the intrusion, Major. I am Jiber Kidath of the Jibetian High Council." She could see the man from the waist up. He bowed slightly as he addressed her. "I am inquiring about a mission we believe your commander has undertaken. A mission looking for our ship the *Nibix.*"

"The lost ship?" Kira asked. She hated diplomacy. It went against every blunt bone in her body. Yet she knew that each word she said now was important. It was equally important to satisfy the official without lying to him. If possible.

"Yes," Kidath said, nodding. "The lost ship. We

understand your commander has led an expedition to
find it."

"I am not at liberty to discuss Commander Sisko's
activities, Councilman. Perhaps if you went through
regular Federation channels . . ." She let her voice
drop off.

"I intend to, Major," Kidath said. "I had hoped
that you might cut through the official red tape. I
understand your people have a deep religious faith
and know what it means to have other cultures
interfere with your beliefs."

"The Bajoran religion accepts other cultures," Kira
said, unable to let the misconception through. "I
wouldn't be on this station if it didn't."

"Forgive me, Major. I had presumed much on little
knowledge." Kidath bowed again. "Perhaps it would
be best if I spoke with your commander."

"I think you need to go through Federation channels," Kira said, her palms flat on the desktop. A
trickle of sweat ran down her spinal column. He was
trying to trick her, to force her to tell him that
Commander Sisko was gone.

"You are free to speak with me, but your commander is not?"

Kira smiled her most charming smile, thankful that
she had had a few hours to read about the *Nibix*
before this contact. "I had thought that your communication had something to do with *Deep Space Nine*
business. The Federation takes a dim view of any
discussion about your lost ship. They are quite protective of it. Any type of communiqué about it must
be referred to them. Commander Sisko could tell you
no more than I could. I'm merely trying, as you say, to
cut through the official red tape and save you some
time."

"Thank you, Major." Kidath smiled back at her. "I appreciate your help—and your surprisingly deep knowledge of my people's greatest tragedy and greatest hope."

His image winked off her screen. She clenched her fists and then opened them again, biting back a curse. She hadn't fooled him at all. He had made that clear from his last remark. He knew that Commander Sisko had taken the *Defiant* in search of the *Nibix*. She would have to let Odo know there was a leak somewhere.

She reached for her comm badge when the computer screen filled, letting her know that a special security-coded message was coming in from Starfleet.

She responded to the hail with the proper code, and Admiral Wolfe's face appeared.

"Major Kira," he said without preamble, "I understand that Commander Sisko has taken the *Defiant* on a mission to find the *Nibix*. Is that so?"

Kira felt like a child caught with her hands in someone else's mess. "Yes, sir," she said.

"His timing couldn't be worse," the admiral said, looking at someone beyond the screen.

"Commander Sisko believed that he had to act before anyone else did," Kira said slowly.

"I am not questioning his decision," the admiral said, "although I do wish this had waited a year or two. What are his chances of success?"

"I know little about the *Nibix*, sir," Kira said, "except what I learned this afternoon. However, the commander and Lieutenant Dax have a great deal of knowledge about the ship, and they are convinced—"

"That's enough, Major. You've answered me. Have Commander Sisko contact me when he returns and not before. We can't even trust secured channels on this thing."

Clearly, Kira thought. "Admiral, a moment before I received your communiqué, Jiber Kidath, a member of the Jibetian High Council, contacted me. He wanted to know if Commander Sisko was searching for the *Nibix.* I did not answer him, sir, but he took the fact that I had any knowledge at all about the *Nibix* as an affirmative."

Admiral Wolfe nodded. "He would with the information I'm sure he has."

"To be honest, sir," Kira said, "I have no idea how he or you even knew to ask the question. Commander Sisko and I thought we had this mission under wraps."

"You obviously have a security breach, Major. I suggest you find it."

"Yes, sir," Kira said.

"We are sending three starships to your area. They are to be used as you and Commander Sisko see fit. Lock down the station and be prepared for anything. Understood?"

"Yes, sir," Kira said.

"And one more thing," the admiral said. "If you have not contacted the *Defiant* since they arrived at their destination, do not do so now unless absolutely needed. No point in taking any undue chances."

Kira nodded. "Understood."

"Good luck," the admiral said. "There is a lot riding on the outcome of this."

The screen blinked out, and then the files on the *Nibix* returned. Kira took her hands off the desk. Wet palm prints marred the surface. The leading edge of the storm had just hit. She had no idea how the news got out, but it had. It was time to get prepared. If the admiral ordered her to lock down the station, then she'd lock it down tighter than it had ever been locked.

She stood and went through the door into Ops on a run, shouting orders as she went.

CHAPTER
8

JULIAN BASHIR never expected to find himself in the commander's chair of a starship. Heading sickbay, yes, but the commander's chair, never. He'd had the training in the Academy—they all had—but medical officers were allowed to cut some of the niceties of command short while they concentrated on six semesters of rudimentary alien anatomy and two years of starship medicine, or, as it was called among the medical students, six ways to save a dying captain using a tricorder, a thermometer, and a comm badge.

His first forty-five minutes in the chair had been astonishingly easy. The ensigns Commander Sisko had assigned to the mission seemed to know the routine. Bashir had only to sit nervously in the chair, monitor the life signs on his scanner, and wait for his next order.

The calm was too good to last.

"Sir?" Ensign Coleman's cautious voice drawled the word. Long and low and uncertain. "I think we have a problem."

"What is it, Ensign?" Bashir leaned back in the chair. At the word *problem,* his heart rate had increased and his respiration became shallow. Panic, in layman's terms. Something he could not allow in this chair any more than he could allow it in the infirmary. He forced himself to breathe deeply.

"I've been monitoring the Cardassian border, sir, and well, something strange is going on."

No time for panic reduction. He'd have to run at full adrenaline. "Ensign, by the time you tell me what's happening, the crisis will be over."

"Ah, yes, sir. Sorry, sir. But it seems—"

At that moment, Commander Sisko's voice boomed over the open channel. "Doctor, I need you here immediately."

"Commander, just a moment. We seem to have a situation here." Bashir glanced at Ensign Coleman, waiting for an answer. Commander Sisko did not respond, which Bashir took as the moment he had requested. "Well, Ensign?"

"A fleet of Cardassian ships is massing on the border. Sir. I think," Ensign Coleman said.

"You think?" Bashir's voice rose a notch too high.

"I have the reading, too, sir," Ensign Kathé said. "There's no doubt. We have a fleet of Cardassian ships on that border. They're combat ready. They seem to see us."

"Doctor!" Sisko's voice boomed from below. "I said now."

"Forgive me, sir," Bashir said. "We have a slight—"

"Ensign Kathé can handle the *Defiant* for a few minutes. I need you here."

"With all due respect to Ensign Kathé," Bashir said, nodding at her, "I believe someone with more experience needs to be on the bridge. A fleet of Cardassian warships are gathering on the border. They seem to be interested in us, sir."

"The Cardassians?" Bashir could hear the frown in Sisko's voice.

"Sir," said Ensign Coleman, "they're changing position."

"Should we cloak?" Ensign Dodds asked.

"Not yet," Bashir said. He needed time to think, and he had no time. Maybe he should have taken only five semesters of rudimentary alien physiology.

"Doctor," Sisko said, "I still need you down here with all the equipment you can carry. Bring anything you need for cold-sleep revival. Ensign Dodds, I want you to assemble and beam down three days' worth of supplies to Dax's coordinates, along with heating equipment and warm cloths. I need that immediately. I assume it will take you a few minutes, Doctor."

"Yes, sir, but the fleet—"

"I'll beam aboard in two minutes. Ensign Kathé, be prepared to leave orbit. Doctor, I expect you to be down here in three. Sisko out."

And that was how command decisions were made. Bashir could speak that quickly only in the infirmary. He was already moving toward the lift. It would take him nearly three minutes to gather his equipment. Ensign Dodds was ahead of him, running at full speed. Fortunately for her, the survival gear, including dried food, was all kept in one place.

"Ensign Kathé," Bashir said, "you have the comm

until Commander Sisko arrives. Ensign Coleman, keep an eye on that fleet."

And then Bashir left the bridge.

Three minutes and eight seconds later he beamed into the dead ship below.

Kira hadn't stopped moving since she spoke to Admiral Wolfe. She hadn't located the leak, but then she hadn't really tried. She needed to prevent anything else from happening first.

She had had brief contact with Odo before whipping up a storm in Ops. Fortunately the day crew included Tappan, O'Brien's right-hand man. Kira was terrified that with her luck the last few hours, everything in the station would break down as well.

She had stopped at the science station and was double-checking the space around the station herself, not trusting anyone else to this task, while giving orders to the crew around her.

"Are all the ships locked into docking clamps?" she demanded.

"Major, you just gave the order a moment ago," Ensign Sneed said from his post near Communications.

"They should be locked by now, Ensign," Kira said. "This is all high priority. We have no time for mistakes or for daydreaming."

"They're locked," Sneed said.

"Good," she said. "Mr. Tappan, have the crews returned to their ships?"

"Except for a group of Caxtonians that won't leave one of Quark's holosuites," Tappan said. He was hunched over the communications panel, his brown hair curled around his neck. "I've sent Security to pull them out."

"Tell Security I want those Caxtonians on their ship in five minutes."

"Already done, sir," Tappan said.

She missed the regular crew. She missed Dax, if truth be told. But Dax was on the *Defiant,* exploring lost ships for treasure, while Kira had the entire station to deal with.

She brought the screens up. "Mr. Tappan, I want this station to stand at yellow alert. Notify me the moment the *Defiant* returns."

"Yes, Major," he said. The lights around Ops came on, and the yellow alert sounded.

The hair rose on the back of Kira's neck. She was hoping for the *Defiant* at any moment now, hoping against hope that they hadn't found anything, that this was a false emergency, and that the Caxtonian lied. But judging by Quark's interest, Dax's silence, and Sisko's ill-disguised excitement, this sighting was probably not a false emergency.

Two ensigns were monitoring interstation activity. Tappan was helping Kira monitor all communications. Odo was doing the same from Security. Three starships were on the way, and Kira would wager an entire month's pay that the Jibetians were as well. If Sisko didn't return, she would have to be the diplomat. Odo wasn't capable of it, and there was no one else with the knowledge to do so. Kira wished she had time to return to Sisko's office and finish her studies on the *Nibix.* But she didn't.

Time had run out.

She hit her comm badge. "Odo?"

"Yes, Major?" Odo always managed to sound as if he were doing nothing, as if he had all the time in the world. She envied that trait.

"Is everything locked down?"

"We got the Caxtonians out of Quark's holosuite. They're going to their ship now. I've posted guards on every major intersection, and of course, I put a security screen around Quark's. He and Rom are locked inside, out of harm's way."

Kira laughed. "Good thinking," she said. "Let me know when everything is buttoned up tight."

She wished she could ask him if he'd found the source of the leaks, but that had better wait until she reached a place where they could talk in private.

Odo signed off. Kira scanned the entire station, verifying what he told her. Then she turned her scans on Bajor. Everything looked normal there.

"Major," Tappan said. He, too, managed that calm drawl. But, of course, he didn't know all that was at stake. She wasn't sure if she did either. "I just ran a long-range scan and picked up something odd."

She stiffened. More trouble.

"A fleet of Cardassian warships are massing on the Cardassian border."

"A fleet?" Her old battle instincts rose. "Where are they? Are they headed for Bajor?"

"No, Major. They seem to going away from Bajor as if they're going to head into deep space. But there's nothing in that direction."

Except a red-star system filled with asteroids. Kira cursed softly. "Any sign of those Federation starships?"

"None, sir."

She leaned against the console. What would it mean to the Cardassians to discover the *Nibix?* The wealth? Or were they simply monitoring the *Defiant?* But that made no sense. If they were just monitoring the *Defiant,* they wouldn't have an entire fleet pointed in its direction. Maybe control of the *Nibix* would give them some power in their dealings with the Federation. It would clearly give them power in this quadrant. Power they didn't need.

Unless she was making too much of the *Nibix*. Maybe the Cardassians were taking this moment, without Sisko on board, without the *Defiant,* to make a move against the station.

Her mouth was dry. They should know by now that Kira Nerys was more than match for them.

Maybe they thought she was on the *Defiant,* too.

None of this made any sense. Better not to think. She had learned that a long time ago in the resistance. It was better to act.

"Major," Tappan said, "the Cardassian fleet is moving and has changed course. It's heading this way."

"Battle stations," Kira said. "Red alert."

At last a fight. Something she understood. Something she did very, very well.

CHAPTER
9

IT HAD TAKEN Jake and Nog a few wrong turns in the maze of narrow passageways and crawl spaces that led over, under, and behind rooms along the Promenade before they found a small spy area looking into Quark's Bar. The cleanliness of the passageways bothered Jake. He almost wished for the gray dust to return. He hoped these passageways had a different ventilation system because they overlooked the main part of the Promenade, although part of him wondered if they weren't clean because they overlooked the part of the Promenade still in use.

As they wound their way toward Quark's, he had mentioned, in a whisper, that perhaps they should find Chief O'Brien and report this maze of tunnels. But this time, Nog was the one who wanted to go on. He had become enamored with the idea of finding a place to spy on his uncle, a place that would guarantee

Nog would never go home to too much work or too much fighting again.

When they found the room, its size surprised Jake. After that much work, he had expected to find a room the size of the first spy hole. This one was no bigger than a storage closet, and it had only one gratelike spy hole. A small stepladder led up to it. The spy hole smelled like Romulan ale and Caxtonian sweat, a nauseating combination.

"This has got to be it," Nog whispered gleefully.

"I think we should find Chief O'Brien." Anything to get away from the smell. Jake was willing to bet that this tiny room trapped all the noxious odors from Quark's.

"Of course you do," Nog whispered. "Now that I've finally found something good about this place."

"That's not it," Jake whispered. "I'm getting nervous."

"Maybe because you're making too much noise." Nog climbed on the ladder. When he reached the top, he stood on tiptoe, trying to see through the grate. He couldn't even reach it. He braced himself to jump, but Jake stopped him, figuring a crash of Ferengi and ladder would probably bring the entire station to the room.

"Someday," Nog whispered, "I'm going to build a place built for people my height."

Jake frowned. Another detail fell into place. This was clearly Cardassian built then. If Quark had made the tunnels, everything would have been Ferengi height. "Let me see if I can look out this one."

Nog climbed down, and Jake climbed up. The ladder was sturdier than it looked. A bead of sweat ran down his face. The room was hot and had grown hotter since they arrived. It was clearly built for one spy, not two.

Even with the ladder, the spy grate was too high for Jake to see through. But he could reach the top with his hands.

"Boost me up," Nog whispered. "If you hold me, I'd be able to see."

Jake didn't relish balancing Nog on the ladder top, but the quicker he tried, the quicker they could leave and inform the chief of the maze behind the Promenade.

Nog climbed the ladder. Jake backed to the edge, braced himself against the wall, and cupped his hands. Nog stepped in them, his heavy shoes digging into Jake's palms. Nog pulled himself up to the spy grate and hung there for what seemed like an eternity before he spoke.

"This is some kind of trick."

"What is?"

Their whispers had grown softer, as if they both expected someone to overhear them.

"My uncle's bar is empty. It's never empty at this time of day. This is a trick."

Jake wished he could see.

"What's going on?" he whispered.

"Nothing. There's not even a Dabo girl by the table. No one's—" Nog stopped speaking suddenly as the voice of his uncle filled the spy hole.

"They can't keep my bar closed forever. And to keep us prisoner! I'll complain to Commander Sisko when he returns. Maybe then he'll do something about Odo."

"I thought this had nothing to do with Odo." The second voice belonged to Nog's father, Rom. "I thought it had to do with that statue—"

Quark's gasp echoed in the enclosed space. "Who did you mention the statue to?"

"No one, brother."

Nog signaled that he wanted to get down. When Jake lowered him, Nog didn't meet his gaze.

"You had to have told someone."

"I didn't, brother. But there were a lot of people in the bar at the time."

"Well, I don't like this," Quark said. "It's interfering with my profits. I'll have to take it out of your salary . . ."

Their voices faded. Nog had reached the floor, his head bowed. Jake climbed down.

"Something's wrong," Jake whispered. "My dad would never close the bar. Or trap your uncle inside."

"Well, he did," Nog whispered back. "They'll kill each other in there, trapped together like that."

Jake put a hand on his friend's back. "No, they won't. They grew up together. Your uncle needs your dad. They'll be all right."

"I hope so," Nog said. "What do you think's going on?"

"I don't know," Jake said, "but I think we'd better find out. Let's go back."

They left through the same door they had entered. Nog led the way, jogging through two rooms and one crawl space. The boys emerged into a small gray room with no spy holes and two identical passages heading off in two different directions. Jake remembered coming through here but hadn't paid much attention.

"Which one?" Nog asked, the panic starting to creep slowly into his voice.

Now Jake wished for the dusty corridors where following their tracks would have been no problem. But in these tunnels and rooms, there was no dust, and he wasn't sure which tunnel they had come out of the first time.

"Doesn't matter," he said, shoving past Nog and leading down the tunnel to the right. "If we pick the wrong one we just come back here and take the other."

"I'd like to get out of here today," Nog muttered.

"We will," Jake said. "There has to be more than one way out of this place. We just have to find it."

He closed his eyes, imagined the layout of the Promenade and then tried to insert it near the tunnels. Then, making his best guess, he followed the tunnel to the right.

At first the way looked familiar. Then they passed through two unfamiliar closet-sized rooms and a long crawl space. Jake was almost convinced they hadn't come this way the first time.

"Why does it always take longer to leave than it does to arrive?" Nog asked.

"Because we're paying attention this time," Jake said.

The crawl space opened into a large, well-lit room. As Jake levered himself down, he promised himself that they would turn around if the room proved unfamiliar.

As Nog landed beside him, Jake surveyed the room.

He had never been there before. He knew that the moment he examined it. The room had no view holes, even though it did have a chair and what appeared to be a supplies cabinet. Three narrow passages lead from it, counting the one Jake and Nog had just come from. The air here was cool and filtered. It had the processed scent of some of the maintenance areas in the lower decks.

But that wasn't what made it different. The wall directly across from Jake made the room different.

He tapped Nog on the shoulder and pointed. Nog turned.

"Oh, no," he whispered.

They both stared at the bank of panels lining the wall. At least ten of those panels were viewscreens. Jake walked up to them. They didn't appear original to the station, although they were of Cardassian design. They appeared almost new.

"This is a Cardassian spy hole," Nog said. "I've seen holos of these in my uncle's programs. There's one he's kept for Cardassian use: The Secret Conquerors of Bajor, where—"

"I don't want to know," Jake said. He tried to ignore most of the uses of the holosuites. He stared up at the empty viewscreens, his own image reflecting back at him. A streak of dirt ran along his face, and his clothes looked like he'd been playing in the mud.

"We're the only ones who know about this," he said, and that knowledge made his heart thump. "We've got to get out of here."

"Where is out?" Nog asked.

"Let's go back to the room over your uncle's bar. The second tunnel out of there should take us back." And the sooner the better. Jake crouched and cupped his hands so that he could boost Nog back into the crawl space.

The light overhead suddenly turned red. Then, with a cranking noise that filled the room, steel panels slid from the walls and slammed closed all three entrances. The echo of the booms made both Nog and Jake cover their ears.

Then the wall of monitors flickered into life. One

showed the Ops center. Another two screens were different views of the Promenade. Another was of Jake's father's office. Screen after screen popped on, revealing all the important areas of the station. And only Ops had people in view.

"We're trapped!" Nog shouted. He ran for the steel walls and began examining them, looking for a way out. Jake frowned at the monitors—something was wrong about them—but he didn't have time to think about it. He went to the steel walls, too, and looked for an opening mechanism.

The red light made everything seem as if it were bathed in blood. His own skin had a reddish cast, making it appear unfamiliar, not like his skin at all. He got metal splinters in his fingers as he worked the edge of the walls.

He found nothing.

Nog had moved to the monitors, looking in all the panels. "There's got to be a way to open these walls," he said. He could be clever about mechanical things when he wanted to be. Jake took out the tricorder he had slung around his neck and did a quick reading to see if it showed anything. From what he could tell, there were only monitors here. The controls for the door were somewhere else. Probably outside the room.

"If we could figure out how we triggered it, we can get out," Nog said.

Jake watched his friend, then his gaze was drawn to the monitors. They looked like they were running on real time, not some kind of tape. That meant the system tapped into the station's existing communications systems to get this kind of picture. If it happened all the time, O'Brien would have found it by now. This place only ran at odd moments, moments of crisis, moments when . . .

Jake studied the scenes in the monitors. Odo's office was empty. So was his dad's. And Kira was running across Ops, shouting orders. "I don't think we triggered it," Jake said slowly.

"We must have," Nog said. "Why else would it trap us?"

"The red light," Jake said.

"A warning system?"

Jake nodded. "Our warning system. The station's on red alert."

That statement made Nog stand up. "It can't be."

"It is. Look at Ops."

"So that's why my uncle's bar is empty."

"And why everyone looks so busy in Ops."

They stared at the monitors for a minute.

"Where's your dad?" Nog asked quietly.

"I don't know," Jake said.

Nog went back to the panels near the monitors and began to open the ones that he could. "Come on," he said. "Help me. We'll die in here if we don't find a way out."

"I don't think so," Jake said, sinking in the chair. "I don't think we'll die unless they blow up the station. I think we've found the safest place of all."

And somehow that thought terrified him even more.

CHAPTER
10

COMMANDER BENJAMIN SISKO strode on deck of the *Defiant*. He had discarded his deep-cold gloves and stripped his uniform to its essentials. Still, he felt the chill that had gone into his bones on the *Nibix*. It felt as if he would never be warm again.

Ensign Kathé vacated the commander's chair the moment she saw him and returned to her post. Ensign Coleman nodded a welcome, his features tight with fear. Ensign Dodds was staring at her monitor, her fingers moving on occasion. Ensigns Harsch and Ba'M'eel watched him from battle stations.

Sisko took the commander's chair, wondering if his reluctance showed. It had taken all his personal strength to leave the *Nibix* especially after discovering that the Supreme Ruler was still alive. His stomach jumped at the thought, and he thanked all the gods on all the planets that Dax was still down there. She at least understood—on a deep level—the importance of the discovery. O'Brien saw the entire thing as an engineering challenge, and Bashir would look upon it as a medical curiosity, not the potential intergalactic disaster it was.

"Is Dr. Bashir on the surface?" Sisko asked.

"He arrived a moment ago," Ensign Dodds said. "The supplies arrived just before him."

"Excellent," Sisko said. Cardassians. He hated the sound of that. And he didn't know what had tipped them off. Obviously, Kira and Odo hadn't been able to seal off the station quickly enough. It meant potential disaster if Sisko couldn't hold them off.

"Ensign Coleman, have the Cardassians noted the *Defiant?*"

"I'm almost certain of it, sir," the ensign said. Almost certain was the best Sisko would get from this cautious ensign. "As you were beaming up, sensors picked up a long-range scan. It came from their direction."

"Good," Sisko said, and Ensign Kathé looked at him in surprise. Of all the ensigns on this voyage, she was the one with the most hope of taking a leadership position in Starfleet. He noted the way her sharp features caught every nuance of his command. "Ensign Kathé, plot a course back to *Deep Space Nine.*"

She whirled, her rainbow mane flickering in the light. Her fingers danced across the console. "Done, sir."

"Ahead warp factor five." He leaned back in the chair as the ensign followed his command. The *Defiant* responded immediately. She was a wonderful ship, with tremendous capability. He only wished he had more opportunities to use her. Although he could have forgone this one. His heart and his dreams were back on the *Nibix* with that green glowing staff.

He forced himself to concentrate. As the stars whizzed by on the viewscreen, he mentally charted the coordinates himself. Sometimes he felt as if he had this part of space memorized.

"In ten seconds, Ensign Coleman, I want you to cloak us."

"Aye, sir," the ensign said.

"Commander," Ensign Harsch said from his battle station, "the Cardassian fleet has crossed the border. They're pursuing us."

Sisko nodded. They would do that. The only logical place he could run to was *Deep Space Nine.* They would expect him to go there. And they would pursue at leisure. Losing him on this voyage would be something they expected.

Their presence made him nervous. If they went after the *Nibix,* they would be in violation of the peace treaty.

"We're cloaked, sir," Ensign Coleman said.

Sisko turned to Ensign Kathé. "Swing us in a wide arc and place us between the fleet and the *Nibix.*"

"Aye, sir," she said.

The screen in front of Sisko showed the change of direction as the *Defiant* moved around into position. No one spoke on the bridge and the tension seemed to grow with the silence. Sisko was pleased with his young crew. He had picked five of the best. They were responding well to an unusual situation.

"Sir," said Ensign Ba'M'eel, the only Orion on the crew. His uniform clashed with his green skin. "The Cardassians are continuing toward the station."

"Mr. Harsch, conduct a full-range scan of the

asteroid belt. I want to know if any ships are hiding there, waiting to find the *Nibix*. Assist him in his efforts, Dodds."

Both ensigns bent over the task. They worked furiously—a little too quickly actually—but that was to be expected from such a young crew as this one.

"No, sir. The system is clear," Harsch said. He was barely out of the Academy, a thin blond human who had chosen a deep-space assignment over working his way up the ranks of a starship.

"My readings are the same, Commander," Dodds said.

Sisko hoped his spur-of-the-moment decision was the right one. He also hoped Kira was ready for a fleet of Cardassians to descend upon her. It amazed him that the station could go from calm to near disaster in a few short hours. He hadn't even had a chance to tell Jake he was leaving.

Someone would bring him up to speed.

"Ensign Kathé, follow the Cardassian ships to a point exactly halfway between the *Nibix* and the station."

"Yes, sir." She frowned as she plotted in the coordinates. The *Defiant* turned sharply and then righted itself. "Done, sir."

"Good," Sisko said. "Hold this position. Mr. Harsch, continue monitoring the asteroid belt. I want to know if anything changes nearby."

The crew bent over their tasks. Now the tough part of the mission would occur. These young ensigns would realize that they were part of a space battle, and they would learn that the fighting was easy. Waiting was hard.

And Sisko was prepared to wait days if he had to.

Protecting the *Nibix* was his top priority. Kira would take care of the station, and the Supreme Ruler's life was in Dr. Bashir's hands.

What Sisko wouldn't give to still be on the *Nibix,* walking the corridors while Bashir did his work. Sisko could still remember the glow of the green staff beneath his gloved hands. He had read thousands of articles over the years about what would occur when the *Nibix* was found. Almost all of them had assumed everyone aboard would be dead. The handful of other articles, written by less reputable scholars, speculated that the *Nibix* had found its planet, and a long-removed descendent of the Supreme Ruler lived there, awaiting discovery. But not one article speculated that the same Supreme Ruler who was overthrown eight hundred years ago would still be alive.

And if Bashir was half the doctor that Sisko knew him to be, the Supreme Ruler would be up and moving around very shortly. What would they do then?

Sisko had no idea.

And he wouldn't even allow himself to think about the possibility of the Supreme Ruler dying as Bashir tried to revive him.

Half an hour ago, Sisko had thought finding the Supreme Ruler alive was his worst nightmare. Having the Supreme Ruler die on them would be much, much worse.

Bashir had expected a lost ship to be dark. The bright light over the cold-sleep chamber was a bigger surprise to him than the chamber itself. He had seen a hundred cold-sleep chambers, some in the Federation's space museum and even more in the rudimentary ships he'd practiced on in his training.

In his sophomore year of medical school, he had devoted an entire semester to the science of cold and cold sleep to fulfill his history of medicine requirement.

Nothing had prepared him for the grandeur here.

Nor the cold.

O'Brien was crouched near the side of the cold-sleep chamber. Dax was holding a tricorder next to him, pointing it sideways in a most unusual manner. They hadn't unpacked the supplies that the commander had beamed down for them.

Bashir shivered in the chill, reached into the supplies, and pulled out deep-cold jackets for all of them. With the Cardassian threat above, there was no telling how long they would be down here. He would make certain they rationed their three days of supplies.

"Well, here you are, Julian," O'Brien said as if they hadn't seen each other in days instead of hours. "This chamber is still working."

Bashir picked up his equipment. He glanced at the two cold-sleep cocoons near the platform. One look at the occupants told him they had died a long, long time ago.

"Is it empty?" Bashir asked.

"If it were empty, do you think the commander would have sent for you?"

"Well, he should know that the odds of reviving an eight-hundred-year-old cold sleeper are about as good as you winning two dart games in a row." Bashir mounted the platform.

"I won twice this afternoon," O'Brien said.

"Thanks to a riot and a few other distractions." He set his equipment down on the opposite side of the cold-sleep chamber and then pulled out his tricorder. His hands were freezing. He pulled gloves out of his pocket, gripped them with his teeth, and tugged them on finger by finger.

Dax had turned her tricorder toward him. "Forgive me, Julian," she said, "but the commander insisted that we record all our efforts here."

"Including my first statement, I suppose," Bashir said, feeling a flush creep into his cheeks.

Dax smiled. That soft smile always made her a vision of loveliness. "I'm afraid so."

He shook his head slightly, then glanced at the opaque lid of the cold-sleep chamber. The man inside belonged to a race Julian had never seen before. On the trip, he had brushed up on Jibetian physiology, but his material was on current Jibetian anatomy, not anatomy from eight hundred years before. He didn't remember much about the shallow-ridged cheek-bones, although he did remember reading about the redundant internal organs that had been common among the royal family. Some scholars claimed those organs were responsible for the family's longevity.

"Dr. Bashir," Dax said, "You'll have to explain each procedure. This tricorder isn't set up for in-depth recording."

"I'm not going to talk my way through each stage," Bashir said. "It would take too much time."

"But you'll at least have to give us an overview."

He glanced at her, biting back his annoyed comment for the sake of posterity. She was positioned well behind the tricorder, and so when she shrugged, she added a bit of mischeviousness to her movements.

She was amazingly joyful for a woman trapped on a crashed space ship, eight hundred years old.

Bashir didn't want to think about that. If he were Dax, he would be exploring the ship. She didn't know the great luck she had, being able to see all these new places. He beamed down for crisis after crisis, rarely got a chance to explore his surroundings, and usually had to concentrate on some new type of medical emergency.

Like this one.

Something bothered him about this cold-sleep chamber. But the technology was just unfamiliar enough to his Federation-trained eyes that he couldn't quite pinpoint the problem right away.

He flicked on his medical tricorder, then nodded toward Dax. "I am going to do a basic medical scan of the man inside this chamber. I need to make an overall assessment of his condition."

O'Brien had almost disappeared on the side of the chamber. He seemed to be working on something as well, probably examining the technology to see why it was still working. Bashir couldn't concentrate on that, nor could he think about the reasons behind Dax's intensity or the commander's unusual order to record their proceedings.

Instead, he focused on the readings from his medical tricorder. He hit a button that would record the readings for later use. If the commander could be that cautious, so could Bashir. The findings were just as he suspected, but for the sake of the unseen people who would review this case, he reached into his bag and pulled out a different tricorder, running the scan all over again.

Then he shook his head. "This man has massive cell damage from eight hundred years of cold sleep. I doubt anyone will ever be able to revive him."

Dax's expression changed from mischievous to one of pure horror. O'Brien popped his head up from the side of the chamber. "You can't make that kind of diagnosis from two tricorder scans, Julian," Dax said.

"I'm afraid I can, Lieutenant," he said, keeping everything formal. "Cells are cells, whether they belong to Jibetians or Trills. Everything in the universe does run along the same plan. Cells have a particular life span. A cold-sleep chamber slows that span, but it does little else to lengthen it. Had this man slept the requisite number of years planned for the mission, he would have awakened aged only a few months. I dare say he's been here much longer than they ever planned for. His cells have the equivalent of freezer burn."

"Doctor," O'Brien said, "that's not *any* patient. That's the Supreme Ruler of eighty worlds."

Bashir started. They could have warned him about this before he came down. "Nonetheless," he said, "my analysis stands. It will take nothing short of a miracle to revive this man."

"Well," Dax said, her voice jaunty even though her expression was haunted, "time to add miracles to your repertoire, Doctor."

"This would be much simpler if we could beam this chamber onto the *Defiant* and take the whole thing back to the station," Bashir said. "If we did that, I might have a chance at saving this man. As it is, you're expecting me to do delicate work with thermometers and comm badges."

"With what?" Dax asked, stunned.

"It's just an expression," Bashir said. He rummaged in his bag, hoping he had brought everything he needed.

"I'm sorry, Julian," O'Brien said, "but I've been examining this chamber, and even if we wanted to beam it to the *Defiant,* we couldn't. This platform only carries half of the systems that are keeping this man alive. The rest are imbedded in the floors and walls of the room, and this room would take up more space in the *Defiant* than we have available. Even if we had the opportunity to beam it aboard, we simply couldn't. You'll have to work with the equipment you brought along."

Despite the cold, Bashir felt nervous sweat form on his back. He felt like he had when he took the final test for his medical license, the day after he had finished his finals at the Academy. He wanted to practice frontier medicine. It didn't get any more frontier than this.

"Then, Chief, please get the cold-sleep equipment I brought with me. I'll need your help rigging this up." Bashir glanced at Dax's tricorder. "We may have already had our miracle," he said, addressing his remarks to the tiny piece of equipment in her hand. "No cold-sleep system was ever designed for this many centuries. The fact that it even works is astounding."

"I'll say." O'Brien's voice echoed from below the platform.

Bashir removed three devices he hadn't used in a long, long time. Time to forget the impossibility, forget the expectations, forget the importance of his patient. It was time to get to work.

"Well, your highness," Bashir said softly, turning back to the cold-sleep chamber. "Let's see what I can do to save your life. All eight hundred years of it."

CHAPTER
11

THE BAR WAS UGLY when it was empty. Quark could see the ripped felt on the Dabo table, the jagged edges where the chair legs had been repaired, the missing paint on the walls. Rom was on his hands, scrubbing the floor. It hadn't been cleaned since the riot. When Dax returned, Quark would charge her for every single drink.

And then some.

The red alert lights flashed in the empty hall. The force field shimmered across the door. That hadn't been necessary. Quark would have stayed in the bar if someone asked him. But no one asked him. They had imprisoned him. With Rom. And no customers. They'd even let the Dabo girl go.

"Where do you suppose Nog is?" Rom asked.

"If I knew, I'd bring him here and have him scrub the bar with an ear pick. We needed that boy this afternoon. I can't believe you allow him to come and go as he pleases."

"He's almost an adult," Rom said. "He's going to go to the Academy."

"Which is the dumbest thing I've ever heard. Where's the profit in that, Rom? His exposure to humans has taught him the wrong values, despite everything I've done for him."

"I'm proud of Nog," Rom said. He had his back to Quark, his arm moving frantically as he worked at getting spilled sweet nectar off the floor.

"You would be. You haven't a profit-making bone in your body. If you did, this bar would do better."

"This bar is yours, Brother. I merely help you."

Quark sighed and sat on a barstool. He put his chin in his hand. "It's not fair that they've trapped us in here. Odo only did it because Commander Sisko is gone. It has nothing to do with the red alert. It's just Odo. And I won't stand for it."

Rom sat on his haunches. He didn't say anything, but Quark recognized the warning expression on Rom's face.

"What? I figure they can use my services. The red alert probably has something to do with the discovery, right? So they'll need my knowledge. They just don't realize it yet."

"Brother—"

"And they'll be grateful. Very grateful."

"Brother—"

"Yeah," he muttered. "Grateful." He reached across the bar and tapped the comm switch.

"Odo, listen. You can't imprison us in here. We have valuable knowledge that could—" He stopped and frowned. His voice sounded wrong. "Odo?" He flicked the switch again. "Major?" Again. "Odo?" And again. "Anybody?"

Quark stood and examined the panel behind the bar.

"I was trying to tell you, Brother," Rom said. "They isolated us when they turned on the force field."

"They can't do that. What if we were in trouble? What if they needed our help?"

"I thought you said they did need our help." Rom was standing now, his scrub brush on the floor near his feet. A large sudsy puddle pooled beneath a table and began to trickle toward the stairs.

Quark pounded the intercom one more time and got no response. He slapped his hand on the bar.

"That does it." Quark went around behind the bar and pulled open a drawer. "I let more wealth than any Ferengi's ever seen slip through my fingers, and as a reward I get locked up here with you. I don't care what Commander Sisko threatened. Nothing is worse than this."

"Brother, you gave your word," Rom said.

"A Ferengi's word is worth nothing without profit," Quark said. "If I get the wealth off that ship, I will be more powerful than the Grand Nagus. I won't need this silly little bar and I won't have to listen to Commander Benjamin Sisko."

Quark riffled through the drawer and finally pulled out a pistol-shaped object covered with Ferengi designs. He slid it across the bar.

"Take that," Quark said. "We're getting out of here."

The puddle had pooled around Rom's boots, but he didn't move. "I don't believe in violence, brother."

"I'm not saying you should," Quark snapped. "Who are you going to shoot anyway? Me?"

"I can't help you," Rom said. "It's not right."

Quark glanced at the tool on the bar. "It's a cutting torch, you idiot. Now pick it up and come with me. I'm going after that treasure ship."

"If I help you, will I get a share of the profits?"

"You'll get the bar," Quark said. "Now take the torch."

Rom crossed his arms. His hands were red and puckered from the strength of the soap. "I don't want the bar. I want a share of the profits."

"For what?" Quark asked. "You don't know how to invest. You'd just waste the money on frivolous things."

"I want it to pay for Rom's schooling."

Quark gaped at him. The entire world had turned around. Schooling? The next thing Rom would tell him was that he had found a good Ferengi woman and was to dress her and give her a home on DS9.

"See?" Quark said. "I told you that you'd spend it on something frivolous. You can have the bar. It's worth a little bit of money. And I won't be needing it any more."

"If you give me the bar," Rom said, "I'll sell it."

"I won't care what you do with it, dimwit," Quark said. "I'll be the richest man in the galaxy."

He grabbed the cutting torch himself and tossed it at Rom. Rom caught it with both hands. Quark went to the wall near the Dabo tables, then glanced at Rom to make certain he was following. Rom was. He was leaving boot-sized footprints on the sticky floor. Quark winced and then remembered that it wouldn't matter once he escaped. Nothing in the bar would matter.

When Rom reached his side, Quark pointed to a plain metal bulkhead. "Cut a small hole in there, chest high, but big enough for us to crawl through."

"We can't tunnel our way to the docks," Rom said. "It'll take weeks."

"We don't have to tunnel, dear Brother," Quark said. "The Cardassians already did that for us. There's a series of spy tunnels behind this wall that extend all the way through the Promenade, into the main guest quarters, and around Ops. The first rule of Cardassian life. Trust no one. They used to spy on their own through that grate up there." He pointed up at what looked to be a return air duct.

"How did you find out about it?" Rom asked.

Quark laughed. "I've always said knowledge equals profits, Rom. You'd do well to remember that. And it's my business to know everything about this bar."

Rom still held back, clutching the cutting tool. "What if we see Cardassians in there?"

"We won't, you idiot. Those tunnels have been deserted since the Cardassians left. And it's not like the Federation to use them, even if they did discover them." Quark pointed to the wall. "Now cut. And don't make the hole too big. I want to cover it up with a chair when this is all done."

The atmosphere on the bridge of the *Defiant* was tense. Sisko hadn't worked with a crew this young since he trained cadets years before. He had forgotten the terror new crew members felt when doing new tasks and facing new challenges.

He rarely felt terror any more.

He was too experienced for it and had too much control. Now he knew that new challenges were inevitable, and mistakes were part of learning. A good commander faced the challenges and moved beyond the mistakes.

There had already been more challenges than he wanted on this mission and not quite the normal number of mistakes with a rookie crew. That knowledge made him nervous. Something would change, and when it did, he was afraid it wouldn't be in his favor.

"We're at full stop," Ensign Kathé said. She had maneuvered the *Defiant* halfway between the *Nibix* and *Deep Space Nine*. They were under cloak, monitoring the Cardassians bearing down on the station. So far the Cardassians had assumed the *Defiant* had returned to the station. Sisko hoped they would continue to believe that.

"I want the entire bridge crew to be scanning for anything unusual out there," Sisko said. Had it been his normal staff, he wouldn't have told them. But he had to reaffirm everything here for his own peace of mind.

He did feel a little out of control on this one. Kira and Odo were responsible for the station now, for everyone on it, including Jake.

Dax, O'Brien, and Bashir were responsible for the *Nibix,* for the Supreme Ruler, and for future relations with the Jibetians.

And Sisko, the man nominally in control, was the one stuck in space, a glorified bodyguard, waiting.

"Sir," Ensign Dodds said, "two starships are approaching *Deep Space Nine* at full warp."

"Federation ships?" Sisko asked, his mouth dry.

"Aye, sir," she said.

"Sir, they're hailing the station,' Ensign Coleman said. "The *Starship Madison* will arrive in about a half an hour, followed by the *Starship Idaho* an hour later. They expect to rendezvous with the *Starship Bosewell* in a few hours."

Sisko let out the breath he had been holding. The ships arrived too soon for Kira to have contacted them. The Federation had sent them. But he didn't know why.

"Any communications as to their mission?" Sisko asked.

Ensign Coleman shook his head. "No, sir. But Major Kira just informed them that the station was on red alert."

So she had seen the Cardassians. Good. Sisko felt his shoulders relax. He could leave this mess to her for the moment.

"Commander," Ensign Dodds said, "there's something else here, something odd."

"What is it, Ensign?"

"A ten-ship fleet of Jibetian warships has just entered the space near the station. They'll arrive within the hour."

After the *Madison* was at the station. Captain Higginbotham had been on Utopia Planetia with Sisko. He was a good man, a savvy judge of character with excellent diplomatic skills. He would balance Kira well until Sisko arrived.

Sisko stood and paced the bridge. He had several options himself. He could return to the station and get in the middle of the diplomatic tangle; he could stay here, guarding the *Nibix;* or he could return to the asteroid to help the crew below.

Kira would know the situation soon enough. *Deep Space Nine* would be a powder keg, with Cardassians, Jibetians, and three starship captains. Too many cooks, as his mother used to say. Sisko would only be one voice among many. Kira knew how to deal with the Cardassians, and Higginbotham would have control over the situation since he was the highest-ranking officer to arrive on the scene.

They didn't need Sisko.

He swallowed, beating down nerves. Normally he would head right back to the station to protect it, the wormhole, and Jake. But this wasn't a normal situation.

Because if Bashir, Dax, or O'Brien made any mistakes on the *Nibix,* the entire Federation would have to answer for them.

"Ensign Kathé," Sisko said. "Take us back to our former coordinates over the *Nibix* asteroid. We will remain cloaked. As such, our shields will remain down, and we will not send or receive communications."

"But, sir," Ensign Coleman said, "the station seems to be in trouble. Won't Major Kira need to reach us?"

"There's a leak on *Deep Space Nine,*" Sisko said, not caring that Coleman breached protocol. "The last thing we need is for those two fleets of warships to converge over the asteroid. Any communication with the *Defiant* will show the Jibetians and the Cardassians where the *Nibix* is. Major Kira is a capable officer who has handled far worse situations. She will be fine."

"Aye, sir," Coleman said, but his tone remained unconvinced. All five ensigns were experienced enough to know that two different fleets and three starships hovering over a space station was a diplomatic nightmare at best, a holocaust at worst.

But nothing would happen until Sisko returned with news of the *Nibix.*

He hoped.

CHAPTER
12

KIRA PACED THROUGH OPS. She walked from the turbolift across the front, up the stairs, around Sisko's office, and back down again, all the time pretending to monitor the Ops crew. Instead, she was thinking. The Cardassians wouldn't dare touch the station. They had signed a treaty with the Federation. They had to be here as a warning.

Because of the *Nibix?*

They hadn't contacted her to say, and that bothered her more than anything. Tappan was monitoring them. Beth Jones now manned the science station in place of Dax. Three other ensigns were working the boards. Odo was checking the docks, making certain all the ships were secure. He would arrive shortly, and then she would have someone to talk to. Someone to confide in. Someone who understood.

Odo knew what it was like to face down Cardassian

warships. Odo knew how difficult it was for her to follow Starfleet protocol when all her instincts urged guerrilla attack. Sometimes she thought she was happier in her rebel days, fighting for her people in the most creative way she could.

Not defending some wrecked ship that might hold the head of a religion she didn't understand.

And certainly not facing down Cardassians to do so.

"Major," Ensign Moesta said. She was monitoring communications. Deep shadows marred her eyes. She had been asleep when the red alert sounded, and Kira had sent for her, knowing that Ensign Moesta was one of the most invaluable members of Ops. "There's an incoming message from the *Starship Madison.*"

The *Madison* was one of three ships that Admiral Wolfe had sent to assist her. The *Idaho* and the *Bosewell* would also come to the station soon. She had been relieved to hear which ships were coming. She had met both Captains Higginbotham and Kiser before, a number of years back.

"Put it on screen," Kira said. She stopped in front of the closed door to Sisko's office, spread her legs slightly, put her shoulders back, and raised her chin. "Captain Higginbotham, this is Major Kira Nerys, first officer of the Federation Space Station *Deep Space Nine.* I understand you'll be joining us soon."

"And I wish it were a pleasure trip, Major." Captain Higginbotham's lean face appeared on the screen. Some gray had crept into his beard since she last saw him.

"So do I, Captain," Kira said.

"We're reading some unusual activity in your sector," Higginbotham said.

"We've dealt with Cardassians before, Captain," Kira said.

His smile was faint. He had heard her war stories all those years ago. "Indeed you have, Major, but that's not what disturbs me. It's the fleet of Jibetian warships that will join them in a few hours that has me the most concerned."

A chill ran down Kira's spine. The *Madison*'s long-range sensors were more sophisticated than hers. She had known the Jibetians were going to come, but she hadn't realized they would arrive so soon. This drama would play out long before Sisko ever returned.

She gripped her fists behind her back. If she survived this, she'd give him a piece of her mind for going treasure hunting while she had to deal with the biggest diplomatic crisis of her career.

"I spoke with the Jibetians earlier," Kira said, deliberately keeping her voice calm. "They had said nothing about coming to the station."

"Jibetian politicians are rarely direct, Major," Higginbotham said. "I've dealt with them before. Their presence does not surprise me."

"The fact that they're bringing a fleet of ships has me rather concerned, Captain," Kira said. "The Cardassians are quick-tempered. Having two sets of warships near *Deep Space Nine* could create an incident if one lowly officer is trigger-happy."

"Certainly no one on your staff or mine fits that description, Major," Higginbotham said, clearly reading her concern about both groups, even though she had been less than honest about the cause. He knew, as she did, that the Jibetians and Cardassians were both after the *Nibix* and had no interest in the station at all. But in case one or both groups were monitoring, she had to play along with this scenario. "I estimate our arrival to be in twenty-two minutes. We will not dock, but instead will patrol the space near the station. The *Idaho* and *Boswell* will do the same."

That solved one of her problems. She could continue the station lockdown. "We are on red alert here, Captain," she said. "And we are prepared to take any steps necessary to protect the station."

"A prudent move," he said steepling his long, thin fingers, "despite the fact that the Jibetians are allies and the Cardassians have signed a peace treaty with us."

If they were monitoring, they would hear his warning.

"Sometimes contracts don't mean much to the Cardassians," Kira said, allowing some bitterness into her voice.

"Let's hope it means more to them than you believe it will," Higginbotham said. "I suspect the Cardassians know, as we do, that there is little worth risking a fragile peace over."

"Ever the optimist, Captain." Kira said with a smile.

"I prefer to think of myself as a realist, Major. We'll see you shortly." His image winked off the screen.

Kira relaxed her stance. She wasn't as tense as she had been a moment before. She had forgotten how much she liked Captain Higginbotham. At the dinner he had attended on DS9 several years ago, he had regaled them all with stories about Sisko when the two of them served on Utopia Planeta years before. At that time, she had only known Sisko a few months and couldn't imagine the mischievous man that Higginbotham described. Now sometimes she saw that imp peeking out of Sisko's eyes, and she always knew she was going to enjoy the joke.

Right now she missed him. He was much better at subtlety than she was. She felt as if she had been about as subtle as a phaser when talking with Captain Higginbotham. Any Cardassians or Jibetians listening in would have known most of that interchange was for them.

Kira took a deep breath. "Ensign Moesta, put a schematic on the big screen. I want to see the location of all the ships heading toward the station at this moment."

"Yes, sir," the ensign said. Within a moment the screen showed a targeting diagram of the station and nearby space. The station was a white dot in the center. The starships were small gold dots heading toward it, two close, with a third lagging behind. The five Cardassian ships appeared in red, and the ten Jibetian ships appeared in blue. The *Madison* would definitely arrive first, followed shortly by the *Idaho*. Then the Cardassians would appear. The Jibetians and the *Bosewell* would arrive at the same time.

At the far edge of the screen, a green dot streaked toward the station.

"What's that other ship?" Kira asked.

"I can't identify it," Moesta said.

"It's still too far away," Jones clarified. "But at its current speed, it should be here in three hours."

The thought of one more problem was too much for Kira. "Let's keep an eye on it," she said, "and see if you can get it to identify itself. But three hours is a long way away."

And in three hours, the identity of the new ship might not matter. By that point, nothing might matter at all.

* * *

The small room had grown uncomfortably hot. Jake no longer sat in the chair. He stood and watched the screens, mostly Ops, as the situation in the station grew worse. Nog was sitting—resting, he claimed—but Jake could feel the fear coming off his friend in waves.

They hadn't located the panel that governed the steel doors yet, but they had discovered the sound switch. They used it to turn up the volume in Ops, and Jake wished that they hadn't. He didn't want to know that two military fleets were descending on the station, that his father had taken the *Defiant* on some undisclosed mission, that Starfleet was so concerned about the events at *Deep Space Nine*, they had sent three starships to protect it.

To make matters worse, the long search of the tunnels had left him thirsty, and the supplies box they had found was mostly empty. Nog wanted to eat the dried rations immediately, but Jake figured they could only use them in an emergency, which he defined, quite loudly, as not being found within a day or so.

That thought had depressed Nog completely and sent him into the chair where he stared at Ops and occasionally wondered aloud if he would handle the situation with as much aplomb as Major Kira.

Jake knew that his father would use more finesse, but his father was gone. Chief O'Brien was also nowhere to be seen in any of their scans. Rom and Quark had been busy arguing in the bar until they disappeared from the screen. Jake's greatest fear—and the one he couldn't admit to Nog—was that no one would notice they were missing until it was too late.

He had been wrong about this section of the station

being the safest. It was clearly the most secure, but there was nothing safe about it. The lack of dust and the low rations made him uncomfortable. Perhaps someone else knew about these tunnels. Someone dangerous. Someone who would be very unhappy to learn that Jake and Nog had invaded this little room.

"Who swore?" Nog asked, suddenly sitting up. "I thought it was against Starfleet protocol to swear during a crisis."

"I didn't hear anyone swear," Jake said.

Nog held up his small hand. "There it is again. Hear it?"

Jake did, a voice reciting a whole string of curses, first in Cardassian, then in Ferengi, then Klingon, and ending with a Romulan epithet that was commonly considered to be the crudest and most descriptive in the galaxy.

Nog stood up, his head cocked and his huge ears focused. Then he crossed to the wall and reached into the sound panel, turning down all the sound.

The curses were louder. They continued in English, then followed with Caxtonian, and ended in premodern Vulcan, an arcane language that Mrs. O'Brien had insisted Jake and Nog learn to read along with Latin as one of the building blocks of interspecies linguistics.

"I don't like this," Nog said. He glanced around the room, looking for a place to hide.

"If that person knew we were here," Jake whispered, "they wouldn't be making so much noise."

"They'll know we're here when they see those doors slammed shut," Nog whispered back.

Jake shook his head. "We don't know if that's a normal response to a red alert. If it is, we have the benefit of surprise."

"Yeah, right," Nog whispered. "And what will it gain us?"

"If we play it right, we might be able to escape." Jake's heart pounded with the thought.

"You think so?" Nog asked.

"Yeah," Jake whispered.

The cursing had stopped. Jake thought he heard the rumble of another voice. He held up his hand.

"What are we going to do?" Nog mouthed.

Jake put a finger to his lips. He gestured Nog to stand near the door. Jake grabbed the chair and stood behind it.

The cursing started again. This time Jake didn't recognize any of the languages. He used the words as a cover for his own.

"Stand there when the door opens," he whispered. "Whatever you do, don't look at me. Just smile."

"Smile?" Nog's voice rose as the metal plate pulled back. He glanced at Jake, a wide, fear-filled look, and then plastered an unconvincing grin on his face.

Jake lifted the chair and got into position. The only advantage they would have was surprise. He doubted the spy who used this tunnel expected to find anyone in the room. They would attack him and run, yelling as they went and hoping that they found an exit before the spy found them.

The door opened part way, and a body came in, going sideways.

Jake brought the chair down on the movement, his fear giving him strength, just as the intruder said, "Nog? What are you—?"

The rest of the sentence was lost in the crash.

"Hey!" Nog yelled, and another voice joined him.

Jake stood over the chair. The body below it belonged to Quark.

Rom came in, wringing his hands.

"You've killed him," Rom said. "Oh, dear. What are we going to do now?"

"We'll get help," Jake said. He started for the door, stepping over Quark. But as he did, he realized the door was closing.

Quickly.

He reached for it, but it was too late. His fingers brushed the edge as it slammed into the wall.

"What's going on here?" Rom asked.

"We're trapped, Father," Nog said. "And now we'll never get out."

CHAPTER
13

DAX'S KNEES ACHED. She'd been kneeling on them since Julian arrived a half an hour before. Her hands were cold, and her nose even colder. She could see her breath.

But she didn't want to move for fear that she would miss something. She felt it her duty to keep both men in line. They didn't know what was at risk here. Oh, perhaps they did on a superficial level. But not to the degree she did. Not to a level of concern that went deeper than the cold.

She kept the tricorder focused on Julian. He was intent in his work, using all sorts of equipment she didn't even recognize to get the exact condition of the Supreme Ruler's tissue, to read his blood chemistry levels, and even to see if his eyeballs had shrunken into his head.

Some of the tests were inconclusive. And most were showing what his initial scan had: that the Supreme Ruler was technically alive but would never really regain consciousness. Julian would impart this information in a dry terse voice, as if he were speaking into his medical log on the station. After the initial tussle over speaking aloud, he didn't even seem to notice that the others were near him. He was completely absorbed by the task before him.

Dax had seen this level of concentration in Julian before. It both worried and heartened her. She had seen Julian perform miracles—keeping Vedek Bareil alive during Bajor's negotiations with the Cardassians had been one of them—but she also knew that no man could do everything. And this task might just be too big for him.

Not to mention what it would do to his career.

If he succeeded, he would be the man who saved the Jibetians' Supreme Ruler. And if he failed, he would be the man who let the religious leader of eighty worlds die. The protections Dax had set up—the tricorder, the redundant record keeping—would only fuel the debate. They wouldn't change the overall facts of what would happen here.

And only she and Sisko understood the implications.

O'Brien had worked his way around the platform and around the room. Occasionally, he, too, would speak to Dax's tricorder, explaining his actions. Essentially, he was checking the systems to see if there was a way to safely beam the Supreme Leader to the ship.

She could have helped them, she supposed, but she felt as if her presence were needed here, beside Julian, protecting her friends and the Supreme Ruler from a threat she wasn't even sure existed. Something felt wrong on this ship. Very, very wrong. And once Julian was done, she would try to find out what that was.

Finally, Julian sighed and straightened. He put a hand on his back and winced at the obvious stiffness in his muscles. He had been in the same position for a long time and had cramped up in the cold. It wasn't like Julian to ignore his own body's needs. He was fanatical about health—his own, the crew's, and his patients'.

He looked at her. His cheeks were ruddy with the chill. The lines showed beside his mouth. "Here's the official word, Lieutenant," he said. "Make sure your device is working."

Dax glanced at the tricoder. It was working. O'Brien came up to the side of the platform and stopped beside Julian. The tricorder would pick up both of them.

"The cold-sleep chamber is keeping this man alive, if that is what you want to call his condition. He has been in this state for eight hundred years. The decay I've found is normal for this kind of machine working at this level of efficiency for this long. I might be able to reverse some of the decay, but I cannot do so here. It would be better for all concerned to wait until we have better facilities before we attempt to revive this man." Julian's eyes looked hollow. Sometimes his enthusiasm and naïveté made Dax forget how truly brilliant he was. He did know the importance of saving the Supreme Ruler and of doing it properly.

And then she corrected herself. He knew, of course, and didn't care. This was Julian Bashir, a man who prided himself on his commitment to life. He would give any patient from his greatest enemy to his closest friend the same kind of treatment.

"Well, Chief," Dax said, "that puts all of this on you."

O'Brien shook his head. "It actually will take all of our resourcefulness," he said. "I've double-checked everything. We could beam the entire room onto a ship if that ship were big enough to hold it, but I doubt we have anything in the Federation that could carry such an unusually sized load."

"We'd have to check," Dax said. "What about beaming the platform onto the *Defiant?*"

"I've looked at that option as well," O'Brien said. "If we move the platform, we disconnect the cold-sleep chamber. If we disconnect the chamber, its own fail-safe system comes on. The reawakening process will start. If it doesn't start, then we'll lose the Supreme Ruler."

"You're certain?" Dax asked.

"Believe me, if there was another way to do this, I would have found it by now." O'Brien ran a hand through his curls. "I'd be happiest if we had an entire fleet of specialists helping me on this project."

"I agree," Julian said.

Dax sighed. "I doubt that we'll ever get that chance." Unless the Jibetians wanted to do it. She could imagine the scenario: a Jibetian team loses the Supreme Ruler because reviving him is simply impossible, and then eighty worlds at the edge of Federation space are involved in a massive civil war. She shook her head. The image was too much. Jadzia Dax wished they had never found the *Nibix*, no matter how excited Curzon would have been.

"All right, gentlemen," Dax said. "I'm going to leave the tricorder running at all times facing the Supreme Ruler's chamber. I think we should examine the rest of the ship."

She stood and led the way out of the ruler's room. As she passed a pile of supplies, she picked up the nearest box and carried it into the corridor. She couldn't sleep near all those bodies. She doubted the others could either.

"If you're thinking we might find more working chambers, I can guarantee we won't," O'Brien said. He picked up a box as did Julian. "I've looked at the other sleep chambers. None are as elaborate as this one."

"Although there must be a place for the rest of the royal family to lie in state," Julian said. "I'm sure that they would have equally sophisticated systems."

The door closed behind them as they stepped into the corridor.

Dax shook her head. "Everyone in that period of the Jibetian dynasty was considered expendable. The Supreme Rulership was a patriarchal system, and the Jibetians believed that a man could always father children. The only person of any consequence at all was the ruler himself."

"Although it wouldn't hurt to check," O'Brien said.

"If we're here long enough," Dax said.

Bashir set down his box and pulled from it Starfleet's regulation portable heater. An older version of one of these had kept Curzon Dax and Sisko alive for two days in an ice cave. They'd had to evacuate the cave when it became clear that the heater was cracking the ice.

"Let's get that thing running," O'Brien said. "I've been cold long enough." He bent over and started the heater, then warmed his hands over its early heat as if it were a campfire. "The thing I've never been able to understand about cold sleep is how the survivors ever felt warm again. Just knowing that my metabolism had been slowed by the cold for eighty years would give me a permanent chill."

"It wouldn't work that way, Chief," Julian said. "Your system would warm gradually . . ."

Dax dug in the other two boxes as Julian explained the psychology of cold sleep. She found blankets and pillows. She went back into the main room for the rest of the supplies, moving box after box. Both men offered to help, but she turned them down. She had watched them work. Now they could watch her.

". . . rather like a long night's sleep. Some veterans of cold sleep even claimed that they had dreams," Julian said, his voice rising with excitement. Once he started on a topic he loved, there was no stopping him.

Fortunately O'Brien seemed to be interested in it as well. "I'm simply glad for the development of warp technology. Cold sleep had too many hazards, not the least of which this ship met with."

"You mean crashes?" Julian asked. "All ships run that hazard."

"No, they don't." Dax had finished carrying the boxes. She took out a pillow and sat on it. This part of the corridor had warmed up considerably. In another half an hour, she would be able to remove her deep-cold jacket. "Most ships have living pilots in addition to their computerized navigational systems. This one didn't."

"Cold-sleep ships were usually designed so that someone would wake up at the first sign of trouble," Julian said. "I wonder if someone woke up here."

"I doubt it," Dax said. "They'd been traveling a long time when they reached this asteroid belt."

"You're right about that, Lieutenant," O'Brien

said. "But Julian's also right. The system should have attempted to revive one, maybe two pilots. And everything should have been working well enough to at least make the attempt. But I see no signs that type of system kicked in at all." He rubbed his chin. "How long do you think we have until the commander returns?"

Dax grabbed a blanket from one of the boxes and spread it around the floor to ease the chill of the metal. She didn't want O'Brien to see her face. While they'd been working on the Supreme Ruler, she had forced all thought of the Cardassians from her mind. But she couldn't ignore that threat forever. The Cardassians hadn't massed on the border at that time for some other undetermined threat. They had arrived because they knew that the *Defiant* had found the *Nibix*.

The Cardassians were wily. They would take what advantage they could. With proper use of the *Nibix*, they could destroy the heart of the Federation.

She hoped that relations between the Federation and the Cardassians had improved beyond that point, but she didn't know. She was afraid they hadn't.

"Lieutenant?" O'Brien asked, his tone showing his curiosity at her inability to answer.

"The Cardassians were just something I didn't expect," she said.

"You don't know how long the commander will be gone, do you?" Julian asked.

She shook her head. His three-day estimate might be long. It might be right. Or, if things went really poorly, he might not return at all.

"Good thing Odo knows where we are," O'Brien said. "I wouldn't want to end up like one of those fellows." He pointed toward one of the cold-sleep chambers. Vivid memories of those skeletons rose in Dax's mind. So little left of lives so filled with hope.

"Well, there's nothing we can do about them," Dax said. "And you two believe we're better off not touching the Supreme Ruler. Benjamin thought he might be gone for days. I suppose we should make ourselves comfortable."

Julian grinned. "We could treasure hunt."

Dax did not meet his grin. "If anything's missing from the *Nibix* when the Jibetians arrive, they'll blame us for the losses."

"I wasn't suggesting we take anything, Jadzia," Julian said. "Just look."

O'Brien shook his head. "I think the lieutenant is right. I think we should hold off looking for treasure. But I would be curious to see the control room. I'd love to know why the emergency revival system broke down while the Supreme Ruler's system didn't."

"We don't know if it broke down," Julian said.

"If the emergency revival system didn't break down, that would be even more interesting, don't you think?" O'Brien asked.

Julian stood and grabbed his cold-weather gear. "Ah," he said. "An age-old conspiracy."

"It might be age-old," Dax said as she stood, too, "but it might be more relevant than you think."

O'Brien shook his head. "I can't believe that an eight-hundred-year-old wreck would cause so much controversy." He stood, dusted off his trousers, and grabbed his cold-weather gear. "Since we'll be here a while, Lieutenant, do you think you could find it in your heart to tell us the true story of the *Nibix?*"

"All the details?" Julian added.

Dax smiled. "I'll tell you so many details, you'll wish you'd never heard of this ship."

"Too late," Julian said, gazing around the dark corridor. "I already do."

Every muscle in Kira's body was tense. She paced around Ops. The team with her studied their monitors. The air felt hot, even though she knew the environmental controls kept everything at an even temperature.

The *Starship Madison* had just taken its position around *Deep Space Nine*. The *Idaho* wasn't far behind.

"Major," Tappan said, "the *Madison* is hailing us."

"On screen," Kira said. She stopped in the same position she had been in before. In front of Commander Sisko's office, as if the remnants of his presence gave her more power than she really had.

Captain Higginbotham's lean face filled the screen. "Major," he said. "The Cardassians are only a few minutes away from the station. Our sources believe Gul Dukat is leading the fleet."

"Gul Dukat?" Kira felt herself go cold. Commander Sisko had established a passing relationship with Gul Dukat. Her relationship with him had remained fiery.

"I seem to remember that your station has had dealings with Gul Dukat before."

Kira nodded once. "Gul Dukat used to head *Deep Space Nine* when it was a Cardassian station. We've dealt with him more than once."

"I suggest that you initiate the contact with him. I will monitor. If need be, I'll help."

Kira frowned. She had thought Captain Higginbotham would be the diplomat on this trip. "Captain," she said, allowing a bit of worry into her tone, "Gul Dukat and I aren't exactly friends."

Captain Higginbotham's smile was almost merry. His eyes twinkled. "I know, Major."

And, she finally understood, he counted on it. He wanted her to stall Gul Dukat until the Jibetians arrived. Of course, he couldn't say so, not with the Cardassians so close.

"I can't promise I'll be civil to him," Kira said, more as a warning to herself than to him.

"I'm sure you'll treat him as you normally would," Captain Higginbotham said. "The *Bosewell* is nearly here. We'll have a full contingent of starships shortly."

"And some Jibetians."

He nodded. "It promises to be an interesting afternoon," he said and signed off.

Interesting didn't begin to describe the situation. Tense, terrifying, exasperating. Kira might have used those words. And Higginbotham wanted her to engage Gul Dukat. Higginbotham was capable of Sisko-style negotiation, but he didn't want that. He wanted the fireworks of a Bajoran against a former Cardassian warlord. He wanted her to stall.

Stall she would.

She went to the science station and looked over Jones's shoulder. The Cardassians would arrive at the station momentarily. The *Bosewell* was almost here, as were the Jibetians. As of yet, though, no one had figured out what that other ship was, the one that was streaking here at a speed that was dangerous to most ships known to the Federation.

Her only solace was that it hadn't come through the

wormhole. The ship belonged to this sector. No Changelings in the mix.

As the Cardassians approached, she straightened. "Mr. Tappan," she said. "Hail Gul Dukat."

"Aye, Major," Tappan said.

In a moment, Gul Dukat appeared on the screen. He never seemed to age. His lizardlike features had a fire to them that instantly put Kira on guard.

"Gul Dukat," she said in the only voice she could use with the Cardassians—one that was slightly sarcastic, one that barely hid the anger she had toward them—"you hadn't told us you were favoring us with your presence."

"Major," he said, "we saw the *Defiant* near our border and believed you had trouble here. We have come to assist you."

"The *Defiant* is not here," she said.

"No? But we saw it head this way." Gul Dukat seemed genuinely surprised.

Sisko must have seen the Cardassians and led them away from the asteroids, which either meant he was cloaked and nearby or that he went back. If he saw the starships, he probably would have returned to the asteroids.

She hoped.

"You are mistaken," Kira said.

"You seem prepared for trouble, Major," Gul Dukat said, his voice at its softest and most dangerous. "Two Federation starships and one more on the way. I am sure something must be happening."

"We are having a meeting between the Federation and some applicants to the organization." Kira smiled her sweetest smile at him. "Clearly this has nothing to do with you. Or your fleet."

"Obviously," Gul Dukat said and looked as if he were about to sign off. Then he frowned. "Major? We recently heard that the Romulans provided the Federation with a cloaking device."

"You've known that for months, Dukat," Kira said. "I thought you were here to assist us."

"Since I'm here, Major, I thought I'd check on the device." He shrugged. "Do you have the plans available?"

"Dukat," Kira said, "what do you want?"

"A little honesty, Major."

Kira clasped her hands behind her back. "You know exactly what I think of you, Dukat."

"Major—"

"And while we're talking about honesty, tell me what brought you across the border."

He leaned back away from his screen. She could now see the silver of his breastplate. "I told you, Major."

"Good. Now that you know what's going on, you're free to leave."

He shook his head. "I think I'll stay awhile, Major. You have no understanding of the internal workings of the Federation. Neither do I. But I have observed them. Never before have they sent three starships to conduct a negotiation. Not even as sensitive a negotiation as a treaty with the Cardassians." He smiled. "I think you might be happy for my presence, Major."

"I'm never happy for your presence, Dukat."

"Perhaps that will change in the next few hours," he said, and his image winked out.

"Do you want me to hail him again, Major?" Tappan asked.

"No." Kira growled the word. Dealing with Cardassians always left her feeling furious.

"How long until the Jibetians arrive, Mr. Tappan?" she asked. She wanted to know if she had a moment to go to Sisko's office and smash something to get rid of this foul temper she was in

"One hour, ten minutes, Major."

Time enough then. She whirled, headed toward the office, and had opened the door when Ensign Jones spoke.

"Major?" she said, "I've identified that ship."

Kira stopped, sighed, and let the office door close. She came back into Ops. "What is it?"

Jones pushed away from the station so that she could face Kira. "It's the Ferengi flagship."

"The Grand Nagus?" Kira asked. She clenched her fists. "I sure love the way this station keeps a secret."

CHAPTER
14

As THE *DEFIANT* drew near the asteroid, Sisko tensed. He sat in the commander's chair, hands gripped on the armrests, and watched the monitors.

The asteroid looked as it had when he first saw it, a pockmarked ball floating among a dozen other pockmarked balls in the darkness of space.

No ships. No one had followed them. No one had preceded them. The *Nibix* was safe.

For the moment.

"Ensign Coleman," he said, "are we alone?"

Coleman had been monitoring the other ships in the area ever since they left the space around the station. Even so, his cautious nature demanded that he double-check. Sisko waited a beat too long as Coleman ran the scans again.

"No one followed us, sir."

"Good." Sisko leaned back in his chair. Even

though no one followed them, they had to be cautious. The asteroid belt itself bothered him. Ships could hide easily here—he had used asteroid belts for that himself. "Keep an eye out. We don't want anyone to sneak up on us."

"Yes, sir," Ensign Coleman said.

Sisko stood. The immediate danger had passed. Now he had to discover how the away team did in reviving the Supreme Ruler. He didn't want to risk a subspace transmission, even encoded. But he would risk a quick transport beam. Besides, if he were going to be honest with himself, he had to admit that he wanted desperately to return to the surface. No amount of justifying would change that.

"I'm going to beam to the surface to see how we're doing," he said. "Ensign Kathé, you have the conn. I want you to decloak only during the time it takes me to get to the surface. Then stay cloaked. Keep the transporter locked on me at all times. If there are any problems at all, I want you to beam me back to the ship immediately."

Ensign Kathé stood. Her long rainbow hair wrapped around her like a shawl. The colors shimmered in the bright light of the bridge. "Yes, sir," she said, her tone reflecting her pleasure and terror at being in charge. "I'll do everything I can, sir."

"I know you will." He made sure he spoke gently, wishing that he had brought one more crew member, someone else he could trust. It surprised him that there were so few members of the DS9 crew that he trusted on this deep level. Kira and Odo had to remain at the station. Jake wasn't qualified. And the others were on the surface below.

If he told that concern to Dax, she would laugh at him and tell him to be thankful he trusted so *many* people on his staff. They both knew that some leaders had no one to trust but themselves.

He took the turbolift. On his way, he grabbed his cold-weather gear. Then he walked into the transporter room and smiled when he saw transporter veteran Vukcevich at the controls. Vukcevich had been a member of the DS9 crew from the beginning, but he usually worked in the docks. When the *Defiant* came to the station, Vukcevich petitioned Sisko for a position on the ship, saying he had always wanted to work a transporter, and the luck of the draw had put him on a space station instead. Sisko had put Vukcevich in charge of all the duties concerning the transporter ever since and had not once regretted it. Seeing the slight man hunched over the control pad made Sisko revise his earlier thoughts.

He trusted his crew. All of his crew. Some, though, had earned a deeper trust than others had.

"Commander," Vukcevich said, speaking so softly he was hard to understand, "I have the coordinates for the away team, but they are not where they should be."

Sisko stopped, one foot on the step leading to the transporter pad. He leaned in, hoping he had heard incorrectly. "Where are they?"

"Using the ancient schematic Lieutenant Dax superimposed over the wreckage, I would guess that they're in what used to be the control room."

The worry that had dogged Sisko all day grew worse. A chill ran up his spine. "Are there problems at their previous coordinates?"

"No, sir, not that I can tell."

"And they're alone on the surface?"

"According to my scans, sir. You might want to check with the bridge."

He had checked with the bridge. And double-checked with the bridge. And didn't want to check with the bridge again. He stepped onto the pad. "Beam me down there."

"Aye, sir," Vukcevich said. Sisko watched. Vukcevich manipulated the controls and that slightly warm, slight prickly feeling of transport began. A second later, Sisko was standing in a poorly lit, freezing cold cavernous control room. He pulled on his gloves and his deep-cold jacket, wishing he had some sort of protection for his face.

The control room had a high domed ceiling open to the stars. Some type of clear material—probably the same glasslike substance used for the cold-sleep chambers—arced overhead, unbroken by the crash. Faint starlight filtered in. Sisko looked up first, half searching for the blip that would be the *Defiant* in orbit, even though he knew the *Defiant* was cloaked.

Then he made himself look down. The control panels glowed a soft but insistent green, the same green as the Supreme Ruler's glowing staff. An overhead light spotted on the center control panel, a thin black board in a boomerang shape that filled the center of the room. Dax stood beside the board, one hand on its panels. Bashir was in the chair beside her, arms behind his head and his head tilted back as he gazed at the stars. Sisko couldn't see O'Brien anywhere.

"It would be nice if you said hello to your commander," Sisko said softly and smiled as Dax and Bashir started. They hadn't heard him beam down. A large bang echoed in the room, followed by a soft curse. Then O'Brien emerged from beneath the boomerang. Black particles filled his curly red hair and dotted his face.

"Benjamin," Dax said, "we didn't expect you for another day, maybe more."

"I can see that," Sisko said with a smile. He walked over toward them. The air was so cold that it made his boots squeak. "At least I didn't catch you treasure hunting."

"Something far more interesting," O'Brien said.

"I trust the Cardassians are no longer watching us," Bashir asked.

"We lead them to the station," Sisko said, "where they were greeted by three Starfleet starships and will soon be joined by a fleet of Jibetian warships."

"Poor Kira," Dax said softly. "She was hoping to avoid diplomatic duty for a while."

"Sounds like she'll put in enough diplomatic duty to be promoted to ambassador," Bashir said. "How did all those groups converge so quickly? I thought this was supposed to be a secret mission."

"So did I," Sisko said. "Their presence makes our actions here even more important. I am surprised you're not with the Supreme Ruler."

"We don't dare touch the Supreme Ruler with the equipment we have here," Bashir said. "His cells have deteriorated, and while he's technically alive, I'm not certain he's revivable. I would like to take him to the station's medical facilities before I proceed any further."

"We don't always get what we want, Doctor," Sisko said.

"Well, sir, I'll be blunt. It's my belief that should I attempt to revive him here, he will die. Totally and irrevocably. At the station, I'll have the equipment to give him a fighting chance."

Sisko's stomach tied itself in knots. Dax smiled at him, her look understanding. She knew, as he did, that to lose the Supreme Ruler now might not just destroy the careers of the people around him, but it might have serious—and fatal—repercussions for the Federation as well.

Sisko took a deep breath, hoping to calm himself. "Let's beam him aboard the *Defiant*, then, and post a guard here to prevent scavenging."

"I'm afraid it's not that easy, sir," O'Brien said. "We can't remove him from his sleep chamber, and if we tamper with the chamber itself, it'll stop working. We'll have to move the room itself."

Sisko closed his eyes. A slight shiver ran through his system, brought on, he hoped, by the cold. He needed a few moments to think. "Tell me what you're doing here," he said.

"Now that's the question, isn't it?" O'Brien said with more enthusiasm than he had ever shown for the *Nibix* or the Supreme Ruler. "We got to talking about what made this ship crash on the asteroid. Cold-sleep ships have fail safes—"

"I'm familiar with them, Chief," Sisko said gently. Not only was he familiar with them, he had made them a special point of study during his early interest in the *Nibix*. Some of the theories of the *Nibix* were that its fail safes had been improperly constructed, allowing the ship to disappear without awakening any of the crew.

"Good then." O'Brien glanced at Bashir. He had sat up in the chair, and looked in this light like a spotlit piece of Renaissance art.

Dax was watching O'Brien, a frown on her face. "You found something, Chief?" she asked.

"Just when the commander showed up. I was about to call you down, Lieutenant." O'Brien took a deep breath as if to control his emotions, and then he grinned. "Forgive me, sir. Dax explained how important all this is. It's just I feel like Sherlock Holmes. The clues are so subtle, and yet they're there, clear as anything."

"What clues?" Sisko asked. His stomach had knotted so tight it felt as if he had swallowed a rock.

"The *Nibix* was sabotaged." O'Brien rocked back and forth on his feet as if he couldn't contain his excitement.

Sisko let out the air he'd been holding. "You're certain, Chief?"

"As sure as I am of anything, sir. This ship was never intended to reach its destination. From what I can tell, as soon as it left Jibetian airspace, all its navigational systems went off-line. Then the automatic awakening systems were disconnected."

Bashir stuck his hands under his arms, an obvious defense against the cold. "If someone did all that," he said, "why not just shut off the cold-sleep chambers?"

"That would activate a different fail safe, Doctor," Sisko said. "It was simpler to do this."

"That's my theory," O'Brien said. "Besides, this way the saboteur didn't commit actual murder."

"Because the cold-sleep chambers should have kept everyone alive as long as the ship ran." Bashir shook his head. "Ingenious."

"And nearly perfect." Sisko rubbed his hands together. They would have to go somewhere warm, too. "If the ship hadn't passed through this asteroid belt, no one would have found it."

"The *Nibix* would have stayed a part of history," Dax said. She looked at Sisko. "This means extra trouble for us, doesn't it, Benjamin."

"I don't see how it couldn't," he said. He understood her concern. He felt it, too. The sabotage was important. The *Nibix*'s influence had always reached through history. The sabotage wouldn't be any different.

Jake sat on the only chair in the room, his arms crossed over his chest. The little surveillance room had grown stiflingly hot, and he worried that air wasn't circulating through it. He didn't tell his worries to Nog, though.

Nog hadn't spoken to him since Jake kaboshed his uncle.

Nog and Rom hovered over Quark, who had only recently regained consciousness. He had been out over thirty minutes, during which time Nog had repeatedly berated Jake for his stupidity. Jake had let him; he had been around Ferengi long enough to know such verbal abuse was a way of blowing off steam and tension. Besides, it was safer for Nog to blame Jake than to take the blame himself. Quark's punishments could be bizarre and severe.

Jake's stomach growled. Their situation had grown desperate. The hunger wasn't that bad. The heat and the lack of water concerned him the most. The red alert showed no signs of abating. Jake had hoped that Kira would shut off the alert quickly and then the doors would open, but so far that hadn't happened. During Nog's beratement, Jake had watched the screen showing Ops and realized that the situation there was growing worse, not better.

Which meant that the red alert might continue indefinitely.

Quark moaned. Rom was murmuring soothing words, and Nog was hovering over both of them, occasionally throwing helpless glances over his shoulder at Jake. It felt as if Nog wanted Jake to make

Quark better. Jake didn't have that skill. The only thing he could do was figure out a way out of here.

He had tried to talk to Rom about how they had opened the door from the outside, but Rom had said Quark had done that. And Quark wasn't answering any questions. Yet.

Jake stood and walked to the panel of screens. Watching Ops would get him nowhere, and he had already apologized to Nog. Jake had to go back to what he was doing before the other Ferengi arrived. Studying the panel.

The setup made no sense to him. It seemed to be some sort of surveillance system made to spy on the station, but who set it up and why? And where was the information going out? And for that matter, how? Jake didn't know that much about station security, but he couldn't imagine Chief O'Brien, Odo, and his father not discovering some sort of signal leaving the station from this panel.

Jake stood back from the panel and tried to really look at it. Chief O'Brien had taught him a lot about machinery. A general rule, he said, was to examine the pattern. Anything that didn't fit into the pattern bore investigating. So Jake stared at the panels and let what he was seeing form patterns.

It took a moment, but then he saw it. The screen in the lower corner really didn't show a strategic area of the station but showed instead a hallway just outside a docking bay. And the main focus of the picture wasn't the door to the docking bay, but a communications wall unit near it.

"Why would that be?" he said to himself.

"Why would what be?" Nog asked.

Jake started. Nog was standing beside him. He hadn't even heard his friend approach. And Quark had stopped moaning. He was still holding his head, but now he was watching Jake. Rom crouched beside him, his small eyes bright.

"Did you find a way out of here?" Quark asked. He didn't sound like he was in as much pain as he had been in a moment before.

"I don't think so," Jake said. "But this screen is focused on only a communications panel near a docking bay while the others show main areas of the station."

"So?" Nog said.

"It's a relay station," Rom said.

"Shut up, Rom, and let Jake work on this," Quark said. "We don't need your stupid comments."

"He wasn't being stupid," Nog said. "He knows more about machinery than all of us put together."

Jake frowned. He remembered his father mentioning that. Rom had wanted to use his mechanical skills. He had never wanted to go into business. Such an attitude was sacrilege for a Ferengi, but it had worked to Nog's advantage. It had given his father enough courage to fight for his son's desire to go to the Academy.

"What makes you think it's a relay station?" Jake asked Rom.

Rom glanced at Quark. Quark waved his free hand dismissively. "You brought the subject up. You defend it. And no long-winded theories. We need to get out of here."

Rom swallowed. "I think it's a relay station because that's how I would have set it up."

"But you're not known for your intelligence," Quark said.

"Give him a chance," Nog said fiercely.

"He's the only one with an idea," Jake said in his most placating tone. "Let's hear it out."

Rom twisted his hands together. He wouldn't look at the boys. "A relay station near a docking bay is in the perfect position," he said. "It can send the information to a nearby ship—and it doesn't have to be the same ship every time. Just one that knows the right band. Then the ship can send the information out without the station sensors picking it up."

"That makes perfect sense," Jake said.

Nog smiled at his father.

Quark shoved Rom. "Why don't you come up with something like that for me?"

"You need spy equipment?" Jake asked.

"No, not exactly," Quark said. "I just meant that we should be able to use his expertise to help the—"

"You don't want to hear my theories, Brother," Rom said. "You always tell me to be quiet."

"Yeah," Nog said. "Maybe you should listen to him more. He's a lot smarter than you give him credit for."

The last thing Jake wanted was to be trapped in this tiny room while a Ferengi family quarrel raged. He had to focus the three of them. "Do you think the relay is working while the station is in red alert?" he asked Rom.

Rom glanced at Quark, then at Nog. When neither of them said anything, he came forward and studied the screen. "I can't tell," he said. "But I would design the relay to dump its information on an exact schedule, every few hours or maybe twice a day. It wouldn't be logical to not have information going out while the station is under alert. But if I were designing this—"

"Which you aren't," Quark muttered.

"—I would make sure everything is being recorded

very carefully while under alert, more so than normal."

Jake studied the screens for a moment. Whomever was monitoring this would learn that Kira and Captain Higginbotham had planned strategy before the other ships arrived. They would hear confidential conversations from Ops to Security. Jake didn't know what had been discussed, but whatever it was had been important enough to cause the station to go to red alert. Having anyone learn about station business at a time like this had to be dangerous. And who knows when the information would dump next.

"If this works the way you say it does," Jake said, "then we need to get out of here and make sure no information leaves the station."

"How do you expect us to do that," Nog asked, "with us locked in here and my uncle mortally wounded?"

"I'm not mortally wounded, Nog," Quark said. "That would mean I'm dying, and I'm not." He touched his head gingerly. "Although I wish I were."

"I'm sorry," Jake said for what seemed like the thousandth time.

"I'm just glad you're on our side, kid." Quark grinned. "You pack a mean chair." Then he snapped a finger at Rom. "Help me up."

Rom put a hand under Quark's arm. Nog did the same on the other side, and together they heaved Quark to his feet. He swayed for a moment, rolled his eyes, and sagged against them. They staggered under his weight.

"I'm all right," he murmured. "I'm all right."

He stood again and shook them off, swaying for a moment and then using the wall to catch himself. He kept one hand on the wall for balance as he made his way to the door he and Rom had entered. Quark studied it for a moment, then put his free hand against his head.

"Not a chance," he said, and sat down against the steel plate. "At least until someone cancels this emergency."

"And when they do, it might be too late," Jake said.

"Yes." Rom managed to get a lot of worry into that one word.

"But," Quark said, "I doubt if it will help the Cardassians."

"Cardassians?" Jake and Nog both asked at once.

Quark nodded and then flinched. "Who do you think built that panel? Little space ghosts?"

"Hasn't this been here since we came to the station?" Jake asked. He couldn't reconcile that thought with the efficiency of his father's team. The chief wouldn't allow random signals and strange energy feeds in his station. Neither would his father. And if they failed to notice it, they had Dax. She always saw what was different.

"No, it hasn't been here that long. It wasn't here six months ago, I can tell you that." Quark tapped the door he was sitting against. "And neither were these."

The lump on Quark's head had to be more severe than it looked. He was imagining things. "I don't see how the Cardassians could install these doors and this kind of surveillance system under Odo's and Chief O'Brien's noses," Jake said.

Quark laughed, then winced, touched his forehead, and moaned. "First," he said, his voice small as if he were in pain, "I said the equipment was Cardassian. That doesn't mean they installed it. Anyone could have done it for them at the right price."

Jake gave him a harsh look.

Quark opened his hands. "Why does everyone suspect me first?"

"There's profit in it," Nog said.

"Not for my brother," Rom said. "He doesn't know a laser bolt from a light tack."

"Right," Quark said. "I think." He glanced at his brother and nephew as if he knew they had said something unusual, but he didn't know what it was.

"But people can't just crawl around the station without someone noticing," Jake said.

"You have," Quark said. "We just did. No one's hurrying to our rescue. No one thinks about these tunnels."

"Chief O'Brien does," Jake said.

"And where's he, hmmm? Off on the *Defiant* searching for treasure."

"Treasure?" Nog asked.

"But he's not always gone," Jake said.

"He's been gone a lot this year," Quark said. "And so has your father and Dax and Odo, for that matter. All it would take is a few afternoons. I think there's been plenty of time to install this little spy shop."

Jake glanced at the wall. Kira was pacing around Ops. The red alert was still sounding, and his father was nowhere to be seen. Quark knew something about the mission they were on, and he still hadn't explained his own presence in the tunnels.

"How did you get here?" Jake asked.

"I crawled, same as you," Quark said.

"Why?" Jake couldn't keep the suspicion out of his voice.

"I forget," Quark said, closed his eyes, and leaned his head back. And no matter how many times Jake tried to rouse him, Quark refused to utter another word.

CHAPTER
15

HIS FAMILY'S GREATEST NIGHTMARE looked as if it were about to become true. Hibar Ribe stood in the center of the bridge on the largest warship in the Jibetian fleet, his hands clasped behind his back, his long black robe heavy and oppressive on his shoulders.

His assistants were watching him warily. They recognized his foul mood and didn't understand the cause of it. They had rejoiced when they heard of the chance that the *Nibix* had been discovered.

Everyone would.

The warship's main deck crew worked tirelessly, pushing the engines at full power to arrive at the Federation deep-space station as quickly as possible. Ribe, who was head of the Jibetian Council and who had never even been on a warship until that morning, watched in complete fascination.

Gone was the ornamentation of his usual starship.

No observation decks, no domes open to space, no high-backed chairs. Everything on this ship was built sleek and long. Built for efficiency and maximum firepower and nothing more.

Here, on the main deck, black walls rose. They were covered with equipment, computer panels, and small dividers separating each work station. No distractions. No thoughts allowed other than the ones the generals wanted the troops to hear. It had been this way in warships for nearly eight hundred years. The revolution, once it ended, would never happen again.

His ancestors had seen to that.

He shuddered and returned to his command chair. General Caybe had given him a position on the main deck, but it was only honorary. He could not give orders to the crew. Too many chances for confusion. If Ribe wanted changes made, he spoke to the general, who then issued the orders.

But the command chair gave Ribe a good view of the crew. It also had its own screen, which he had left running. The screen showed, with the flick of a finger, a three-dimensional map with the fleet's trajectory plotted on it. The map showed the ship nearing the Federation space station. He then flicked the screen and saw the blackness of space punctuated by the light of nearby stars. It told him nothing. So he magnified the image ten thousand times.

And froze.

A fleet of Cardassians, which he had expected.

Three Federation starships already docked, which he had not.

"General," he said, "we must consult."

His advisors moved closer. He used to joke that they were a small army trying to operate as one brain. It never worked. If it hadn't been custom for the head of the Jibetian Council to surround himself with advisors, he would have cut his loose a long time ago. But tradition and the past on which it was based were the foundation of Jibetian culture.

It was his job as head of the Jibetian Council and the senior member of the Ribe-Iber-Bikon family to make certain that the past—the official, government-sanctioned past—was never challenged.

"Forgive me, Lord High Sir," the general said, "we're nearing the station. I—"

"You'll come here," Ribe snapped.

The general's mouth thinned, but he whirled and took his place beside Ribe.

Ribe gestured at the screen. "Explain this."

"Our sensors just picked it up." The general lowered his voice so that only Ribe and the advisors could hear. "The station is at priority alert. It appears to be under some sort of threat from the Cardassians."

"I thought that treaty was settled."

"As did I, Lord High Sir."

"But they are expecting us."

The general nodded once.

"And they have not told us to turn around."

The general nodded again.

"How much firepower does a Federation starship have?"

"More than three of our ships combined," the general said.

Ribe tapped his lip with his index finger. Strange. Very strange. But he didn't pretend to understand the Federation. It was a complex organization made up of dissimilar peoples. To ascribe it one cultural attitude was to underestimate it. "Then, in your estimation, they don't need us for firepower."

"No, Lord High Sir. I don't believe they do."

Ribe nodded. "You may return to your post. Keep me informed on our proximity to the station and its own status."

"Yes, Lord High Sir." The general's tone had an edge of disrespect. He managed it in the repetition of Ribe's title, but technically the man had done nothing wrong. He was merely allowing his resentment of Ribe's usurpation of his ship and his fleet to show in a subtle, unpunishable manner.

Ribe hoped that the resentment would go no farther than this. He could not command a fleet on his own, and his advisors, useless in political matters, were dangerous with weapons at their disposal.

He stared at the screen, thankful for the military efficiency of the vessel. No one would interrupt him. His advisors knew better, and the crew could not even make eye contact with him. He needed a moment to think. His emotions had been in turmoil since he received the news about the possible discovery of the *Nibix.*

Children learned about the *Nibix* in Siberan religious classes. It was the great ship that took the Supreme Ruler to his destiny, and God saw fit to lose it among the stars. He had loved that story until he came into his majority.

Then his father told him the truth. Told him about the past.

Ribe snapped his fingers. His senior advisor, Concar, leaned over his shoulder. "Any news as to the *Nibix?"*

Concar shook his head. "The ship's name has not been mentioned nor any search mission. Could our information be faulty?"

Ribe pointed to the screen. "Three Federation

153

starships and a station on alert would seem to say otherwise."

Concar nodded but obviously did not agree. "Unless our security is not as tight as we might like to think."

Ribe templed his fingers, a sign for Concar to remove himself. Concar leaned back, keeping a reasonable distance from the chair. Ribe studied the ships.

The search for the *Nibix* and its wealth had entranced this entire sector for generations. In the rule of his great-great-grandfather, a possible *Nibix* had been discovered. The old man had visited the ship himself, even though he knew it was not, could not, be the *Nibix*. This cold-sleep ship had weapon burns on its sides, and its crew had died awake and fighting.

The crew on the *Nibix* went to sleep one night and never woke up. Bikon had seen to that.

Bikon, family legend held, was brilliant and charismatic, a man everyone trusted. Ribe had always doubted that part of the legend. Bikon may have been brilliant, but he would have been the only member of the Ribe-Iber-Bikon family to have charisma. The family had held its power all these centuries, not through love, but through complete and absolute control of history, resources, and information. The existence of the council itself was a mere formality. The religion had evolved into harmless pap, a mixture of legend, stories that made the people feel good, and common wisdom.

The discovery of the *Nibix* would change all of that. The clear death of the Supreme Ruler would challenge his presence in Siberan as an immortal. The wealth on the ship would cause great internal and external chaos.

And the sabotage.

The evidence of the sabotage could never get out. Bikon had always been smart, but even he had not been able to hide his method of escape. Eight hundred years ago, no one had ever heard of a transport beam. Eight hundred years ago, he had to use an escape pod.

It would become clear to anyone with half a brain that Bikon had planned his betrayal carefully. All of the work the Ribe-Iber-Bikon family had done since then—eight hundred years of maintaining peace, expanding Jibet's economic and world base, and improving the Jibetian way of life—would be discounted with that one piece of news.

For Bikon, believing his rival gone forever, had allowed the Supreme Ruler to live in the people's imaginations. He had used the Supreme Ruler's image to defeat the revolution, and then he had used the Supreme Ruler's family history, its supposed lineage to the Jibetian pantheon of Immortals, to maintain stability.

It must have seemed so brilliant at the time.

And it was.

But it was Ribe's curse now.

His only hope was to destroy the ship and to make it look as if someone else did it.

Preferably the Federation.

The starships might make that easy for him.

"The station is hailing us," the general said.

"Let them," Ribe said. "I will talk with them when I am ready. Spread the ships into standard defense positions and hold your location."

The general turned and gave Ribe a puzzled look. Ribe had not given a direct order about the fleet before. Ribe ignored him and continued to stare at the ships hanging around the space station.

After a moment the general turned away and did what he was told.

The Jibetian fleet had reached the station. The ships were unlike any Kira had ever seen. Instead of the birdlike Cardassian ships or the mounted saucer starships, the Jibetian ships were long, sleek, black ovals built for speed.

She hated them on sight.

She hated even more the fact that they were not responding to her hails.

"Mr. Tappan?" she said for the fifth time.

"I've tried every frequency, Major," he said.

"They are receiving our transmissions, aren't they, Ensign Jones?"

"So far as I can tell, Major." Jones had tucked a strand of hair behind one ear. She was bent over her console, her fingers flying. "I think they're not responding on purpose."

"Great." Kira let out a huge sigh. She couldn't be a diplomat if she couldn't even talk to the parties. Combat was easier. Then a person knew why ships had arrived and how to respond.

"Major, the *Madison* is hailing us," Tappan said.

"On screen."

She whirled, deciding to let her frustration show. "Are they responding to you?"

"I haven't tried, Major." Captain Higginbotham smiled. "We agreed that you'd handle this."

"Obviously, they don't want to talk to me."

"For the moment." Higginbotham looked relaxed except for the tightening around his eyes. They had to have a class at the Academy to teach Starfleet commanders the art of looking calm under pressure. "Captains Kiser and Mouce will join me in a meeting on *Deep Space Nine*. We would like to consult with you as well. I want you to beam us all aboard on my mark."

Kira almost reminded him that to beam him aboard, she would have to drop her shields. But he knew that. The Cardassians would as well. But the Jibetians might not.

Their silence was affecting her more than she had realized.

His image winked out.

"Ensign Moesta," Kira said, "when the captain gives his mark, drop our shields. Raise them the moment the captains beam aboard."

"Aye, sir," Ensign Moesta said.

"Mr. Tappan," Kira said, "Hail them and let them know we're ready."

Tappan nodded. His fingers flew across the pad. "We hailed, and they acknowledged. Another hail from Captain Higginbotham."

"On screen," Kira said.

Higginbotham's image winked on again. Behind him, she could see the bright lights of the transporter pad. "Now, Major," he said.

His image broke up as the screen winked out. Ensign Moesta followed her instructions. Kira held her breath.

The three captains appeared in a triangular formation in Ops.

"Shields up now," Kira shouted.

Ensign Moesta hurriedly obeyed her commands.

Captain Higginbotham smiled. He was taller than the other two captains. Rangier, too. Captain Kiser was shorter and heavier. His wedge-shaped face was grimmer than she had ever seen it. Usually his dark humor and subtle teasing brightened any gathering.

And in the far corner, Captain Mouce stood. Kira had never met the captain of the *Bosewell* before. She was small and lean but had a lot of power in her petite frame. Her hair was a mixture of gray and white, and her eyes were a wide bright green. She had the exotic look of humans raised in the outer colonies.

"Welcome to *Deep Space Nine,*" Kira said, and never had she given a more sincere greeting in her life.

A bead of sweat ran down the side of Jake's face. The back of his throat was dry. The heat in the room was up considerably. Quark had moved away from the door, but he still kept his eyes closed. Nog sat beside his uncle, and Rom was examining the side of the equipment, as far away from Quark as he could get.

Jake was studying the screens, hoping for a clue, anything to help them escape.

Then he saw Kira speak briefly to one of the starship captains. The captain's image winked out, and Kira snapped a command to one of the ensigns.

"Looks like something is about to happen," Jake said.

Quark sighed. "Something is always about to happen," he said. "Let me know when it does happen."

Suddenly the light in the room brightened for a moment and then a scraping sound filled the area, cutting through Jake's ears and making his teeth ache.

"What—?"

On one screen Jake could see three starship captains beam into Ops.

"The doors!" Quark shouted as he tried to scramble to his feet, but Nog, in his haste, bumped into Quark and sent them both tumbling. Rom launched himself toward his family instead of turning toward the door behind him.

All three doors were opening at once. Kira had to drop the screens on the station to let the three captains aboard and the automatic doors were somehow linked to the screens. Cool air entered, relieving some of the heat. The doors had made it half open and then started to close.

"No!" Jake shouted. He sprang for the sliding metal plate. His thin body somehow made it between the closing metal and for only a flash he thought maybe he should stay there and try to hold the door open for the others. But it became quickly clear that he wouldn't even be able to slow the door down. Its weight would crush him.

At the last second he slipped on through, barely pulling his arm and fingers out of the way as the panel slammed shut.

On the far side he could hear the distant shouting of the three Ferengi.

"I'll get help!" he shouted back, but he doubted they could hear him.

He turned and looked down the dark, narrow corridor. A short distance away, the corridor forked. He was back to the same problem he and Nog had earlier.

Which way was out?

CHAPTER
16

Sisko could see his breath. The cavernous control room of the *Nibix* seemed colder than it had even a moment before. The domed ceiling, open to the stars, added to the illusion of chill. Sisko felt, if he glanced up, as if he were standing on a platform in open space.

Bashir had his hands under his arms and was rocking back and forth. Dax had crawled under the control panel with O'Brien to see the sabotage for herself. When they came out a moment later, she was covered with the same black specks that dotted O'Brien's skin and uniform. She confirmed his findings and added that the sabotage was both thorough and subtle.

It had been done by someone completely familiar with the ship.

Sisko ran a gloved finger over one of the green glowing control panels. The ship still seemed alive and vital, just as he imagined it would. But, with all his study, he had not been able to foresee how many problems the discovery would cause. And how many of the problems would fall on his shoulders.

"What do you think, old man?" he asked Dax softly. She was standing beside him, looking beautiful despite the cold. He still wasn't used to his old friend's new look, new beauty. He still felt Curzon's presence, the old man's vitality and quick mind, even though Jadzia was a completely different person.

"The word is out, Benjamin. The presence of the Jibetians as well as the Cardassians proves that. The moment we communicate with those starships, everyone will know where the *Nibix* is. And judging from Quark's reaction to the ship, not only will there be political trouble, we'll have trouble with scavengers as well."

"Couldn't we post some sort of guard around the ship?" Bashir asked.

"We could," Sisko said. The writing on the console was faint, almost unreadable. He had forgotten most of the ancient Jibetian he had studied anyway. "But this ship is big. We'd use a tremendous amount of manpower to watch over it, and that still wouldn't prevent some determined treasure hunter from getting in here."

"Then we have the Supreme Ruler to worry about." Dax put her hand beside Sisko's. The green glow reflected off her gloves. She didn't touch any of the panel, but she appeared to be examining it, as he was. "He's the nearest thing Jibetians have to a god."

"That should protect him, shouldn't it?" Bashir asked.

"Julian, sometimes I think you skipped all the important stuff at the Academy," O'Brien said. He was still near the sabotaged control panel. "One man's god is another man's demon."

"And sometimes," Sisko said, "it's not as black and white as that. Sometimes it's as simple as the destruction of a belief. The believers themselves might go after the Supreme Ruler once they discover his youth or his actual physical form. Not to mention what someone with actual power might do to prevent the ruler's existence from becoming known."

"You're right, Commander," O'Brien said. "We can't defend the ship here. So that leaves us with only one choice."

"If we remove the chamber with the Supreme Ruler in it, we still have the problem of the valuables," Dax said.

"That wasn't the choice I was thinking of," O'Brien said.

"Obviously, Chief, you have something in mind that we haven't thought of. What is it?" Sisko asked. He took his hand off the panel and turned so that he could see O'Brien's face.

"I think we'll have to take the *Nibix* to *Deep Space Nine.* We can defend it there."

"And you're calling me unrealistic," Bashir said. "You propose to haul this ruined piece of equipment through Jibetians and Cardassians and somehow hook it up to the station."

"It's not a ruined piece of junk," O'Brien said. "It's in remarkable shape for its years and for all that has happened to it."

"The Supreme Ruler is in remarkable shape for his years and for all that has happened to him, but I wouldn't put him through the middle of a potential battle right now," Bashir said.

Sisko held up his hand for silence. His initial

reaction had been the same as Bashir's, but he also knew O'Brien well enough to understand that his chief wouldn't suggest anything completely impossible. "You believe that the *Defiant* can pull the *Nibix* to *Deep Space Nine* without doing any damage to the *Nibix.*"

"I know it can," O'Brien said.

"But the Jibetians. The Cardassians. Surely they count," Bashir said.

"You're five steps ahead of us, Julian," Dax said. "I want to hear how the chief believes he can get the *Nibix* off this rock first."

"That's the problem, isn't it?" O'Brien said. "Even the tractor beam is useless if we can't get the *Nibix* back into space."

"But you have a plan," Sisko said.

"I've been thinking about it since we got here," O'Brien said. "You're interested in this ship for its historical mystery. But it was giving me a technical mystery as well. One that I'm only now discovering all the answers to."

"You could share them," Bashir said.

O'Brien gave him an annoyed glance. "I was about to. You see, the fact that the *Nibix* still exists is amazing all by itself. When the ship hit this asteroid, it wasn't a direct blow. Probably what happened is that the ship and the asteroid were going in the same direction and they were pulled together."

"Of course," Dax said. "I've been so interested in the contents of the ship that I hadn't thought of the ship's presence at all. If it had been a direct hit or even a glancing blow, we would only have a crater to explore."

O'Brien nodded in agreement and went on. "So I did some more scanning and determined that this ship is structurally sound. In a few places the hull has been ruptured, but in ways that affect life support, not structural integrity. If I placed a dozen or so freight antigrav units in strategic positions around the hull of the ship, it would give this thing just enough of a boost that the tractor beam on the *Defiant* might be able to pull it free."

Sisko glanced around the ship. Here, in the control room, such a thing sounded possible. But he remembered the destruction in the chambers near the Supreme Ruler's chamber, and that made him skeptical. "You think we can do this without ripping the *Nibix* apart?"

"I wouldn't suggest it otherwise," O'Brien said. "This old ship has given us enough troubles without adding one more into the mix."

Despite himself Sisko shuddered. The last thing he wanted to imagine was the accidental destruction of the *Nibix*. He clasped his hands behind his back and walked away from the group. He needed a moment to think.

There were so many factors here, each one spelling disaster and each one hinging on decisions he made. He still felt as if he wasn't thinking like a commander, but like an excited kid. Of course he would like to bring this toy back to his station. But was that the best thing for the *Nibix,* for the Federation, and for the station itself?

He wished, more fervently than ever, that he had never seen the statue, that the *Nibix* still remained a legend, a myth, a figment of a collective imagination.

He walked back to the group, still undecided.

"Dr. Bashir, if you have use of the station facilities, can you save the Supreme Ruler?"

"There's no guarantee, sir," Bashir said. His slender features had a haunted look. "But at least we'd have a chance."

"Not to mention three other doctors from Federation starships," O'Brien said.

Bashir nodded. "The consultation would be very helpful and very welcome."

"And it would show the Jibetians that we're doing all we can," Dax said.

"They'll have to understand that nothing like this has ever been tried before," Bashir said. "That must be a factor."

"You're asking for logic in religion, Doctor. Some races can't combine the two at all," O'Brien said.

"That's very cynical," Dax said.

"I'm sorry," O'Brien said. "I'm not usually that way. I've just been thinking what would happen to the O'Brien clan if I suddenly went back eight hundred years. The history of Ireland on Earth is rife with all sorts of religious misunderstandings, some logical and some not."

"But we're talking about the Jibetians," Sisko said, "who, after their revolution was quashed eight hundred years ago, have been stable ever since."

"That concerns me, Benjamin," Dax said softly.

He glanced at her. He didn't need more concerns.

"Jibetian history says that the Supreme Ruler's main assistant had this ship built. But he was also the one who quashed the revolution and ruled while he waited for word of the Supreme Ruler."

Sisko frowned. "I thought scholars decided that the Supreme Ruler had been hasty in leaving Jibet. That if he had waited, he would have continued to rule Jibet instead of his assistant, Bikon."

"That was the theory," Dax said. "But that was before we knew of the sabotage."

"A double-cross?" Bashir asked.

"Possibly," Dax said. "It was a conundrum with no real answer. The Jibetians always sort of skimmed over it in the history. No one ever thought to consider that Bikon might have betrayed the Supreme Ruler."

"Although they did acknowledge a small betrayal if I remember right," Sisko said. "They claimed that Bikon erred in leaving the Supreme Ruler's side. If Bikon had insisted that the Supreme Ruler stay, he would have."

"That's an old political principle," Dax said. "Admit a small mistake so that you don't get blamed for the large one."

"Now whose being cynical?" O'Brien asked.

"I don't understand why this is important," Bashir said.

"Because," Sisko said, "Bikon's family has ruled for eight hundred years."

"Discrediting him is like discrediting the entire government," Dax said.

"And you expect us to take this ship into the middle of a Jibetian fleet knowing all of this?" Bashir asked.

"We're the only ones who know about the sabotage," Sisko said. "It's not likely that Bikon let that information out. To anyone."

"That still doesn't make this safe," Bashir said. "You listed a number of reasons that this ship is in danger."

"But no one dares destroy it near the station," Dax said.

"I hope you're right," Bashir said.

Sisko did, too. He met Dax's gaze over Bashir's shoulder. Her eyes were twinkling. She loved taking risks as much as Curzon had.

As much as Sisko did.

This mission might end both their careers and could cost them their lives. But the thought of flying the greatest lost treasure ship of all time right into port was a thought neither of them could let go of.

Sisko grinned at her, and Dax grinned back. The grins soon became chuckles, and the chuckles turned into full-blown laughter, the first laughter to echo down the cold halls of the *Nibix* in eight hundred years.

CHAPTER
17

JAKE HURRIED THROUGH the tunnels. Sometimes he was able to run. Sometimes he had to crawl. And at each intersection, he ripped off a piece of his shirt, leaving it as a marker in case he got lost again.

He was terrified that he would never find that room again. Then Nog and his family would be trapped forever.

From a logical standpoint, Jake knew that would never happen. Eventually the red alert would end, the shields would go up, and they would get out. But all the terror he felt while trapped had built into an overwhelming force since he escaped. Not only was his friend's life on his shoulders, but the station's might be as well. He had to find a way to get out of here before more information was relayed off the station.

He missed Nog's assistance and his company. Even

though Nog didn't help Jake into the elevated tunnels, his constant babble had kept Jake preoccupied. Now, when he encountered a tunnel so high that he had to grab it with his fingertips and pull himself up, he worried that he would never get to the top.

He didn't know how his father did it all, bearing this much responsibility every day of his life.

Jake had long since lost his sense of direction. He only knew he had never been in these tunnels before because the dust was undisturbed. It rose around him, like a cloud of smoke, getting into his mouth and throat, making him even thirstier than he already was.

A drink would be heaven. A shower would put him in ecstasy.

He felt as if he had been running for hours, but he knew he had only been outside the room for a matter of minutes. Each minute was valuable, though, and now that he was outside, he didn't know if the red alert had ended or not.

He couldn't hear anything except his own ragged breathing. And it was so loud, he was afraid that the Cardassian who set up the spy system could hear it, too. Even though Quark and Rom believed the system to be entirely automatic, Jake wondered. The lack of dust in the area around the equipment meant that someone checked on it.

The Cardassian, phantom or not, was his first fear. His second fear was that he would discover another room with automatic doors. These, his imagination told him, might be tied to motion or intrusion, and he would be trapped forever.

His third greatest fear was that he would be crawling through this tunnel for the rest of his life.

And his fourth greatest fear was that he would die of thirst before ever reaching a way out.

He wasn't even sure he would recognize the way out when he saw it. When they had come in the grate near the Promenade, Jake hadn't really looked at it from the inside. He was afraid it would have blended into the wall on the inside, looking like a normal part of the tunnel instead of a way out.

He wasn't even really sure if it was a way out. Those bolts were on the outside. He still had his tools, but he wouldn't be able to remove a bolt from the inside unless it had the proper fittings. He wished he had looked at things more closely. He wished he knew.

Finally he saw a light ahead.

His heart pounded. His breath was coming even faster than it had before. This was the first room he had seen since he got out of the spy chamber, and it could be another trap.

Still, he had to go in it and see if he could escape through the peephole.

There had to be a way out. There just had to be.

The light ahead looked the same as it did in other rooms with peepholes. It provided just enough contrast to illuminate the darkness. Jake was able to stand upright in this part of the tunnel. He ran toward the light, pausing only briefly to place a piece of his shirt against the side of the entrance.

This room was half the size of the one he had been trapped in. It had no equipment—for which he was very thankful—and a short ladder leading up to the grate.

He climbed up the ladder and looked through the grate.

Right into the security office.

Odo sat at his desk.

Finally, Jake would have help.

"Odo!" Jake shouted. His voice rang in the small room.

Odo didn't even look up from his screen. He wasn't even doing anything interesting. Jake could see the entire screen from here, and all Odo was doing was checking the outgoing messages from the last two days. Dull stuff. Not the kind of stuff that took concentration.

"Odo! Help!" Jake shouted.

Odo always responded to a cry of help. But this time, he didn't even look up. He couldn't hear Jake. The room was soundproof.

"No," Jake whispered. He wasn't going to let this opportunity slip by, soundproofing or no soundproofing. He jammed his finger through the grate and yelped when he smashed against a hard, crystal-clear shield. No wonder the grate was soundproof. And no wonder that little room where he had been trapped with Nog had become so hot.

The grates weren't always used for listening. The one in Quark's was. The one here was used to spy on Odo's computer. Jake had learned from O'Brien a long time ago that Odo's computer had more security protections than the computers in Starfleet headquarters. Breaking into Odo's system was not an option— except through good old-fashioned eyesight.

Figuring out the purpose of the grate didn't really help him now. He had to get Odo's attention.

Jake shouted Odo's name again and then banged on the wall.

This time Odo looked up, as if he had heard something that disturbed him. Jake banged again, and Odo glanced at the wall. Jake stuck his fingers against the sound shield in the grate and kicked the wall again as hard as he could.

Odo came over to the wall and looked up at the grate.

Jake wiggled his fingers, hoping that Odo could see them. Then he banged twice again.

Odo moved away from under the grate, grabbed a chair, and pulled it under the grate. As Odo stood on the chair, Jake pushed his hand against the shield and then put his face as close as he could to the inside of the grate.

Odo frowned, then Jake could see him mouth the word "Jake?"

Jake wanted to jump up and down for joy. Odo had seen him and recognized him. Jake gave the wall two quick kicks and Odo nodded. Odo mouthed the words "Stand back" and then made a motion for Jake to move away from the screen.

Jake leaned back, although he remained on the ladder. A moment later a slim thread of liquid poured through a thin crack at the base of the grate. The liquid gradually spiraled upward and reformed into Odo.

They both stood on the ladder, which groaned under their weight. Odo put one hand on the wall for balance and glanced around the tiny empty room.

"A Cardassian spy tunnel," Odo said without surprise. "I thought we had all of these sealed. How did you get in here?"

"That's not important," Jake said. He was both relieved to see Odo and terrified it was too late. "Is the red alert still on?"

"Yes, of course." Odo frowned. "What does that have to do with this?"

"Nog and I, we discovered this room filled with spy equipment. Nog's trapped in there now with Quark and his father, and if we don't get out of here, the relay will—"

"Slow down," Odo said. "Who is trapped?"

"Nog, Rom, and Quark. But that's not as important as the relay," Jake said.

"What relay?"

"The one that has been sending information off the station. Rom thinks it sends information to a nearby ship at regular intervals."

"Everything that's said on the station gets relayed to the Cardassians." Odo shook his head. "I should have known they would reestablish this system. Do you know what information they have?"

"All I know is that the monitors are focused on Ops and your office and every other important place. Including what Rom thinks is the relay."

"Well done," Odo said. "Do you think you can find your way back to that main panel or do we need to launch a search party?"

"I think I can find it," Jake said, holding up the bottom of his tattered shirt. "I left markers."

Odo nodded his approval. "Stay right here. I'll be back shortly. I need to report what you've found. It might make a difference."

Jake didn't argue. Odo's word was always good. He would be back. Odo slid into a pool of liquid, which flowed up the wall and through the grate.

Jake took a deep breath and dropped to the floor. He had never felt so much relief in his life. At least someone knew where they were now. And soon he would rescue Nog and his family and escape this place.

He leaned his head against the wall. He never realized how truly exhausting adventure could be.

* * *

Kira hated the meeting room off of Sisko's office. Its vaguely oval shape and its Cardassian design made her think of all the failed war councils the Bajorans had held with the Cardassians over the years. Usually she could set the feeling aside, but not today. Not with a Cardassian fleet outside *Deep Space Nine.* A Cardassian fleet lead by Gul Dukat.

The three starship captains had all taken seats in the room. No one took the head chair, and Kira, a major, wasn't about to. She also didn't want to sit by any of them. As a group, they made her nervous. She had the distinct impression that they made each other nervous. And she supposed it made sense. Starship captains were used to making decisions on their own at lightning speed in the far reaches of the galaxy. Sometimes they followed orders, but often they were the supreme commanders of their own tiny empire.

The problem with three captains was like having three Vedeks controlling one tiny area of Bajor. Each would think he was right, and none outranked the other.

And they all outranked Kira.

She remained standing. She leaned against the cool metal walls and watched as the captains settled into their places. Higginbotham sat alone on the side nerest the wall. He was a tall, lean man whose length was in his torso. He towered over the group.

Kiser was also tall but not as tall as Higginbotham. He was imposing, though, in his own way. All traces of his humor were gone. When he said hello to Kira, it was as if she were looking at a different man than the one she had met a few years before. That Captain Kiser had been relaxed. This one looked like he would be a formidable opponent if crossed.

Mouce was about Kira's size, and she moved with power. She took the chair beside Captain Kiser and, although he was much bigger than she was, seemed almost to dwarf him.

Apparently Higginbotham had been the brains behind the idea. The others appeared to let him run the meeting, although Kira knew that appearance would change should any of them disagree with him.

No one even seemed to remember Kira was in the room.

Until Odo came through the door.

Kira pushed away from the wall. Odo never let himself in a private meeting. All she needed was this sort of gaffe in the middle of the crisis.

Unless something else happened.

"Odo," she said as she hurried to his side, "this is a private meeting."

"I'm sorry to intrude, Major, but we have an urgent problem."

"Handle it," Kira said.

"I would," Odo said, "if it were within my capabilities, but it is not. It depends on you. On all of you, I suppose."

Mouce stood, her hands flat on the table top. "And just who are you?"

Kira turned. Of course, Captain Mouce didn't know. She had never been on the station before. "Odo is our chief of security."

Odo nodded at her, then turned his attention to Captain Higginbotham. "No one contacted Starfleet about the discovery of the *Nibix,* right, sir?"

Higginbotham smiled. "I don't know, Odo. Admiral Wolfe contacted me."

"What's this all about, Odo?" Kira asked.

"I believe we found the leak, Major. But if so, we may have another problem. I trust the Federation discovered the *Nibix* by overhearing Cardassian and Jibetian communiqués?"

"Forgive me, Odo," Higginbotham said. "But to give you any information at all would violate Starfleet protocol. You are not an officer. You aren't even a member of Starfleet."

"Neither am I," Kira said, "and you've been talking to me."

"The Federation has an understanding with the Bajorans," Kiser said. "This man is a Changeling, aren't you, sir?"

Odo took a step back, his movements jerky as they often were when confronted with his heritage.

"Odo was raised in this quadrant," Kira said. Her face was warm. She could feel the tension, bottled up inside her all day, turn to anger. "He didn't even know who his people were until last year."

"That's right," Kiser said. "On a mission in which both you and he were held by the Changelings for a short time, isn't that correct?"

"Are you implying something, sir?" Kira said. "Because if you are, you should know that I hate implications—"

"Major." Odo's voice was soothing. "This will get us nowhere."

"Perhaps, Mr. Odo," Mouce said, "you should give us the facts, and we can make whatever decision you believe is so important."

Odo nodded at her with what seemed like gratitude.

Kira clenched her fists. It took a physical effort to keep quiet.

Odo glanced at her, then addressed his remarks to

Higginbotham. "We have discovered a Cardassian spy system within the station. The information is gathered from points all over the station, including Ops, my office, and this room. We think the information goes to a relay, which sends it regularly to a ship docked at *Deep Space Nine.*"

"You're sure about this?"

Odo nodded. "The system is in some old spy tunnels. Commander Sisko and I cleared out the electronics and sealed the spy station when he came to *Deep Space Nine* three years ago. Within the last few months, someone must have reopened the system, put in new equipment, and set up the relay."

"Why haven't we noticed this before, Odo?" Kira asked.

"We haven't had need for this kind of secrecy since—"

"—the treaty negotiations," Kira said and sat down in one of the empty chairs. The negotiations between Bajor and Cardassia, conducted here on *Deep Space Nine,* at the cost of Vedek Bareil's life. "You think they were established then?"

"No," Odo said. "I checked the tunnels at that time. But afterward, I think the Cardassians did not want to be at a disadvantage again. My guess is that whoever got the information first about the *Nibix* broadcast it far beyond just the Cardassians."

"The history of the relay doesn't matter," Mouce said. "What matters is whether or not Mr. Odo is telling us the truth."

"He is," Kira said.

"Until we can disable that relay," Higginbotham said, "we can't beam out of here."

"Who's your chief engineer?" Kiser asked Kira.

"He's on the *Defiant*," she said.

"Then who would be your second choice, Major?"

"I'm fairly handy with laser tools," Odo said.

"And you're a Changeling," Kiser said. "I know Ben Sisko trusts you, but he and I have been known to have differing opinions. I think that—"

That was too much. She couldn't let this go on, starship captain or not. "I think that you had better stop maligning Odo's honor, Captain," Kira said. "He's done more for this station and for Starfleet than half the officers in your fleet. There are a dozen people, admirals among them, who would vouch for this man's decency and his loyalty. Don't question it."

"So you would have him do it?"

"I most certainly would," Kira said.

"That's good enough for me." Higginbotham stood in an attempt to end the conversation.

"But you're not the one in charge here, are you, Paul?"

Higginbotham looked at Kiser. "Are you suggesting, Jim, that we need someone to take charge?"

"Captain," Mouce said, the word covering both of them, "we're not dealing with Changelings here. We're dealing with a near ally and a planet with whom we have a treaty. To throw in another conflict is to lose track of where we're at. Major Kira, the situation exists on your space station. Remedy it and quickly. We'll stay here for the moment, but none of us want to be separated from our ships for long."

"Thank you, Captain," Kira said. She nodded to Odo, who left before someone could countermand Mouce's order. She wiped her hand over her face. The Cardassians' spy system was set up again. And someone had sent information about the *Nibix* all over the galaxy. No wonder the Ferengi had shown up. Others would show up soon, too.

Between the mercenaries, the opportunists, and the two war fleets, *Deep Space Nine* would soon be chaos.

CHAPTER
18

HE FELT LIKE he was sitting in a crypt. Julian Bashir climbed the stairs to the Supreme Ruler's sleeping unit. The man's face hadn't changed. He still looked serene. It seemed odd to Bashir that the man before him *looked* younger and was actually hundreds of years older than Bashir was. If the Supreme Ruler ever did wake up, the shock of being so far into his own future might just kill him.

Bashir smiled at the thought. Earlier O'Brien had told him he was thinking five steps ahead. Now he was thinking twenty steps ahead. If the *Nibix* lifted off the asteroid, if they made it back to DS9, and if they managed to revive the Supreme Ruler, then the shock of surviving might kill him.

Seemed ridiculous to worry over.

But then it might be the cold.

He hadn't ever been this cold, and except for a

small unit on the effects of temperature in medical school, he didn't know much about it. Perhaps it made a man find humor in situations that were essentially humorless.

Or perhaps that was simply the mind's way of dealing with too many stresses, too much information.

That seemed more logical.

He sighed and sat on the platform. Its chill soaked through his deep-cold pants. O'Brien's words about never being warm again after cold sleep returned to him.

No one had ever been in cold sleep for eight hundred years. No one knew the effects. Maybe Bashir could revive the Supreme Ruler only to discover the man had permanent frostbite or that the cold had gone to his head, literally.

He sighed. It wasn't the cold or the number of events that made his black humor appear.

It was fear.

Dax had told him his entire career would be on the line when it came time to wake up the Supreme Ruler. His future, his post at *Deep Space Nine,* his ability to face challenges like this one, might all go away if he failed here.

And even that wasn't as important as the Supreme Ruler's life.

Bashir put his gloved hand on the cold-sleep chamber. He could do nothing to guarantee the man's condition if he lived. He remembered this twisting in his stomach from prolonging Vedek Bareil's life unnecessarily, turning a warm and generous man into a machine, bit by bit, for the political benefit of the Kai.

Bashir wasn't sure whom the Supreme Ruler's survival benefited. Not the Jibetians, because his presence would cause internal turmoil of unparalleled degrees. Not the Federation, because they would have to deal with that turmoil. Not even the ruler himself, who would be a man out of time, a man whose life was literally centuries in the past. Even if he were resilient enough and flexible enough to survive that change, to expect him to rule over a world so changed from the one he left would be complete folly.

Yet Bashir had taken an oath. And even if his career and his own future did not depend on saving this man, he would do so. He had learned and he deeply believed that each life was important.

Somehow, though, he would have to find a way to make the Supreme Ruler's life worth living.

If the ship got off this asteroid.

If they managed to sail past the warships.

If the Supreme Ruler could be revived.

If. If. If.

Bashir sighed and waited. He would monitor the Supreme Ruler and make certain that liftoff did not disturb the sleep chamber. His equipment was nearby in case something went wrong at this early stage. Although he knew, Dax knew, and Sisko knew that if it did, the Supreme Ruler would not survive.

His comm badge chirruped. He hit it. "Bashir."

"Doctor." The voice belonged to Sisko. He had arrived on the *Defiant* then. "How's the patient?"

"I can safely say that there's been no change at all."

"And you?"

He sighed before he answered. "I'm as ready as I'll ever be."

"Good," Sisko said.

"Commander?"

"Yes, Doctor?"

"Go lightly. I don't know how liftoff will affect my patient."

"I'll relay your concerns to the chief," Sisko said and signed off.

But the chief already knew his concerns. They all did. Bashir just had to voice them one final time.

Because he truly believed that this ship would never rise from this asteroid. His patient and his career would die here in the cold barren darkness, on a ship that should have remained a part of myth forever.

Dax finished setting the antigrav unit to full spread and force and crawled out of the tight passageway. Her hands were shaking as she finished but not from the cold. The entire passageway was lined with jewelry, all of it contained behind the same glasslike substance that formed the top of the cold-sleep chambers. The jewelry had traditional Jibetian settings, some in gold and some in that glowing green, and all of them were priceless. The Curzon part of her cited rarity and begged to touch one. Just one.

She ignored it as best she could.

And that meant allowing her hands to shake, because they needed to move. If she allowed them any more movement, they would touch a glass panel and all would be lost.

The passageway opened into a wide sleep chamber. The dead in this room had a completely different appearance than the other dead. Here, her tricorder told her, the sleep chambers had stopped functioning centuries before the *Nibix* landed on the asteroid.

She wondered who was in here and when—or if— the saboteur had planned for this entire room to fail early. Probably not. It was beyond anyone's reason-

able expectations for the cold-sleep chambers to survive as long as they had.

She climbed around a few chambers to the wider
aisle in the center. Still, she couldn't prevent herself
from looking through the clouded glass. The clothing
was formal and as rare as the jewels in the hold. Most
of it was made of a velvetlike material, deep and thick
and beautifully embroidered. The dead looked as if
they were going to a party instead of planning a
seventy-year nap.

Until she looked at their faces. The faces had
mummified. The skin was wrinkled and dried. It
adhered to the bones. The eyes were sunken inward,
and she was glad they were closed because she didn't
want to see the condition of the eyeballs. The lips
were pursed in a mock pucker as if they were all
waiting to be kissed.

She was glad that she didn't believe in ghosts. This
ship would be ripe for such things.

She tapped her comm badge. "Chief, I've got my
two set."

Her voice echoed in the room. No one had spoken
in here in eight hundred years. She could almost see
the dead opening their eyes in surprise.

The comm line made a faint hiss. Then O'Brien
said, "I'm ready here, too."

She was glad he was still on the ship and would be
throughout this. She had a lot of skill but not nearly as
much as Miles O'Brien. Julian was guarding the
Supreme Ruler, even though they all knew that one
mishap in that area would be a disaster not even
Julian's talents could ease.

"Let's meet back in the control room, Chief," she
said and signed off without waiting for his answer.

She had moved one of the heaters to the control

room earlier. She hoped it would be warm there now. Or warmer. This cold was deadly.

As she made her way to the corridor, she tapped her comm badge again. "Benjamin?"

"Sisko here," he said in his command voice. He had to be on the bridge of the *Defiant*. She could hear the dampened excitement in his tone and knew that his movements were a little sharper, his features a little more fluid, than normal. She felt the same way.

"The chief and I will be in the control room in one minute."

"Good," Sisko said. "We're nearly ready here. But I want you to do one more thing."

"Yes?"

"There seems to be power around here. See if you and the chief can get any systems running in the ship. Especially the communications system. If that doesn't work, rig one up. It might come in handy."

"We'll do what we can," Dax said. She didn't want to make many promises. The systems hadn't been used in eight hundred years.

"And Dax?"

"Yes?"

"Stay away from the controls for the cold-sleep chambers."

He didn't need to tell her that. She already knew to stay away. But this was a delicate mission, and each word, each order, was being recorded into the logs. If something happened to the cold-sleep chambers and that command was missing, the blame for this entire mission would fall on Benjamin's shoulders.

"Absolutely," she said. Then she signed off.

Dax flashed her light around for one last look at the cold-sleep chamber. Deep black shadows wavered as her light moved. She could almost imagine the cold-sleep chambers popping open and the desiccated bodies getting out. She blew out a deep breath of frosty air and made herself relax. She was getting fanciful in her old age.

Still, she couldn't shake the feeling that they were trying to move an entire graveyard.

And the dead didn't want to be moved.

Instead of sitting in the command chair, Sisko paced back and forth in front of the screens showing the asteroid and the *Nibix*. At the moment the *Defiant* was still cloaked, having only decloaked long enough to get him back on board and to send down the supplies needed to secure the *Nibix* for lifting. Even that had felt like too long. He had Ensign Coleman monitoring the space around them, looking for any sign of mercenary ships, Cardassian warships, or Jibetians. So far, no one.

But that didn't mean they were safe.

He would conduct this mission as if the *Defiant* were already discovered. He would use that much caution. Although *caution* wasn't the word to use in describing this mission. A cautious commander would have notified the Jibetians of a possible discovery of the *Nibix* and let the cards fall where they may. A cautious commander would never attempt to haul the ship back to Federation space with an eight-hundred-year-old sleeping man aboard.

Of course, if he hadn't taken this action, no one would have learned that the Supreme Ruler survived. The treasures would have been lost to treasurer hunters and private collections, and the *Nibix* would have become the biggest political crisis since—since—

Well, that part was no different. He at least was preventing this from becoming an even bigger disaster than it already was. The actual discovery of the *Nibix*, no matter how it happened, was bound to create problems.

He could feel the ensigns watching him surreptitiously, all except Coleman who was studying the scanner as if it were the final fifty-point question on the Academy entrance exam. His pacing made them nervous. But he had too much energy to contain. Only Dax knew that. Dax, who felt the same way. Dax, who had thought their days of outrageous adventure over.

His senior team was all geared toward taking this risk. He didn't much like the thought of leaving crew on board that old ship as they tried to pull it free of the asteroid, but both Chief O'Brien and Dr. Bashir had argued that he had no other choice. And even Dax had agreed. Sisko needed to be on board the *Defiant*, and they needed to stay on the *Nibix* if this was to work at all.

Sisko turned to Ensign Harsch. "On my mark, trigger the antigrav units at exactly the same time."

Ensign Harsch nodded without turning from the board. Sisko had been over the process with him detail by detail. He had chosen Harsch because he had specialized in tricky antigravitational maneuvers in his Academy days. Harsch knew more about the units than anyone else on board. Sisko should have had faith in this—his team on the *Defiant* was young but among the best in the station—but he didn't.

The survival of the *Nibix* wasn't just important to the Jibetians and the Federation. It was important to him and not for any glorified career reasons.

Because he was walking through a dream. A dream that had turned more difficult than he had ever expected. A dream that in his waking hours he never imagined would happen. But a dream nonetheless. He had to honor it and his own excitement. For his own happiness, he had to do this right.

Sisko tapped his comm unit. "Doctor, brace yourself."

"Braced," Bashir responded.

Sisko next tried the control room. "Dax, is the chief with you?"

"In the control room and ready to fly into history. Sir," she said. He could hear the edge of excitement in her voice as well. She felt the same way he did: reckless and cautious at the same time.

"Transport, do you have a lock on the three crew members below?"

"Yes, sir," Vukcevich said from the transporter room. That was the most crucial aspect of all. If the *Nibix* broke up as it lifted off, Sisko wanted to beam his people to safety.

Sisko turned to Ensign Harsch. "Drop the cloak and start the antigrav units."

"Aye, sir," Harsch said.

Sisko watched the viewscreen in front of him, knowing that he wouldn't be able to see anything happening at first. And that if he could see, they had a disaster on their hands. The four antigrav units would never be able to lift that ship on their own.

Without turning, Sisko said, "Tractor beam, wide span. Cover every meter of that ship."

"Done, sir," Ensign Kathé said.

"Ease that ship off that rock, Ensign," Sisko said, wishing he could do every part of this operation himself. Hands on each station from the transporter to watching the Supreme Ruler to running the tractor beam. "Ease it off there."

For a moment nothing seemed to happen. Then

slowly he could see a change in the readings from the ship.

"It's holding together," Ensign Harsch said.

"She's flying, Commander," Chief O'Brien said. His voice rose with exaltation. "And I can't see a single problem down here. Not one. Oh, she's a lovely ship, sir. Just lovely."

"That she is," Sisko said, hoping their luck would hold a bit longer. Sisko let himself breathe as the huge ship lifted from the asteroid.

He punched up the magnification on his viewscreen to show the approaching *Nibix*. He had never seen anything more beautiful in his entire life. The *Nibix* flying again.

"Move us away slowly," Sisko said. And then he watched.

The *Nibix* in flight was a sleek black oval. It actually resembled the sleep chambers within. Its command center, with the clear dome, reflected the ambient light. Sisko felt that if he brought a shuttlecraft over the dome, he would see a giant sleeping within.

The ship had a charm most modern ships couldn't hope to attain. From this distance, none of the damage was visible. The *Nibix* looked as she was designed to be, as he had always imagined her, elegant against the backdrop of space.

"Dr. Bashir," Sisko said as he watched the ship grow in size in the screen, "how is our patient doing?"

"Sleeping like the dead," Bashir said.

Sisko shuddered. "Excellent."

"It's none of my doing, sir. I'm just baby-sitting."

And he would continue to watch, as would they all. The liftoff was only the first hurdle. The rest was yet to come.

CHAPTER
19

THE SOUND OF equipment drilling through the wall made Jake leap to his feet and move into the tunnel opening. The metal wall lit up under the heat of a laser. Sparks flew inside as holes appeared in the metal. Jake could feel the increased heat, even though he was a good distance back. His heart was pounding hard, and his breathing was uneven. He couldn't believe that he would finally be getting out of this place.

He hoped they had stopped the relay from sending information to the Cardassians.

He hoped they would have time to rescue Nog and the others.

After less than one minute, the wall panel under the view hole fell backward with a crash. Bright light from Odo's office streamed in. Two service personnel followed Odo into the tunnel carrying the tools they had just used to remove the panel.

Jake recognized them. He had worked with both of them. Imba was a tough woman whose physical strength was awe inspiring. Ube was thin, wiry and known for his ability to wriggle his way into tight places. Chief O'Brien had used him hundreds of times to repair tiny conduits in the shuttles and in the *Defiant* herself.

"Are you all right?" Odo asked.

Jake nodded. "I could use some water though."

Imba handed him the water bottle attached to her hip. She had an entire tool kit around her waist plus flashlights, a phaser, and a pack of what looked like deep-space rations.

Jake sipped. The water was warm and the most delicious thing he had ever tasted.

"Did you get the relay?"

"No," Odo said, "I just reported in. I need to know exactly where that relay is before we can shut it down."

Jake blinked. He hadn't thought to check. "It could be anywhere. All the screen shows is the wall panel and a bit of a docking bay. There was nothing distinguishing at all."

"I'm sure I'll be able to tell where it is," Odo said. "Come along. We don't have much time."

"This way," Jake said as Odo handed him a flashlight.

They crawled back through the tunnels. Jake was relieved that he had had the presence of mind to mark them. Except for the bits of shirt and some signs of disturbed dust, one tunnel looked the same as any other.

Imba had trouble fitting through some of the panels. Her height enabled them to reach the higher panels more easily, but the narrow ones slowed her down. If Jake wasn't so worried about getting that door open, he would have suggested leaving her behind. But Imba's strength might come in handy soon.

Other than that, the return trip was easier than he expected. What had seemed like an eternity to him actually took them ten minutes to traverse—and that had been slow because of Imba.

When they finally reached the door, Jake stopped. It still looked imposing. Big and metal and blocking the entire passage. He and Nog had approached it from the other side where it had seemed a part of the tunnel system. Here it was clearly a block, clearly a place that was forbidden territory.

Through the door, voices rose in argument.

"Quark is always true to form," Odo said.

"He said there's a way to open the door from the outside," Jake said.

"I sure there is," Odo said. "The key is locating it."

Imba and Ube took one side, Jake and Odo the other. They examined all the paneling until Imba discovered a depression just inside the door's lip. She pushed it, and the door slid back slowly, the metal grating as the door moved.

"Yay!" Nog yelled. "We're free."

"Get back!" Jake yelled and pushed Odo out of the way as Nog leaped through the door, rolling as Jake had done. Rom leaped next, and Quark crawled through, holding his head with one hand. A bluish bruise ran across the ridge of his brow, and a lump the size of his nose grew at the end of it.

Once he was safely outside the door, he glared up at Jake. "It took you long enough. What did you do, stop for a few games of Dabo before you decided to come back here?"

"The bar is closed," Odo said dryly.

"And if you hadn't done that, I wouldn't be here in the first place," Quark said, then he winced. "I need a doctor."

"Dr. Bashir is not here right now," Odo said and walked around Quark into the room.

"Well, he's got to have an assistant," Quark said. He gestured to Rom who came to his side. "Help me up."

Rom did.

Nog hadn't said anything to Jake. When Jake looked at him, Nog turned his back and crossed his arms. Nog seemed to blame him for the whole mess. "Look," Jake said, "I—"

"Mr. Sisko," Odo said from inside, "we don't have much time."

"Right." Jake slipped by Quark and went back into the room.

Its heat was overwhelming. They must have been miserable in here after he left. The panels looked the same, only Ops didn't seem to be the center of activity any more. Kira and three people he didn't recognize were in the conference room, having a heated discussion.

"Is someone going to get me to the infirmary or not?" Quark yelled from outside.

"Rom will take you," Odo said as he stared at the panels. Then, in a softer voice, he said to Jake, "I don't see the relay. Where is it?"

"Here." Jake pointed.

"You don't seem very concerned!" Quark yelled.

"I don't see any cause for concern," Odo said as he crouched. "You seem normal to me."

"I'm not normal," Quark's voice rose. "My head is the size of a Dabo wheel."

"That sounds normal to me," Odo muttered. "Ube, come here. See if you can tell where this relay is."

Jake got out of the way as Ube came closer. He crouched beside Odo. "Jake's right," Ube said. "Could be anywhere."

"Excuse me." Rom peeked his head in the room.

"You come back here!" Quark yelled. "I'm going to fall. Nog, help me or I'll fall. I'll fall!"

"Then fall and be quiet about it," Odo said.

"Excuse me," Rom said again. He came into the room.

"I'm falling!"

"I'm not going to take him to the infirmary, Rom," Odo said. "You do it. We've got more important matters here."

"I'm really falling!"

"No, you're not, Uncle," Nog said in as loud a voice as Quark had been using. "I have you."

"I know where that relay is," Rom said.

Ube and Odo both turned. Jake watched, a half smile on his face. Nog came to the door, Quark abandoned.

"Hey!" Quark yelled. "Hasn't anyone noticed that I'm injured?"

"Where?" Odo asked.

"Docking bay five," Rom said. "On the left-hand side of the bay as you enter. See? That black spot is from phaser fire, and over there is the remains of a Cardassian insignia, the only one still even partially visible in the station."

"I don't care about any dumb relay!" Quark shouted. "I'm going to die out here!"

"Thank you, Rom," Odo said. He spoke carefully, respecting Rom's dignity in a way that he never did with Quark. Jake was amazed. He always thought that Odo treated all Ferengi the same. Apparently his gruff attitude only applied to Quark. Then Odo tapped his comm badge.

The tiny Kira pacing the conference room looked up.

"Major," Odo said, "we have located the relay, and we are heading there now."

"Tell her I'm dying and you won't get me help!" Quark yelled.

"Make it quick, Odo," Kira said. Jake could see her small form talking while the three others in the room talked. She apparently didn't hear Quark's comment.

Odo turned to Imba and Ube. "I want you two to remain here in this room—"

"They should take me to the infirmary."

"—and when I give you the signal, I want you to destroy this elaborate spy system and trace all the links to the hidden cameras." Then he glanced at Jake. "Come along," he said. "We don't have time to waste."

They left the room together.

Nog was holding Quark upright. Quark still had one hand against his bruised head. Odo looked at it. "You might want to have a doctor examine that, Quark," he said.

"I've been saying that."

"And I would do so quickly. I'm sure that the Grand Nagus will want to speak to you when the red alert ends."

"The nagus?" Quark sputtered. "He's here? How'd he get here so fast?"

"The spy system, Brother," Rom said.

"I know about the spy system now," Quark said. "I just thought . . ."

But by the time he finished his thought, Odo and Jake were already hurrying through the tunnels. Jake only caught a quick glimpse of Odo's face, but he swore the edges of Odo's mouth were turned up in a teeny, tiny smile.

The meeting in the conference room was over. They at least had a few plans laid out, working only on what-ifs, but at least talking had made Kira feel better, more like the situation wasn't so out of control.

Kira hurried to Ops, the captains behind her, so that she could be ready. When Odo let her know the spy system was down, she would cancel the red alert and beam the captains back to their ships. And then she expected all hell to break loose.

She felt self-conscious as she stepped into Ops. As she had reminded Captain Kiser, she was not Starfleet, and she had three of the better captains in the fleet watching her every move.

Her every nontrained, nonregulation move.

And then she cursed herself under her breath. She had probably commanded more dangerous missions than the three of them combined. So what if she didn't follow their all important procedure. She knew some effective procedures of her own.

"Major," Tappan said as she moved toward her post, "we've been having trouble with the nagus. He's demanding to speak to Quark. And I can't find Quark anywhere."

"What else is happening?" Kira asked.

"Everything else is exactly as you left it," Tappan

said. "We haven't heard from the Jibetians, and the Cardassians remain near the station."

She sighed. She had wished for a diversion from the nagus. He was impossible under the best circumstances. But, as she had known from the moment Sisko called her to Security, today had not been her day.

"Hail the nagus then," she said.

Tappan did so. Within a second, the nagus's wrinkled face appeared on the screen. At twice life size, the hair sticking out of his ears looked like it hadn't been washed in years.

Kira resisted the urge to grimace in disgust. "Nagus," she said. "Forgive me for taking so long to get back to you. I only now heard that you were here."

"I actually didn't want to talk to you, little lady. I was hoping to speak to your captain or to that rascal Quark. He's not responding to any of my messages." The nagus sounded petulant.

Kira choked back her initial response to "little lady." "I'm sorry, Nagus. Quark is working on a special project for us right now and isn't available—"

"You sent him to the *Nibix?*?? Girl, that's like sending a woman to count the profits." Then the nagus blinked, realizing he had made an error. "If you know what I mean."

Kira put her hands behind her back and clenched her fists. "We're in the middle of some sensitive negotiations, Nagus, and we don't have much time for chat. Is there something we can help you with?"

"I need the directions to the *Nibix.*"

"The *Nibix?*" Kira asked. Captain Higginbotham was standing directly below her, struggling to keep a smile off his face. Kiser had his eyes closed and was shaking his head. And Mouce was showing the outrage Kira felt at the nagus's cavalier treatment. "Really, Nagus, I don't have the time at the moment to discuss lost treasure ships."

"I know you know where the *Nibix* is. I demand to know as well. You can't deny me just because I'm a Ferengi. We've been looking for this ship as long as anyone. There's a profit to be made here, lass, and I intend—"

"If I had the directions to the *Nibix*," Kira said, "I would happily give them to you. But no one has known where that ship is for centuries. That is, I believe, why they call it a lost ship." She couldn't take this any longer. Quark was bad enough—and he was a liberal Ferengi. "Now if you'll forgive me, my station is under red alert and needs my care. When Quark returns from his mission, I'll have him contact you."

"But—"

Kira signed off and the nagus's face disappeared off the screen. She immediately relaxed her stance and let out a huge sigh.

"You said you had no diplomatic skills, Major," Mouce said. "You managed that one admirably."

"I've dealt with him before," Kira said. "Yelling at him only encourages him."

"Major?" Tappan's voice was tight.

She didn't like the caution in his voice. "Mr. Tappan?"

"My screen shows ten more ships heading toward *Deep Space Nine.*"

"Ten more?" Kira shook her head. Her earring rattled. She must have done something to displease the gods. "Are they together?"

"I doubt it," Tappan said. "Three more Ferengi ships are converging from very different directions.

There are three Andorian trading ships and a Federation cargo ship. And the scavenger ship *Soltaires*."

"Jepson's ship?" Kira asked.

"The same."

"Jepson?" Kiser asked.

"Only one of the worst mercenaries in the sector," Kira said. "Who else?"

"I can't identify the other ships yet," Tappan said. Then he frowned. "Add two more."

"Track and identify each one as they come within range," she said. "Ensign Jones, help him."

She stalked to her own post at the controls. When this was over, she was going to resign her commission. No one, not even Benjamin Sisko, not even her beloved Bajor, demanded that she deal with Jepson, the Grand Nagus of the Ferengi, and Gul Dukat all in one day.

Alone.

"Major," Ensign Tappan said, this time not even turning from his board, "Gul Dukat has asked to talk to you."

"He would," she snarled.

Kiser grinned at her. He apparently felt the same way about Cardassians.

"Would you like to conduct this conversation?" she asked him, not pleased at his expression.

"It's your station," he said and bowed slightly.

"Very funny," Kira said. "Mr. Tappan, put Gul Dukat on screen."

She went back to her position before Sisko's office. She liked to imagine that it irritated Gul Dukat to see a Bajoran standing in the position of power on *Deep Space Nine*.

Gul Dukat appeared on the screen. He was at a

slight distance from his monitor. She could see his head and his upper torso. The Cardassian silver uniform was chillingly familiar.

"Haven't you gone home yet?" she asked.

"Testy, testy, Major. And here I thought this was old home week."

She would have none of his snakelike charm. "I told you to leave hours ago."

Dukat smiled. "And maybe I should have. Space around the station is getting limited."

"It would be a lot less limited if there were fewer Cardassian ships surrounding it."

His smile grew. "Of course. You need to make room for the additional visitors who will be here shortly. Apparently you have something everyone wants, Major."

"If I did, Dukat," she said, "I'd give it to them so that they'd all leave."

"Really? I never thought giving in was the Bajoran way."

"Being left alone is the Bajoran way, but Cardassians never learned that one."

"I would say that if you truly wanted to be alone, you wouldn't have all that Federation company."

So he knew that the captains had beamed aboard. How could he have missed it? He was so close to the station she could smell him. "We needed assistance with repairs."

He blinked and his eyes widened—the high-ranking Cardassian version of surprise. Once, just once, she wished their skin and blood vessel structure allowed them to blush. "Really, Major?" he asked a beat too late. "An excessive flow of information, perhaps. Can't you put a stop to it?"

"We can do that, Dukat," Kira said. "We just can't make Cardassians live up to their agreements."

"Indeed, Major? And what agreements are those?"

"The ones that guarantee they'll leave us alone."

"Now, Major. Your commander is away. I would think that you'd be happy for our assistance," Gul Dukat said.

"Then assist me," Kira said. "Go home." She waved her hand, indicating that the communication was at an end. Mr. Tappan severed their connection.

"Perhaps I was a bit premature in complimenting you on your diplomatic skills," Mouce said.

"I've known Dukat forever," Kira said. "He would think I was up to something if I didn't argue with him."

"I hope you're right," Mouce said.

Kira whirled. All afternoon she had been worried about what the captains thought, and when she finally got an inkling, she was past caring. "Listen," she said. "I don't care what you think of my skills as a leader or a diplomat. Just don't second-guess me in front of my crew unless you intend to command this space station."

Mouce held up her hands in the universal sign of truce. "I didn't mean to question you, Major. We're all quite tense right now. Something is going to have to ease."

"I don't think anything is going to ease," Kira said. She glanced at the screen before her, at the blips hurrying toward the station. They'd arrive, then others would arrive, and it would continue. Until Sisko got back.

She couldn't even imagine what would happen after that.

CHAPTER
20

SISKO STARED AT the *Nibix* a full minute longer than he should have as it came into position beside the *Defiant*. His historian's brain told him he was seeing a sight he would never see again in his lifetime, the flight of a ship considered long dead. And one that should have remained buried.

The rest of the bridge crew watched as well. All those young faces turned toward the screen, the awe on them reflecting the feeling in Sisko's chest.

He was the one who had to break the moment. He wished he didn't.

He tapped his comm badge. "Sisko to O'Brien."

"O'Brien here." O'Brien's voice sounded amazingly close.

"How's she holding up, Chief?"

"Beautifully, sir."

202

"Is she doing well enough to hold together at warp two with the tractor beams around her?"

"It shouldn't even strain her," O'Brien said. "I haven't seen starships with this much durability, and that's saying something, sir. I think, if I have enough time, I might even be able to start some of her smaller engines."

"Be careful," Sisko said. "We don't—"

"—want to disturb anything else. I know. Dax has been reminding me of that every five seconds."

"Stay vigilant, Chief."

"Rest assured, Commander."

Rest. Sisko signed off. He wondered if he would ever rest again. "Ensign Kathé, what's the situation at *Deep Space Nine?*"

She wrested her gaze from the *Nibix* on the viewscreen and looked at her scanner. "I count ten Jibetian ships, five Cardassian warships, three Federation starships, and one Ferengi vessel plus at least eleven more ships approaching fast."

Sisko nodded, returning to his post. They had to find that leak as soon as he got back. Instead of closing down the information on the station, it seemed as if the news had been broadcast all over the galaxy.

He tapped his comm badge again. "Doctor, how's our patient?"

"Uncommunicative and stable, sir, but then we like them like that." For all his humor, Bashir sounded a bit strained. Sisko probably would, too, if he were sitting alone in a room with a bunch of corpses and an eight-hundred-year-old sleeping man.

"Good," Sisko said. "Meet me in the control room of your ship immediately."

"And our patient, sir?"

"If his condition is unchanged, then it's safe to leave him, isn't it, Doctor? Your call."

"I suppose, sir, but I don't want to leave him unattended too long."

"This won't take very long," Sisko said. He stepped away from his command chair. "Ensign Kathé, you have the command. Keep a transporter lock on me at all times, and let me know if anything changes."

"Yes, sir," she said, glancing at the screen.

"And, Ensign," he said.

"Yes?"

"I know the *Nibix* is a beautiful sight. Just don't let it distract you."

Her face flushed in embarrassment. "I won't, sir," she said.

By the time Sisko beamed onto the *Nibix,* Dr. Bashir was also arriving in the control room. He looked cold; his cheeks were ruddy and his lips were pale. By contrast, the control room itself was warm. It had changed drastically from a few hours before. The place was brightly lit. The dark corners that had so fascinated Sisko were illuminated, showing some dirt and debris, eight hundred years' worth. The dome was still spectacular. Its view of space made him feel as if he were traveling without a craft. Above the dome, the *Defiant* flew, proud and strong and familiar. It lacked the elegance of the *Nibix,* but the *Defiant* was his ship, his baby, and he loved her a lot more.

O'Brien was standing near the oblong control panel.

"What have you done?" Bashir asked as he walked toward the Starfleet regulation heater. Sisko hurried beside him. The room was light, but it was still cold.

"We just turned on a few lights," O'Brien said, "and got a few power supplies going."

Dax crawled out from under a panel and brushed herself off. She still had dark smudges of dirt on her face, and her hair was coming undone. She looked radiant as she grinned at Sisko. "We should have heat any moment now," she said.

Something clanged behind Sisko. The three men turned.

"That's the heater," Dax said.

"Clanging?" Bashir asked.

She shrugged. "The machinery's old."

The smell of burning dust filled the area, a smell Sisko associated with the old homes of his childhood instead of ships in the depth of space. He smiled. He could almost feel what the *Nibix* had been like in her prime.

He turned to O'Brien. "Were you serious about being able to get one of the engines of this ship running again?"

"I don't think we can get the main drives to go," O'Brien said. "I'd be afraid to try that. But this lady has some pretty solid steering thrusters that would be easy and fairly safe to fire."

"Fairly safe?" Sisko asked.

O'Brien shrugged. "That's as much of a guarantee as I can give you, Commander. At worst, though, we shut them down, no harm done."

"And at best, the *Nibix* flies herself?" Bashir asked.

"Wouldn't that be spectacular?" Sisko murmured. He gazed up at the *Defiant* and the stars beyond. Somewhere out there, the station and all its problems loomed. But for the moment, he was on the *Nibix*, and she was flying.

"Now," Sisko said, "all we need is communication. We can still use our comm badges, but I would prefer to have ship-to-ship communications. Is that possible, Chief?"

O'Brien nodded. "We can do it in less than an hour."

"Good." Sisko turned to Bashir. "Doctor, can you beam the Supreme Ruler directly to the infirmary when we get close to the station?"

Bashir thought for a moment. "It would take me a good half hour to be ready for him. We need to move him to something that would approximate his cold-sleep chamber. I have the equipment for that. If I can set that up, we would be able to beam him across without damaging his chances."

Sisko could sense Bashir's hesitation. He knew that part of it was due to the unusual circumstance. Much of it, though, was simple timing. Somehow, he would have to give the doctor at least a half an hour near the station. He glanced at Dax.

"How good is your salvage law, old man?"

"You're the one who worked at Utopia Planetia," she said, "but I don't do badly on any aspect of Federation law."

That was Jadzia speaking. The brilliant young Trill. It amazed him that he was beginning to tell her apart from the other parts of herself.

"My understanding of international salvage law is this," he said, "any ship abandoned for over one hundred years can be claimed by the finding party."

Dax's smile was wistful. "That would be nice, Benjamin, but this is not abandoned. It still has a technically live occupant."

"Yes," Sisko said, "but no one in the ships around the station knows that."

"So," O'Brien said, "you *are* going to fly this old ship into the middle of that mess."

"Absolutely," Sisko said with a grin. "I wouldn't miss that for the world."

"But what does salvage law have to do with us?" Bashir asked.

"We're going in proudly flying Federation colors. We'll let the diplomats sort it all out after this ship is docked at the station." Sisko turned to Dax. "It seems, old man, that you are about to get your first command."

Dax opened her mouth, but nothing came out.

Sisko laughed. He knew that being on the *Nibix* affected her as deeply as it affected him. Commanding it pleased her more.

"Can you have your ship ready, Lieutenant?" he asked.

Dax nodded. "We'll be ready."

"That we will," O'Brien said. "The Federation ship *Nibix* will make us all proud."

Sisko shook his head. "We can't call it the *Nibix*. At least not when we approach the station. We can't even mention that word at all. We need another name." He turned to Dax. "It's your command."

Dax nodded and then slowly smiled. "The *Long Night*. The Federation Deep-Space Ship *Long Night*."

Sisko smiled. "The *Defiant* and the *Long Night* will jump to warp in ten minutes. We're going home."

CHAPTER
21

JAKE WAS AMAZED at how fast Odo found their way back through the dark tunnels to the opening cut into his office. He never even had to check the markers Jake left. He didn't even pause at the tunnel junctures. He just ran. And Jake had to work to keep up, even though Jake was in excellent shape.

They climbed through the opening to find one of Odo's security guards waiting for them—a woman whom Jake didn't recognize. She gave Jake an odd glance, which he hoped was because of all the filth that covered him, and then the three of them left the security office at full run.

The Promenade was empty. Jake couldn't remember the last time he had seen it like this. Maybe never. It seemed bigger, and the passageways longer. Their footsteps echoed as they ran.

No one spoke. No one needed to.

His throat was dry again, and he wished he had taken more of Imba's water. When all this was over, he would drink a gallon of water and eat two helpings of all of his favorite foods.

He would deserve it. If they were successful.

Jake and the security guard were panting when they reached docking bay five. Odo looked as if he hadn't made any effort at all. They stopped at the opening to the bay.

"We should have brought Rom," Odo said.

That was Jake's first indication that Odo wasn't able to see the panel either.

"He pointed to a laser blast and part of a Cardassian insignia," Jake said. He searched for the insignia. It had looked big in the monitor, but in actuality it might not be. The guard simply waited. She didn't know what she was looking for.

Jake took one side and Odo the other. It felt as if they were losing precious time, as if they would never find the spot. They had to find it. The station would remain on red alert until they did.

Jake made himself slow down and *look*. The diamond pattern in the metal repeated, floor to ceiling, except on the wall closest to the docking clamps. There, a thumb-sized depression showed the remains of a Cardassian insignia.

"Found it!" Jake said.

Odo turned. He glanced up, apparently looking for the laser slash, and then at the tiny insignia. "It is smaller than I thought," Odo said.

Jake nodded. He stood back as Odo and the security guard went to work on the wall. They had the panel on the floor quickly. Behind it was a small transmitter box, a light on top of it blinking red.

The box looked like nothing Jake had ever seen.

Odo studied it for a moment. "Rom was correct. It is set to relay the stored information from the hidden cameras every five hours. From the looks of it, we barely made this in time."

"Do you know how to disable it?" Jake asked.

"Of course," Odo said. "Stand back."

Jake and the security guard did. Odo nodded to the security guard belt, took aim, and fired. The box exploded outward. The sound in the tiny space was deafening. The air smelled of cordite and burning metal.

"I thought you knew how to disable it," Jake said, his hands over his ears.

Odo's odd little smile crossed his mouth again. "I did," he said and pointed at the box.

Jake peered inside. He couldn't recognize the transmitter any more. It had fused into a mass of melted circuits and wires. A tiny fire burned in the center of it. The guard took the extinguisher off the far wall and put the fire out.

Odo tapped his comm badge. "Ube, have you located all the hidden cameras?"

"Yes, sir." Ube's voice came back strong.

"Then destroy that board and everything behind it," Odo said. "Go after the cameras next. We'll take care of the one here on the docking bay."

Jake looked back and up in the direction the camera had to be but couldn't see a thing. He, Odo, and the guard moved down the hall slowly scanning the walls and ceiling until finally Odo spotted it. A small lens, no bigger than the head of a pin, stuck into a tiny hole in a ceiling panel.

Odo pointed to the lens and the security guard leveled her phaser. The small lens, a section of the

ceiling panel, and a small device behind the lens
disappeared in a red glowing mass.

Odo tapped his comm badge again. "Major, we
have destroyed the spy system, but I would like
permission to board and search the ship docked at
cargo bay five."

"Permission granted," Kira said. "Good work."

Odo patted Jake on the back. "Well done," he said.
"Now, shall we see this through to the end?" Odo
headed toward the docking bay door.

Jake's stomach clenched. He wasn't quite sure why
Odo was taking him this far. His father would have
left him behind. If any part of this mission was
dangerous, this would be it.

Then he grinned.

Enough of imagined dangers. He would confront
the real thing. At Odo's side.

Kira let out the breath she had been holding. At
least one thing had gone right. Odo had stopped the
information leak. After this, she would make certain
no area of this station went unexamined for long
periods of time. She hated the idea of the Cardassians
watching her every move. She thought she had gotten
past that a long, long time ago.

"I think we can take our leave of you now," Mouce
said.

Kiser smiled at her. "Anxious to get back to your
ship, Captain?"

She grinned back. "Every moment away is agony,"
she said. Even though the tone sounded light, Kira
could hear the truth behind it. All captains had to feel
that way about their ships.

"Nicely done, Major," Higginbotham said. "Now
let's see how this thing plays out."

"We'll beam you back to your ships," Kira said.

"Ah, Major, excuse me," Tappan said. He was almost cringing as he looked up from his pad.

Kira resisted the urge to roll her eyes. "Mr. Tappan?"

"Commander Sisko is hailing us from the *Defiant*. He says the *Defiant*, with another ship in tow, is approaching at warp two."

"Another ship?" Kira repeated. She felt as if her entire body had gone numb.

"He does know the situation here, doesn't he?" Mouce asked.

"If he's within hailing distance, he's within scanning distance," Kiser said. "He knows."

"And he's bringing the *Nibix* into this mess?" Higginbotham shook his head. "I sure hope he knows what he's doing."

"We don't know whether or not he is bringing the *Nibix*," Kira said. "We're assuming that, but we could be wrong."

Mouce smiled. "I would love to see the expression on the Grand Nagus's face when he learned he had scurried all this way for no profit at all."

"Let's stop the speculation and see what's really going on," Higginbotham said.

But Kira was already ahead of him. She had indicated to Tappan to put Sisko on screen.

When his face appeared, she felt even more relief. He looked normal. Part of her had been worried that he would have been in some strange battle or would disappear into some space anomaly like the *Nibix* herself.

"Hello, Commander," she said, hoping that her relief didn't show in her voice.

"Major," Sisko said. She could see the bridge of the *Defiant* behind him. "I see you have lots of company."

"Yes, sir," Kira said. "And more on the way. *Deep Space Nine* is the most popular place in the galaxy right now, and Quark's isn't even open."

Sisko chuckled. "I'm sure I'll hear about that when I return."

Kira grinned. "I'm sure you will."

Then his smile faded. "Major, the *Defiant* along with the Federation ship *Long Night* will be there in one hour. The *Long Night*'s main drives are out, but it will be able to maneuver in close. You might have a repair team standing by. Sisko out."

The screen went blank. He disappeared before she had a chance to ask a single question. Such as where did he find the *Long Night* and what happened to the *Nibix?* Or was Higginbotham's guess right? Was the *Long Night* the *Nibix?*

Kira might try a stunt like that, but not Benjamin Sisko, Mr. Rules and Regulations himself. Although he had been willing to bend the rules a number of times. Not often enough for her tastes, but on occasion.

"The *Long Night?*" Kiser asked. "I don't think that name is in the Federation registry of approved ship titles."

"I didn't know there was a registry," Mouce said dryly.

"I believe that's the famous Kiser sarcasm, Captain," Higginbotham said. "The Federation prefers rousing names for its ships like *Enterprise* or *Defiant*. In absence of that, the ships are usually named for a famous person, place, or thing."

And then his eyes widened, and his gaze met Kira's.

"The long night," she said to him, "is another name for cold sleep."

"He *is* bringing the *Nibix* in," Mouce said. And then she laughed. "Of all the reckless, wonderful things to do."

"We need to get back to our ships," Kiser said.

"Wait!" Higginbotham said. "He's playing it this way for a reason. We must do the same. As far as we're concerned, this is a Federation vessel."

"Subject to Federation protection," Kiser said. Then he grinned. "Make certain your weapons systems are up."

Mouce laughed. "First thing I do." She returned to the position she had been in when she arrived.

"Drop the shields," Kira said to Ensign Jones. "Let's allow our guests to leave."

The other captains went to their original positions as well. Mouce looked at them, then tapped her comm badge. "Mouce to *Bosewell*. One to beam up."

As her frame dissolved into multicolored light, Kiser hit his badge, requesting a beamup. And when he was gone, Higginbotham did the same.

Finally they were gone. The bridge was empty except for Kira and her crew.

"Ensign Jones," Kira said, "the entire station should be at battle stations, but I want you to double-check. Raise our shields again, and make certain our weapons are ready to go."

"Aye, sir," Jones said.

Kira glanced at the blank screen. She wished she were with Commander Sisko right now. This was her kind of fight. Gutsy, adventurous, and one hell of a good time.

She would make certain he brought the *Nibix* to *Deep Space Nine.*

Or she would die trying.

Sisko clicked off his communication with Kira and sat down hard in his chair. He wished he could send a message to Dax. But to say much more would hurt their ruse.

Ensign Kathé turned to him, her hair swinging as she did so. "Do you think they'll buy it, Commander?"

Sisko smiled. "Of course not, Ensign. But they'll have to pretend they do."

CHAPTER
22

GENERAL CAYBE LOOKED like a caged animal. He had been wanting to take action, any kind of action, for hours now.

Hibar Ribe wouldn't let him, and the general knew better than to question him. Ribe sat in his chair, keeping his expression as neutral as possible, while he watched the events unfold before him.

The advisors were conferring. They had been conferring since he gave his last order. Mostly they were trying to determine what he was thinking. It made him wonder how often they wasted time trying to discover what he was thinking instead of actually thinking for him as they were supposed to.

The rest of the crew on the flagship was working tirelessly. The general had run them through their paces an hour ago, keeping them fresh and alert. Ribe wasn't sure what the general expected, but Ribe knew what he expected.

He expected to see the *Nibix* appear in his viewscreen and then in the dome any moment now. Especially after Commander Benjamin Sisko's last communiqué.

"The Federation Deep-Space Ship *Long Night?*" Ribe asked. "Does such a ship exist?"

The general snapped to attention. The advisors stopped muttering. The crew worked harder at pretending there was no tension around them.

"It seems to," the general said. "But we are checking to be sure."

Imbeciles. The general might believe that Sisko was towing a Federation ship, but Ribe did not. He stood. His lack of control on this ship frustrated him. If he thought he could, he would turn it around and head toward the coordinates of Commander Benjamin Sisko's message, find the *Nibix,* and blow it up.

But he couldn't. He had to wait until it appeared. He had to pretend, for his sake and the sake of his people, that he was overjoyed. He would have to pretend that the *Nibix*'s destruction was an accident.

An accident he would have to devise quickly.

He glanced up at the dome and saw a few ships above him. More had arrived while they waited. The starship captains had also beamed aboard *Deep Space Nine* and made plans. It was no coincidence that after Sisko broadcast his message, the captains returned to their ships and upgraded their status to red alert.

The *Nibix* was coming here.

Ribe glanced at the general and then the rest of the bridge crew. If he couldn't destroy the *Nibix,* he and a few of his most trusted advisors had to take control of

that ship and keep it sealed until his ancestor's
sabotage could be covered.

Somehow.

Kira studied the screen before her. No sign of the
Defiant or the *Long Night* yet.

She had to think of it as the *Long Night*. If she
allowed any other name into her mind, she might
blurt it out at the wrong moment.

"Mr. Tappan," she said, "give me the status on the
other ships."

"The four unidentified ships slowed when they
monitored the commander's message," Tappan said.
"They are waiting just outside scanning range.
Jepson's ship has taken up a position near the
Cardassians. The three Ferengi ships have aligned
themselves behind the negus's ship. All three
starships are in positions around the station and are
at red alert."

The alliances were beginning to show. Leave it to
the promise of wealth to destroy any hope of peacea-
ble terms. She desperately wanted to call Sisko and
ask him just what he was thinking. Then she could
plan her strategy. Instead, she had to work on her
guesses, based on her knowledge of Commander
Benjamin Sisko.

"How long until the *Defiant* arrives?" she said,
knowing she had only asked that question a short
time ago.

Tappan glanced at his screen. "Thirty minutes until
the *Defiant* and the *Long Night* are within range."

Kira leaned against the railing and forced herself to
take a deep breath. Thirty minutes. Thirty more
minutes of waiting. This was the part she had always

hated. When she had joined the Resistance, her cell leader had warned her about her dislike of waiting.

"If you're not careful," he had said, "you'll anticipate every attack, and destroy any chances we have."

She wasn't going to anticipate anything. Maybe nothing would happen. Or maybe she would find herself in the biggest firefight she had seen in years.

The cold had seeped through Dax's gloves. Her fingers moved more slowly than she would like. She hunched over the green panel in front of her, watching the glow grow. The power sources were tied to the green gems that the Jibetians had guarded so well.

The lights had transformed the control chamber from that of a coffin ship to that of a working ship. She could almost imagine what it had been like to work here all those centuries ago. Although no one really had a chance to work here. Not after the ship set off. The sabotage had seen to that.

O'Brien stuck his head out of the panel beside her and grinned. His ruddy skin was streaked with black dirt. Even his teeth had specks on them. He had been working like a madman and had managed to get some of the equipment running, and running well.

"I have the viewscreen hooked up so we're not flying blind," he said.

Dax tapped an auxiliary panel in front of her. O'Brien had rigged it on top of the *Nibix*'s communication controls. A perfect blend of Federation and ancient Jibetian technology. If he continued to do that, the ship truly would become a Federation vessel.

After a moment of sputtering, the small viewscreen winked on. Space zipped by in warp. A familiar sight. Just not one she had expected to see on the *Nibix*.

"Well done," she said.

"I also have a camera on the screen hooked up so you can broadcast," he said.

She wiped her face with the back of her glove, wondering idly if she were as filthy as O'Brien was. Probably. Maybe the extra layer of dirt kept her that much warmer. The tiny heater in the back wasn't helping much, and the heat that O'Brien turned on had made the temperature rise from unbearable to frigid.

She glanced quickly behind her to make sure nothing in the background showed the true identity of the ship. The walls were black, and the paneling wasn't working at all. No green glow. No insignias. Just a polished wall, like ones on a thousand ships. She knew that the ruse of flying in as a Federation ship wasn't really going to fool anyone, but at least she had to keep up the appearances.

O'Brien stood and brushed off his pants. "I don't have enough time to do much more."

She smiled at him. "You've done wonders." The fact that the ship flew at all, that the heat and lights were on, and that she had communications capabilities were small miracles.

Not like the gigantic miracle Julian would have to hope for once they arrived on *Deep Space Nine*.

She tapped her comm badge. "Julian, it's almost time."

"I'm ready," he responded, his voice shaking a little. She could hear his teeth chattering from the cold. It was good, for all of them, that they were nearly to the station.

"Stand by," she said. Then she contacted Sisko, using her comm badge, wishing she could test the board in front of her. "Commander, we have full visual and broadcast capabilities and are waiting for you to give the word."

There was a short pause, then she heard Sisko say, "Well done, Lieutenant. Contact the *Madison* now. We might as well get this started."

"Will do," she said.

"Good luck," Sisko said.

"The same to you," she said.

She took a deep breath and nodded to O'Brien. He flipped two switches and then indicated she should start.

"Lieutenant Jadzia Dax in temporary command of the Federation Deep-Space Ship *Long Night* calling the *Starship Madison*."

Captain Higginbotham's face appeared on the small screen in front of Dax almost immediately. She could barely make out his features. He was holding back a smile. *"Madison* here," Higginbotham said. "What can we do for you, *Long Night?"*

Dax took a deep breath. She and Sisko had gone over what she was to say, but she still needed to be very careful. "We have a medical emergency," she said. "An injured crewman needs care and Dr. Bashir of *Deep Space Nine* has asked that your chief medical officer and the chief medical officer from the *Starship Idaho* confer with him on the station."

Higginbotham frowned. He had clearly not expected that. "I'll contact the *Idaho* for you, Lieutenant," he said. "Both doctors will be waiting for Dr. Bashir on *Deep Space Nine. Madison* out."

The screen went back to showing the white lights of warp speed. Dax let herself breathe for the first time in a minute.

"That man is a pro," O'Brien said.

Dax nodded. "He and Benjamin have some history.

Benjamin said he wouldn't ask any questions. And he didn't."

"It's good he didn't," O'Brien said, "because answering them would have been difficult."

"Oh, it wouldn't have been that bad," Dax said, finally allowing herself to smile. "Unless we had let it slip that the patient had a severe case of frostbite."

CHAPTER
23

KIRA HAD NEVER worked with a crew so tense. Most of the established Ops personnel were off the station or had been off duty when the crisis started. Except for Jones and Tappan, who seemed unaffected by all the happenings around them, the rest of the crew shot nervous glances at both Kira and at the screens.

She wished Captain Mouce hadn't questioned her on the bridge.

She also wished she had Sisko's ability to put people at ease.

She wished she didn't pace when she was nervous. She looked behind her more than once, half expecting to see a path left by her black boots.

"Major!" Ensign Jones said. "The *Defiant*."

Kira whirled. On the screen before her, the *Defiant* and the ship it was towing dropped out of warp at full transporter distance from the station. She had never

223

seen a starship like the one beside the *Defiant*. It was long and sleek and black and five times the size of the *Defiant* herself. The ship had clearly not been made at Utopia Planetia or any of the other ship-building facilities located throughout Federation space.

But the Federation had claimed other ships as its own many times. This could simply be another of those times.

Although she doubted it.

Both the *Madison* and the *Idaho* moved immediately to flank the *Defiant* and the *Long Night* while the *Bosewell* stayed in position near the station. So far, so good.

"Commander Sisko is hailing us," Tappan said.

"Put him through."

Kira clasped her hands behind her back and tried to look calm as Sisko's very serious face appeared on screen. "Major, lower your shields so that Dr. Bashir can beam aboard. *Defiant* out."

"Lower the shields," Kira said to Jones.

Then she took a breath. She could ask Bashir questions when he arrived. Commander Sisko was simply not acting like himself. Kira wanted to know why.

A moment later, Dr. Bashir appeared. He was wearing cold-weather gear, and his lips were nearly blue with cold. His cold-weather uniform was covered with a faint black grit, and his teeth were chattering. "Ah," he said. "Warm at last."

"Shields up," Kira said as she approached him.

Jones nodded.

"Come to the office, Doctor. I need to know what's going on."

"I'm afraid there isn't time, Major." He wiped a gloved hand over his face. He was clearly exhausted, and a stress she didn't understand showed in his face. "Are the other doctors in my office?"

Kira nodded. "They came aboard ten minutes ago."

"Excellent." He took off at a run for the turbolift. "Notify them that I am coming. Then be ready in twenty to thirty minutes to follow the commander's orders exactly."

He got on the lift and, as it disappeared down the shaft, pulled off his gloves. Kira wanted to go with him, to know what the big emergency was about, but she had a situation of her own to deal with.

"It's starting, Major," Tappan said. "The nagus is shouting on all channels that the *Long Night* is actually the *Nibix*, and Hibar Ribe, the head of the Jibetian Council, is hailing the *Defiant*. The Cardassians have gone on full alert, and the Jibetian ships have moved into an attack formation."

Make that an emergency all her own. Kira turned away from the turbolift, her questions forgotten.

"Are all weapons armed and ready?" she asked.

"All ready, Major."

She made herself take a deep breath. This is what she knew how to do. If they wanted a fight, *Deep Space Nine*, the *Defiant*, and all three starships would take them on.

Sisko gripped the arms of his command chair. So far so good. He felt like a space cowboy, the kind he used to read about as a boy. Only this situation wasn't play.

It was deadly serious.

"Hold us here," Sisko ordered as the two starships took up positions near him. Anyone approaching the *Defiant* and the *Long Night* would have to put their ship between the three starships on this side and the station and the *Starship Bosewell* on the other.

"The Jibetian ships are moving into attack formation," Ensign Kathé said. "Their flagship is hailing us.

"On screen," Sisko said.

The man who appeared on screen had long features and the ridged cheeks of his people. His coloring was pale and his green eyes had flecks of white in them. He was older than the Supreme Ruler had been when he left Jibet.

"I am Hibar Ribe, head of the Jibetian High Council," the man said without making the usual diplomatic niceties. "I demand that you turn the *Nibix* over to us."

"Under intersteller salvage law," Sisko said, keeping his voice even, "the *Nibix* has been claimed by the Federation and now flies Federation colors as the *Long Night.*"

"You insult us, Commander. That ship contains the long lost wealth of the Jibetian people. You cannot claim it for your organization's gain." Ribe was clearly a diplomat. He knew how to twist things to put the worst possible face on them.

But Sisko understood the game and wouldn't play. "In case you hadn't noticed, Lord High Sir, the space around *Deep Space Nine* is hostile. Under the agreement between the Federation and the Jibetians, we are sworn to protect the *Nibix* in any way we can. By claiming it as a Federation ship, under salvage law, we make it clear to the hostile forces around us that any attack on the *Nibix* would be considered an attack on the Federation herself."

Got that, Gul Dukat? he wanted to add. Nagus? Jepson?

But he didn't. He was certain they all understood.

And perhaps one of them would explain it to the other ships coming into *Deep Space Nine.*

"This is unacceptable," Ribe said. "The *Nibix* is a Jibetian ship. We have a force here to protect it."

Sisko smiled. "And I trust you will do so. We cannot be too cautious at this moment. When we dock the *Nibix,* we will seal it. Nothing will be touched. Federation officials will arrive in twenty-four hours. I am sure something will be worked out at that time."

"And that gives you time enough to loot it."

"I assure you, Lord High Sir, that no item on the *Nibix* will be touched."

"I would be a fool to trust you with that much wealth," Ribe said.

"I am afraid," Sisko said, "that you already have."

"I demand to put one of my people on the *Nibix* immediately."

"Under interstellar law, sir, this is a Federation vessel. Your people will have access when the Federation says they can."

"You are creating a galactic incident with your stubbornness, Commander," Ribe said.

"Funny," Sisko said softly, "I thought you were by not accepting our very reasonable protections. Surely, after waiting eight hundred years to see the *Nibix,* a few more hours won't make any difference."

"It may be the difference," Ribe said "between peace with the Jibetian Confederation and a long, bloody war."

"That will be your choice," Sisko said. "I am following my orders and the Federation demands for this situation. Until my superiors arrive, I will continue to do so. The diplomats can sort this out. They always do. Sisko out."

He leaned back in his command chair. Ribe's

reaction was worse than he thought it was going to be. The man wasn't being reasonable at all. And he should have been. At least after Sisko told him about the security reasons for bringing the ship in under Federation protection.

His unwillingness to trust the Federation in this matter boded ill for the entrance of the confederacy into the Federation. But some groups were known to place wealth above all else. The Ferengi were one. Perhaps the Jibetians were another.

The thought made him frown. If that were the case, then they wouldn't even be considered for Federation membership.

But, as he had told Ribe, this was a case for the diplomats to sort out. They would understand Sisko's motives when they learned that the Supreme Ruler was alive.

He turned to Ensign Coleman. "Any word yet from Dr. Bashir?"

The ensign shook his head. "But we are being hailed by eleven different ships, including the nagus."

Sisko nodded. "Maintain this position."

"But, sir, what about the hails?"

Sisko shrugged. "I'm not interested in talking to anyone. Let them keep hailing."

By the time Dr. Bashir reached the infirmary, he was carrying his deep-cold uniform. His regular uniform was warm enough. He would have to scrub well before he touched anything, but he didn't mind. It was nice to be warm again.

"Ouch!"

The shouted word made him grimace. He recognized the voice. Quark's.

"Hey! Have some respect!"

That was all he needed.

He steeled himself as he entered the infirmary. His colleagues from the *Madison* and the *Idaho* were both bent over Quark. One was putting a compress on Quark's head, the other was holding a medical tricorder near Quark's skull.

The tricorder doctor looked up. Her long hair was tied back in a ponytail that moved as she did. "Dr. Bashir? I'm Celeste Silverstein of the *Madison*. I trust you didn't call us here to tend to a Ferengi head wound."

"Head wound?" Bashir said, snapping to. Head wounds were always serious. "What happened, Quark?"

"Sisko's son quashed me with a chair. The kid is stronger than he looks. And then Odo wouldn't bring me here. I could have died—"

"From complaining," the other doctor said. He was a slight man with an athletic build. He grabbed Quark's hand and put it on top of the compress. "I'm Dr. Wasner from the *Idaho*."

"Thank you both for coming," Bashir said. He peered at what he could see of Quark's head. A multicolor bruise peeked out from beneath the compress. "We have a matter of some delicacy before us that I can only discuss with you two. How serious is Quark's injury?"

"Nothing some ice can't cure," Wasner said. "He doesn't even have a concussion."

"Ferengi don't get concussions," Bashir said. "They're too thickheaded. Quark, I'm afraid I must confine you to quarters until your skull heals."

"Quarters! I need medical attention, Doc. You need me right here."

"No, I don't, and I'm afraid I don't have time to

dither with you." Bashir set his deep-cold uniform on the other empty chair. "Go to your quarters."

"I can't," Quark said.

"If this is some kind of trick, Quark, play it on someone else. I have a medical emergency to tend to."

Quark grabbed Bashir's collar with his free hand. "You have to keep me here," he whispered. "The nagus is outside the station, and when he learns that I didn't tell him about the *Nibix,* he'll be after my hide."

"Tell it to Odo," Bashir said. "You're jeopardizing a man's life by being here."

"Doctor—"

"Quark, I mean it. If you don't leave, I will call Security and have them remove you."

Quark stood, attempting to look dignified even though the compress had slipped and was resting on his left ear. "I don't get any sympathy at all. I'm a wounded man. I should be allowed to stay here. Commander Sisko will hear about this."

"I can guarantee it," Bashir said, straightening his collar. "Now go away."

Quark did. He lingered near the doorway, and Bashir closed the door. Then he leaned against it. The other two doctors were looking at him expectantly.

"We have a difficult problem before us," he said. "Everything rests on the next few hours. Let me explain . . ."

Ribe strode back onto the bridge of the Jibetian flagship. Discipline had broken down. All the crew members were cheering and hugging each other. The general was clapping his second officer on the back. Even the advisors were grinning.

Except Advisor Concar who was watching Ribe.

They had recognized the *Nibix.* They were ecstatic about the return of the Supreme Ruler, the return of Jibet's wealth, and the fulfillment of all their dreams.

Dreams that threatened Ribe and his entire family.

He had had to contact the Federation commander from a room just off the bridge so that Ribe's sour reaction wouldn't be observed.

"Well, sir," the general said. "Give me the order. We'll take the *Nibix* under our protection."

"I'm afraid that the *Defiant* has made the *Nibix* a Federation ship under salvage law. They insist on docking it and sealing it until their officials arrive."

The general grinned. "I was hoping they would do something like that," he said. "We have a lot of firepower in our fleet, but not enough to hold off all the other ships waiting around us. Although the Cardassians should—"

"Hush," Ribe said. "No one knows that they contacted us. And no one needs to know." He glanced around. The celebration continued around him. No one seemed to notice that last interchange.

"Well," the general said, "waiting a day or so is a small price to pay for Federation protection. And we have the *Nibix.*"

"That we do," Ribe said. But not for long.

He hoped.

CHAPTER
24

SISKO BEGAN COUNTING the minutes after Bashir left the *Nibix*. Bashir wasn't late yet, but Sisko wasn't convinced that Bashir could rig up the proper equipment in the time allotted. And with Ribe's response, Sisko wasn't sure how much time he could give Bashir without opening fire.

On someone.

"We're still being hailed from eleven different ships," Coleman said.

"Any word from Dr. Bashir?"

"No, sir."

"How about the Cardassians?"

"They haven't contacted us either, sir."

The Cardassians worried him the most. He guessed that they were on hand to stir up as much trouble between the Federation and the Jibetians as possible, but that was only a guess. And until they spoke, he would know no more.

Finally, after nineteen excruciating minutes, Coleman said, "Dr. Bashir is hailing us."

Sisko felt the tension in his shoulders lessen. "I want voice only, Ensign."

"Aye, sir. Now."

"Doctor," Sisko said.

"Sir, we're ready here for the injured man."

"Quick work, Doctor. Stand by."

Sisko cut the communication and tapped his comm badge. "Vukcevich, are you ready?"

"Completely, sir," said the man in charge of transporting the Supreme Ruler from one cold-sleep chamber to another. He didn't even sound nervous.

Sisko was. Such a thing had never been tried before. Theoretically, O'Brien had told him, it should work as long as the Supreme Ruler's state remained constant.

Any problem with the transporter, however, a single slip, and the Supreme Ruler would not survive.

"Any changes, Ensign Kathé?" Sisko asked, just to make sure he hadn't missed anything.

"No, sir," she said. "A lot of the ships are talking among themselves on closed channels, but no one is moving."

Sisko took a deep breath. "If things are going to break loose, they are going to do so very soon. Everyone stand by."

He turned to Ensign Coleman. "Hail the station."

Coleman did. A moment later Kira's face filled the screen. "Go ahead, *Defiant.*"

"We are ready to transport our injured crew member to your infirmary."

"Understood," Kira said and cut the connection. She obviously knew the need for haste. Sisko wondered if Bashir had had time to fill her in on the plan.

Probably not.

"The station's shields are down," Ensign Harsch said.

"Mr. Vukcevich?"

"Yes, sir," responded Vukcevich from the transporter room.

"Energize," Sisko said. He then monitored both the *Nibix* and the station from his own screen. Nothing appeared to be happening, not that he would be able to see if anything did.

Only if something went wrong.

The minutes seemed to stretch. The bridge crew had frozen in position. All of them knew the importance of this transfer. If it failed, it would affect everyone's future.

Finally Vukcevich's voice came over the comm unit. "The transport was a success."

"The station's shields just went back up," Ensign Harsch said.

"Good luck, Doctor," Sisko said quietly.

It took them exactly eighteen minutes to rig up a duplicate cold-sleep chamber. They used one of Bashir's diagnostic tables and his frozen injury unit along with parts ordered through the replicator.

Jury-rigged at best.

But it would have to do.

Bashir hoped his luck would hold out. It had so far. His colleagues from the starships were perfect compliments to him. Dr. Wasner had worked with existing cold-sleep cultures on a recent mission. Dr. Silverstein had specialized in ice damage on the cellular level at the Academy. The three of them had enough experience between them to resurrect the Iceman of Sigma Delta Six.

They would need it.

Silverstein had nearly walked when Bashir explained their mission. "You can't really expect us to revive the Supreme Ruler after eight hundred years of cold sleep?" she asked. "If we fail, it will mean our careers."

Wasner had looked at her sharply.

"So I have been told," Bashir said. "So let's not fail."

She had said nothing until the Supreme Ruler beamed into their jury-rigged cold-sleep chamber. "Oh, my heavens," she said. "He's little more than a boy."

"That'll help," Wasner said. "And his condition's stable."

Step one down, Bashir thought. Only a dozen more impossibilities to go.

Ribe returned to the small room off the bridge. He couldn't stand the celebration. Fear made his skin clammy and his palms sweat. He would disappoint his people either way. If the sabotage were discovered, it would destroy the belief in the government his family had so carefully cultivated.

And if the *Nibix* were destroyed, it would destroy his people's hope.

Hope, though, could be rebuilt.

He bent over his own private communicator and sent a scrambled hail.

On his tiny screen, the Grand Nagus of the Ferengi

appeared. He was a hideously ugly man with age-spotted wrinkled flesh, a bulbous nose, and the largest ears Ribe had ever seen.

"What? Unless you can offer me latinum or a place on the *Nibix,* you are wasting my time," the nagus said.

"Then I'm not wasting your time," Ribe said. He shuddered at the raspy sound of the nagus's voice. "I would like to make a proposition to you."

"I'm all ears," the nagus said.

That he was. Ribe swallowed the comment back. "I am Hibar Ribe of the Jibetian High Council. We are prepared to offer you half the wealth of the *Nibix* if you can prevent the ship from docking at *Deep Space Nine.*"

"Couldn't negotiate with Sisko on your own, could you?" the nagus asked. "Doesn't surprise me. He's one of the toughest negotiators in the galaxy."

Ribe didn't care about Sisko. "Are you interested?"

"For ninety percent of the take," the nagus said.

"Ninety percent?" Ribe choked. "Based on what?"

"Based on the fact that we've nearly developed a way to break through the *Defiant*'s shields and confiscate all the wealth for ourselves. You'd get the remaining ten percent for making things easier for us."

"Nearly developed?" Ribe repeated. "Then you haven't developed anything. And you might not before the ship docks."

"We will," the nagus said, but he didn't sound too confident.

"Really?" Ribe said. "It doesn't matter to me if you board the ship or not."

"It doesn't?" the nagus asked.

"No," Ribe said. "Because if you refuse to help us, I'll destroy the *Nibix* myself."

"Destroy?" the nagus said. "You can't destroy it. That's the wealthiest ship in the galaxy."

"Money means nothing to me," Ribe said.

"Clearly," the nagus said. His ears had moved forward in apparent shock. "We'll do it for ninety percent."

"Fifty," Ribe said.

"I need to hire a few other ships," the nagus said, "and I have to make a profit. Eighty-five percent."

"I offer you sixty percent," Ribe said.

"Eighty," the nagus responded.

"Seventy," Ribe said.

"Seventy-five," the nagus said.

"Done," Ribe said.

"Done? Just like that?" the nagus asked. "No wonder you were no match for Sisko. He'd have held firm at fifty percent."

"I can go back to that if you want," Ribe said.

"No, no, there's no need for that." The nagus grinned. "Seventy-five percent will do just fine."

"We have a deal then?" Ribe asked.

"A deal," the nagus said. "We'll make sure the ship never makes the station. For seventy-five percent of the take."

"Excellent," Ribe said and signed off. He had the better part of the deal, although the nagus didn't know that.

Seventy-five percent of nothing was, of course, still nothing.

Nothing at all.

CHAPTER
25

JAKE STOOD BACK and watched while Odo tried to override the security code for the ship's doors. His fingers moved quickly, but Jake was getting impatient. He knew they were still on some sort of time deadline. He just didn't know why.

He was about to suggest that Odo slip under the door and open it from the inside when Odo said, "Got it!"

The door eased back, letting out the overpowering odor of rotting garbage. Jake's eyes burned. "What kind of ship is this?" he asked. "A Caxtonian vessel?"

"No," Odo said. "It belongs to an Andorian trader who claimed he was here for repairs. I suspect the repairs have been done for a long time."

"Do you think we should go in there?" He glanced at the security guard. "I mean, there's only three of us."

"That's more than enough," Odo said and walked through the open door.

The security guard stepped to one side, and after a moment, Jake went in.

The stench was worse inside, and its cause was easy to locate. The trader hadn't dumped his garbage into the recycling system. It sat in bags and boxes near the door, as if it—not the security codes—were meant to keep intruders out.

If so, it nearly worked.

Jake gagged but kept going, waiting until he got past the worst of the smell before he looked around.

The trader's ship was a small cargo vessel. All of the metal walls had been painted, each a different mismatched color. Bright green next to hot pink, pale blue beside canary yellow, burnt orange beside vivid purple. The walls hurt the eyes as much as the stench had hurt the nose.

"They spend all their time in here?" Jake asked.

"The Andorian idea of beauty does not match most of the rest of the galaxy's, I'm afraid," Odo said. He had already crossed through the sleeping compartments and was in the small corridor that led to the bridge.

"Obviously," Jake said. He gathered his clothes tightly around himself, glad they were already ruined. Otherwise he would have to work to get the stink off them, and that would probably be impossible.

The sleeping quarters were a mess of unwashed laundry, filthy uniforms, and half-eaten plates of food. Jake had never seen such slobbishness. He stepped into the corridor with Odo who put a finger to his mouth.

Ahead, on the small bridge, a mauve arm rested on

the pilot's chair. They couldn't see the person to whom it belonged.

"Let me go first," Odo said.

He stalked to the door of the cockpit, opened his mouth, then indicated that Jake should follow.

Jake was surprised that Odo didn't give the Andorian warning. It was only fair. Odo usually did that.

Jake approached the door, and then he realized why from the different smell.

The Andorian was dead.

"Who killed him?" Jake whispered.

"My guess is that he killed himself," Odo said and pointed to the fluted vial on the floor beside the chair. "I think if we test that, we'll find poison. Or something poisonous to Andorian traders."

Jake frowned. He didn't understand why anyone would do that. There appeared to be no clues on the bridge itself. It still looked functional. He stepped farther in. The panels in front blinked bright blue.

"What's this?" he asked. He didn't like what he was seeing. Not at all.

Odo turned and glanced at the panels just as Jake realized what he was seeing.

"It's a core overload," Jake said.

Another blue light flashed on. Then another. Odo pointed to the rest of the paneling. "He dumped the core safeguards before he killed himself," Odo said. "And I don't know enough about these ships to do anything about it."

"An overload doesn't usually take very long, Odo. How long has this guy been dead?"

Odo touched him. "I would say an hour, maybe more."

"That's too long," Jake said, his stomach clamping down into a tight knot. He remembered studying

core overloads during his work with Chief O'Brien.
"We've got to get out of here before this ship
blows."

"Move!" Odo said, shoving Jake toward the entrance.

They ran through the corridor, into the sleeping
quarters, over the piles of laundry, and back into the
room filled with garbage. Jake couldn't hold his
breath. He had to breathe the fetid air, and it made
him choke.

The door was still open, with the security guard
outside. "Get out of the way!" Odo shouted.

She did.

As they passed through the door, Odo hit his comm
badge. "Major, we have an emergency in docking bay
five. The core of the ship is overloading and will
explode at any moment. Release the docking clamps
and jettison the ship on my mark."

"Understood," Kira said as Jake scrambled through
the airlock. Odo slammed his hand on the airlock
button and hesitated just long enough to make sure
both inner and outer doors of the lock were closing.
He shoved Jake and the security guard down the
corridor deeper into the station.

"Now, Major," Odo shouted.

Behind him Jake could hear the sounds of the
docking clamps releasing and then four small explo-
sions as the ship was pushed away from the docking
bay. Ten seconds later a much larger explosion shook
the entire section.

Jake slammed into the wall. Odo flew past him. The
guard landed on her side behind him.

The sound was deafening.

Jake glanced back down the corridor at the airlock
doors, hoping that they had remained closed.

They had.

Odo had landed on his feet. Jake wondered if that was his particular skill. Odo reached over and helped him up. "Are you all right?"

The security guard was scrambling to her feet on her own. She nodded.

Jake could feel the bruises start. He would be sore the next day. "I'm fine," he said.

"Odo?" Major Kira's voice demanded. "Odo?"

"We made it out," Odo said.

There was a short pause. "Good. Join me in Ops as soon as you can. I think we're in for a fight."

Jake took a breath. He had nearly died there. He didn't want to go to Ops, didn't want to know what else could happen. But he had no real idea what was going on. He didn't even know who was fighting whom or why.

Or where his dad was.

"Why don't you go to your quarters?" Odo asked, obviously noting Jake's distress.

Jake shook his head. "You said we should see this through to the end. And I will."

The explosion of the ship startled Sisko. The brilliant orange and blue light spread in all directions. Pieces of the ship flew in all directions, some narrowly missed the docking ring of *Deep Space Nine*.

"Hail Kira," he snapped.

"I have her," said Ensign Kathé, who was already way ahead of him.

"Major, what was that?"

"A discovery of Odo's," she said. "That would have been the docking ring if he hadn't been on top of it."

"Any injuries?"

"Not on our side. Odo said the pilot was dead before they got into the ship."

"That was too close, Major. Have the other ships on the ring searched, and then confine their crew to quarters on the station."

"Sir—"

"Do it, Major." He signed off. He didn't want that explosion to be a dress rehearsal for the *Nibix*. "Ensign Coleman, what kind of ship was that?"

"An Andorian trader vessel. One of the others is hailing us and has been for some time. He wants access to the *Nibix* in exchange for the ship we destroyed."

"We destroyed?" Sisko frowned. "Tell him no access. And tell him to leave this area."

"I don't think he will, sir."

Sisko looked up. The Andorian trader ships had moved in beside the Grand Nagus's ship. So had Jepson's ship. It looked as if they were forming a fleet of their own.

He couldn't believe they would think they could get away with just taking the *Nibix* out from under the noses of the Jibetian fleet and the Federation. They didn't have the firepower.

Unless they were working for the Jibetians, and the Cardassians joined in. The Ferengi and the mercenaries would have the power then to take the *Nibix*. And by so doing would bring a very bloody war to this sector.

The explosion near the station was like the starting gun.

"Hail that Andorian freighter," Sisko said, changing his mind.

"There's no response, sir."

The Andorian ships swung wide of the Ferengi vessels and headed toward the *Madison*.

"Hail them, Mr. Coleman."

"I am, sir."

The Andorian ships opened phaser fire, the shots ricocheting aimlessly off the *Madison*'s shields. So far, the *Madison* was not firing back. Higginbotham was obviously waiting to see what else was going to unfold.

Two Ferengi ships peeled away from the formation, heading for the *Idaho*. They were firing phasers, quick, repeated blasts that made no dent in the *Idaho*'s shields. The *Idaho* swung around and headed toward the Ferengi ships. Sisko grinned. Kiser knew the cowardice of Ferengi was legendary. He would get them to stop the attack if there was no profit in it.

The remaining ships, led by Jepson, made a run at the *Defiant*. They were flying in a Y formation. The last ship, Sisko knew, would sail over the *Defiant* and head for the *Nibix*.

"Double the strength of the shield extensions around the *Nibix*," he said. "And get ready, people. We have a battle on our hands."

Jepson hit the *Defiant* with a barrage of photon torpedo fire. The ship rocked, and Ensign Harsch nearly fell out of his chair. "Sorry, sir," he said.

"Keep your post, son," Sisko said. "Ensign Kathé, keep me informed as to what the Jibetians and the Cardassians are doing. Ensign Harsch, you let me know if anyone gets near the *Nibix*. Ensign Coleman, on Jepson's next pass, I want you to hit his underbelly with full phaser fire. His ship has a weakness in the shields near its engines. You'll only get one shot. Make it good."

"Aye, sir." Coleman's voice was shaking.

Sisko stood. The Ferengi ship in this formation belonged to the nagus. He was wrong. The Andorian ship wouldn't go for the *Nibix*. The nagus would.

The ships had swung around for another attack. This time as Jepson flew overhead, Sisko shouted, "Coleman. Now!"

Coleman aimed the phaser fire and the Jepson's shields flared red. The red swelled, then the shields failed. The ship exploded like a kid's balloon against a pin.

The explosion rocked the *Defiant*.

"Ensign Kathé, get me the nagus."

"He's not answering the hails, sir."

"Then send this message. Tell him his ship is next if he doesn't stop this attack."

"Aye, sir." She hit her panel. "Still no response."

"Ensign Harsch, examine that Ferengi ship for weakness." Sisko glanced up. The *Idaho* had opened fire on the other Ferengi ships, but they were holding their ground. The *Madison* had crippled one trader vessel. The other two had drawn back, outside of fire range. So far, the *Madison* was not pursuing.

And the Cardassians hadn't made a move.

Neither had the Jibetians.

Sisko didn't like this.

The *Defiant* rocked with another blast, this one coming from the Andorian trader ship.

"Where's the nagus?" Sisko asked as he grabbed his command chair for balance.

"Over the *Nibix*. He's firing on it, sir."

"Firing on it! What is he doing? Put me on screen," Sisko snapped.

"They have a channel open, sir, but they're not responding.

"That's good enough," he said. "Zek, this is Commander Benjamin Sisko. If you fire on the *Long Night* again, we will consider your action a declaration of war upon the Federation. Is that clear?"

The nagus's face suddenly appeared on screen. "You owe us the right to examine the *Nibix.*"

"You're not going to get it if you destroy the ship," Sisko said. "And you're certainly not going to get it if you fire upon any Federation vessel. I order you to stop now, Zek, before it's too late."

The Andorian trader ship hit the *Defiant* with a barrage of phasers.

"Our left shield is buckling, sir," Harsch said. "The extensions have weakened it."

"Keep it working, son," Sisko said. "Zek? Did you hear me?"

"I heard you, Commander. I also heard you're in trouble. You can't take me on."

"But the *Bosewell* can. And if they have trouble, we have two more starships here and the station's fire-power. Give it up, Zek."

Another hit from the trader ship.

"Sir, the shields—"

"Ensign Coleman," Sisko said, "one photon torpe-do to the trader's port side."

"But, sir—"

"Do it now, Ensign."

Coleman did. The torpedo connected and demol-ished the trader's shields. It blew a hole in the port side, and all the lights on the vessel winked out.

"What's the ship's status, Ensign?"

"They've lost life support, sir."

"Zek," Sisko said. "Zek, your friends will die without your help. And we'll destroy you if we have to. The ship we're towing is under our protection."

"The Jibetians don't want you to have it."

"The Federation and the Jibetians have an agreement," Sisko said. "And you shouldn't eavesdrop on other people's private communications. This isn't a Ferengi concern."

"It's always a Ferengi concern when profit is involved."

"If you attack the *Nibix*," Sisko said, "it is no longer about profit. It's about profiteering and war. Think how much a war with the Federation will cost your people, Zek. Think about it. Sisko out."

The other two Ferengi ships had stopped attacking the *Idaho*. The third Andorian trader vessel went to help its injured comrade. The remaining trader vessel backed away from the *Madison*.

The nagus's ship didn't move.

"What do you think he's going to do, Commander?" Ensign Coleman said.

"He'll back off," Sisko said. "The Ferengi hate to fight prolonged wars. It eats into their precious profits. Anything he could make on the *Nibix* wouldn't be worth the eventual cost. Zek is a smart man. He knows that."

After a moment, the nagus's ship turned and retreated.

The Cardassian ships hadn't moved. Neither had the Jibetians. The other ships around the station had moved to the perimeter, watching, waiting.

Sisko hit his comm badge. "Dax? Are you all right?"

"We're fine here, Commander," Dax said. "Shaken but no damage."

"Good," Sisko said. "Let's take this baby home."

He wiped the sweat off his forehead. The first fight of the battle had taken less than a minute. Jepson was gone as was one trader vessel. Another was crippled, and the Ferengi, for the moment, were out of the fight. None of the starships had suffered any significant damage. Neither had the *Nibix*.

"Captain Higginbotham is hailing us. He's coming in scrambled," Kathé said.

"On screen."

Higginbotham appeared. His cheeks were flushed beneath his graying beard. "Benjamin, if we take the *Nibix* in close and the Cardassians attack, we won't be able to defend without threatening the station. If the Cardassians and the Jibetians join forces, we won't have enough firepower to defend that ship in close."

"I know," Sisko said, "but I have a secret that will do the trick. But I don't dare play the hand until we're closer to the station."

Higginbotham shrugged. "It's your call, Ben. We'll watch your back. *Madison* out."

He winked off the screen.

Sisko hit his comm badge. "Dax? Chief? Are you ready to fly her into dock?"

"Any time," Dax's voice said.

"How about now?" Sisko said. "Ensign Harsch, drop the shields around the *Nibix* and release the tractor. But stay close enough to shield it again instantly."

"Yes, sir," Ensign Harsch said.

The small thruster jets fired on the *Nibix,* and it eased toward *Deep Space Nine.* Sisko watched on his screen as the long lost ship moved into dock on its own power after eight hundred years in space.

Over twenty different warships from a half-dozen different cultures watched.

And waited for someone to make the next move.

CHAPTER
26

THE DOCTORS SURROUNDED the jury-rigged cold-sleep
chamber. Dr. Bashir stood near the Supreme Ruler's
head, monitoring the diagnostics. Dr. Wasner slowly
raised the temperature on the chamber as Dr. Silverstein monitored the cellular damage. They had just
started injections of nanobuilders designed to help
the cells rapidly regenerate.

Silverstein estimated that the ruler had eighty-five
percent cell damage in the weaker tissues. The
nanobuilders were his only hope.

"He still has brain function," Bashir said as the
temperature rose.

"But his heart isn't going to work. It's not ready yet.
Slow it down, Wasner," Silverstein said.

"I can't slow it down. If I reverse the process, I
confuse his body and he dies."

"It may not be that simple," Bashir said. "The

Jibetians used drugs to induce cold sleep. Some of those might still be in his system."

"After eight hundred years?" Silverstein said. "I don't think so. His cells are breaking down. The chemical compounds would have broken down long before that." She prepared another injection and was about to slide it through the pin-sized hole in the chamber when Wasner grabbed her hand.

"Bashir's right," he said. "We're talking about eight-hundred-year-old technology, Celeste. The chemical compounds used by cultures back then were often harmful combinations that would survive anything natural. We need to scan for them. Only this is ancient technology. I don't know what to scan for."

"I do," Bashir said. He had already started the scan, but so far the results were inconclusive. "Give me a moment."

Silverstein set the injection down. She held her medical tricorder over the ruler's stomach. "He has no liver or kidney damage at all."

"The nanobuilders are working then," Wasner said.

"No," Silverstein said. "I injected them into his lungs and heart, not his bloodstream."

Bashir grinned at her. "That's it then."

She looked confused. "Julian, I don't think his heart is going to make it."

"One more moment," he said. He scanned the liver and kidneys. "I was right. The chemicals are in there. The ancient Jibetians used a screen to slow the organs gently as the person went to sleep. Check the heart, Celeste. It might be there."

"What am I looking for?"

Bashir rattled off the Starfleet equivalents for the Jibetian drugs.

She glanced at him over the ruler, her eyes wide with horror. "But those will—"

"Destroy the nanobuilders, I know."

"Stop that warming process," Silverstein said.

"I can't," Wasner said. "Ancient or modern technology, it doesn't matter. Once the process started, it has to be finished."

Silverstein swore under her breath. Bashir reached behind him. He removed a hypo. "I have a few nanoscrubbers. We could send them in and hope they do the job clearing out the chemicals."

"They won't work, Julian," Silverstein snapped. "Nanoscrubbes must go straight into the bloodstream. His blood isn't moving."

"Straight into the bloodstream so that they can ease into the heart," Bashir said. "We don't have any choice."

An urgent beep made them all look up.

"His heart stopped!" Wasner said.

"Open this thing," Bashir said.

"You'll warm him too fast," Wasner said.

"It doesn't matter," Bashir said. "He's dying anyway."

"If it's not the warmth, it'll be the scrubbers," Silverstein said.

"Have you ever worked with them?" Bashir asked as he quickly filled the hypo.

"Not on cell damage cases."

"Then move. Our only hope is to try." He shoved her out of the way with his body.

Wasner raised the lid on the modified cold-sleep chamber and stale frosty air floated out. Bashir shoved the hypo against the frozen fabric of the ruler's cloak, then made the injection, careful not to

251

put too much pressure on the ruler's fragile body. Since it was frozen, even the slightest movement could cause bones to break.

All three doctors stared at the diagnostic display.

Nothing.

No movement.

The heart had stopped.

"See?" Silverstein said. "It was hopeless."

"His skin temperature's rising too fast," Wasner said.

"It doesn't matter. His heart's not moving."

Bashir held the tricorder over the ruler's heart. "The nanoscrubbers have multiplied. They've sent a contingent through the bloodstream. I don't get any chemical readings from the heart at all now, Silverstein. Try your nanobuilders again."

"It's hopeless, Julian," she said.

He whirled. "You are not going to cost a man's life because you believe we're doing an impossible procedure. This is my infirmary and my procedure. Either you do what I say or I'll make certain you get court-martialed and reported to Starfleet's medical board. You'll never practice medicine again."

"You can't do that, Doctor," she said, squaring her shoulders. "I have decades more experience than you do. I know when something's impossible."

"You don't know. No one's done this before."

"Don't question me, Bashir."

"I'm not questioning you," he said. "I am ordering you."

"Celeste," Wasner said softly, "he's right."

She glanced at both of them, then carefully injected the nanobuilders into the heart. Wasner closed the lid on the sleep chamber and modified the temperature as best he could.

"That was a ten-degree rise in temperature," he said. "It might have been too fast."

Bashir didn't care. He was monitoring the scrubbers. They had cleaned out the liver and kidneys and were now moving into the stomach.

The solid whine suddenly stopped.

He looked up. The ruler's heart was fluttering.

"Silverstein," he said.

"I see it." She began deep-cold procedures for easing the organs into working order. "Can you raise the temperature more, Wasner?"

"As soon as the blood flows evenly, Doctor," Wasner said. They watched as the heart stopped fluttering and began beating several slow even strokes on its own.

"What's the heart rate on eight-hundred-year-old Jibetians?" Silverstein asked.

"Probably not that much different than modern Jibetians," Bashir said.

"Then we've got it."

The blood moved sluggishly through his body and into the brain.

Silverstein shook her head. "There's amazing amounts of cell damage here," she said.

"Will he wake up?" Bashir asked.

She nodded, her mouth in a thin line. "That's the amazing part. Once the heart was repaired, we have him. He's going to make it."

"With his brain intact," Wasner said. "That low brain function, whatever caused it, saved him there."

"I think I know what caused it," Bashir said. He looked at the green glowing staff. Dax had said that it gave Jibetian rulers longer lives and great powers of recuperation. Such stories were often false. But just as often they were true. Maybe at some point in the future, he'd do a project on the powers of the material the staff was made of. Maybe.

Silverstein glanced over the sleep chamber at Bashir. "I'm sorry, Julian," she said. "If you had listened to me, this man would be dead now."

Bashir smiled. "We all make those kinds of errors, Doctor," he said, "which is precisely why I didn't want to do this procedure alone. Logically, we should have quit there. But there are times when logic is not enough."

Silverstein smiled. "Our captain reminds me of that often," she said. "I suppose he has a point."

Wasner kept monitoring the ruler's vital signs. They were steadily improving as the temperature rose.

Bashir hit his comm badge. "Kira," he said, "you need to send a message to Commander Sisko."

"I can arrange for you to send it yourself, Doctor," Kira said.

"I don't have time. Just let him know this: that our patient made it through the procedure. He's still in critical condition, but it is"—he glanced at the other two doctors, and they nodded—"*our* expert opinion that he will recover."

"I'll tell him, Doctor," Kira said and signed off.

Bashir leaned against the nearest chair. The cold, the tension, and the relief were finally getting to him. "One day," he said more to himself than anyone, "I'm going to run out of miracles."

"Nonsense," Silverstein said. "I think this procedure has convinced me that one should never underestimate the power of belief. Miracles happen, Doctor. Sometimes we just help them along."

The advisors were murmuring behind him, their joy muted by Ribe's obvious bad mood. He made no attempt to hide it now. The Ferengi attack on the *Nibix* had failed; he should have known better than to trust those strange little beings who only looked at the universe through their purses.

But he couldn't stop to think now. He had to act.

He stood near his chair, General Caybe beside him. The general had suggested going into the private room beside the bridge, but Ribe would have none of it. If the general didn't do what he wanted, he would shame the man in front of his own troops.

"Lord High Sir, I respectfully disagree. I think you're overreacting. The Federation is our ally." The general spoke in little more than a whisper. Not even the advisors could hear him.

"They have done nothing to show their alliance with us," Ribe said, "except to allow us to apply to their little club. They did this, it is now clear, so that they could take the *Nibix* for themselves."

"But, Lord High Sir, they are only protecting it. And they did. Their weapons are more precise than ours. If we had fired on the trader ships, we might have hit the *Nibix*."

"Then you are incompetent and should be relieved of duty." No one was listening to him. He damned the system that gave him no control over the military. Only the council had control. His ancestor, Bikon, had set that up too, so that a military coup had to happen against the entire government, not against one man as the first revolution had.

A few of the advisors overheard that last remark. They frowned at Ribe.

"What do you suggest we do, Lord High Sir? We don't dare fire upon our own ship."

Ribe leaned closer to the general. "Destroy the

station," he said. "Then they cannot dock the *Nibix*, and we can take the ship for ourselves."

The general took a step backward. "If we fire on a Federation station, the starships will attack us. We'll start a war."

"So be it," Ribe snapped.

The general swallowed. The skin on his ridged cheekbones had turned white. "Lord High Sir, I must remind you that only by unanimous vote of the entire council can we go to war."

"Well, the council's not here, is it?" Ribe leaned closer to the general. "You will do what I say."

The general glanced at the advisors, who shrugged. Ribe suppressed a grin. He would win this. The general knew, as well as he did, that the head of the council could act for the council in the council's absence.

"Forgive me, General," said one of the crew. "But we are getting a message from the *Defiant.*"

The general looked as if he were just granted a reprieve. He turned so that his back was to Ribe so that he couldn't see Ribe countermand the order to answer the hail.

"I'll speak to him," Ribe said. "I'll give this one last try."

"Please, Lord High Sir, rethink your position. The Federation—"

"The Federation is trying to steal our heritage from us. Let me see their traitorous commander." Ribe stepped into the general's normal spot and faced the screen.

"This is Hibar Ribe, head of the Jibetian High Council. State your business, *Defiant.*"

The face on the screen belonged to Sisko, and he looked as intransigent as he had before. "I am Commander Benjamin Sisko of the Federation *Starship Defiant.* It is my duty to formally inform you, under the treaty, that the *Nibix,* which is under our protection as the *Long Night,* will be docking on *Deep Space Nine* shortly. The ship will remain under Federation protection until officials from the Federation can arrive and officially turn the ship over to you. I have said this before, but consider this your formal notification under the treaty."

"I demand that the ship be sealed and that only my people be allowed to board," Ribe said. "Your people cannot be trusted with the wealth of Jibet."

"As I told you in our earlier communication," Sisko said, his voice even, "this ship, under intersteller salvage laws, is owned by the Federation and is a Federation ship. It will be turned over to you in good time without anything missing."

"You are taking advantage of this situation, Sisko. That treaty was made to protect the *Nibix* in case no Jibetian ships were nearby. The ship is clearly owned, and salvage laws do not apply. If you do not turn the *Nibix* over to us, we will consider that a declaration of war. If you have not turned the *Nibix* over to us in five minutes, we will destroy your precious space station."

Sisko smiled. "I don't think you'll want to do that," he said. "You see, your Supreme Ruler, Jibim Kiba Siber, is recovering in our infirmary. An attack might threaten his life, and you wouldn't want that, would you?"

Ribe felt as if he had been shot in the stomach. He gripped the railing behind him.

The hum of the bridge stopped. Every crew member had ceased working and was staring at the screen. General Caybe had taken the tiny replica of the Staff of Life from his pocket and was staring at it in shock.

Ribe's mouth was dry. As a boy, he had believed that Jibim Kiba Siber was one with the gods. Perhaps that belief had been right. Perhaps his family had been wrong.

"No man can survive eight hundred years of cold sleep," Ribe said.

"Your Supreme Ruler has," Sisko said. "Thanks to the technology of the *Nibix* and the skill of modern medicine."

"I do not believe you."

Sisko's smile grew. "I thought you might not. Major Kira, please broadcast from the infirmary now."

Sisko's image winked out and was replaced by the resting body of the Supreme Ruler. He lay on a diagnostic table, his robes wrapped around him. His skin was normal Jibetian white, and he was clearly breathing. The green staff was beside him. A thin human also stood in the picture. He smiled.

"I am Julian Bashir, chief medical officer on *Deep Space Nine*. We found your Supreme Ruler alive when we discovered the *Nibix*. He had extensive cell damage, which we repaired. We expect little long-term damage. He should be awake in a few hours."

Ribe leaned against the rail. The Supreme Ruler looked just as he had in all the ancient paintings. A young man. Younger than Ribe expected.

Only a god could live so long.

Or perhaps Bikon had failed in more ways than one.

They would discover the sabotage and his own betrayals with the Ferengi. They would. Or maybe they already had.

Sisko's face returned to the screen. "So, you see, if you want to be at the Supreme Ruler's side when he wakes up after eight hundred years, you need to stand down your ships."

Behind him Ribe heard the general give the order to stand down and drop shields. The crew was moving in slow motion, as if they were as stunned as Ribe.

Ribe stood, his mouth open, not knowing what to say.

Sisko, after a moment, smiled at Ribe and said, "You're welcome."

Then he cut the transmission.

Odo and Jake had joined Kira on the bridge in time to watch the standoff between Sisko and the Jibetian leader. Jake clearly had questions but waited to ask them, a fact for which Kira was relieved.

When the Jibetian said nothing and Sisko ended the transmission, Kira felt her entire body relax. No war. At least not yet.

"Major," Tappan said, "Commander Sisko is hailing us."

"On screen," Kira said.

Sisko appeared, grinning from ear to ear.

"Good work, Commander," Kira said.

"It's not over yet, Kira," he said, although his tone belied that. "We'll be docking the *Long Night* in a few minutes. As soon as it reaches the station, I want that ship sealed, and I want guards posted from the airlock to the Promenade."

"Will do, sir."

"And Kira?"

"Yes?"

"If anyone attempts to get near the *Long Night,* the guards are ordered to shoot to kill."

The tension returned to Kira's shoulders. Sisko had never given an order like that. Ever. She hoped it was more for the benefit of all those mercenaries listening in than for the guards themselves.

"We'll put the station's shields around it as well," Kira said, "so no one can beam aboard."

"Good thinking, Major," Sisko said. "I also want to record all activity in and near the docking bay. No one is to enter that ship. No exceptions."

"Yes, sir," Kira said.

"Now." Sisko leaned forward. "Did you find that leak?"

"*Someone* reinstated that old Cardassian spy station. The equipment was Cardassian. It was also new," Kira said. "Odo found and dismantled it."

"Actually, Major," Odo said, stepping forward so Sisko could see him, "Jake found the spy system and was instrumental in saving the station when that ship exploded."

"Jake?" Sisko visibly paled.

"I'm okay, Dad," Jake said, also stepping forward. "It was fun."

"Fun," Sisko muttered.

"He helped us a lot," Kira said.

Sisko frowned. "Good work, Son. Just stay out of the thick of things until I return. Okay?"

"I could say the same for you, Dad."

Sisko grinned. "Yeah. I guess you could. We've had more than enough excitement for one week."

"That's for sure," Kira muttered.

"Odo," Sisko said, "over one hundred crew members from the *Madison* will beam aboard the station. They will help with security. Captain Higginbotham says they are among his best people. Use them."

"Yes, sir," Odo said.

"And Kira, please ask the Cardassians their business. And warn all single ships to stay outside of transporter range of the station or be destroyed. Sisko out." His image disappeared off the screen.

"Why does everyone leave the Cardassians to me?"
Kira asked Odo.

"Because you are most effective with them, Major,"
Odo said. "And I must go if I am to coordinate two
security teams. Jake, would you like to come along?"

Jake shook his head. "I think I'll stay here until my
dad returns if you don't mind, Odo."

"I think you deserve a rest," Odo said. "Someday
perhaps the rest of us can get one, too." He made his
way to the turbolift.

Kira turned to Tappan. "Get Gul Dukat."

"I'm way ahead of you, Major."

She smiled at Tappan, thankful for the man's
competence. "Put him on screen."

Gul Dukat was standing beside his command chair,
his hand on its back. His posture made his strange
neck scales stand out. "Major, I see you have the coup
of the century. Not only all the wealth of Jibet, but its
mystical leader as well. You are to be congratulated."

"I asked you to leave more than once, Dukat," Kira
said.

"I know, Major. But I believed that you were doing
so in error. I knew that your commander had a prize
with him, and with all the ships heading toward *Deep
Space Nine,* I believed he might have use of our
services." Dukat put his other hand on the chair back
in a vain attempt to look relaxed. "I was, as usual,
underestimating him. The Federation handled the
crisis with very little bloodshed. Commander Sisko is
to be congratulated as well."

"I'm sure he'll be pleased with such high praise
from you," Kira said. "Now, go home, Dukat."

"You have a strange way of showing your gratitude,
Major."

"And you need acting lessons, Dukat. I don't buy

your I-was-only-here-to-help routine. Especially when we discovered a Cardassian spy station on *Deep Space Nine*."

Dukat smiled. "We've been through this, Major. You know that we sell our technology all through the galaxy. That station could have belonged to anyone. But it does show that you need to tighten security there. Nothing like that would have happened under Cardassian rule."

For the first time since the crisis began, Kira grinned. "Oh, but it did, Dukat. And I do believe I have failed to be polite in that matter. Thank you for all the information you most unwillingly gave Bajor in those years. I wouldn't be here now if you hadn't. Kira out."

Dukat's smile had left his face as his image winked out. A moment later, the Cardassian fleet turned and headed back toward Cardassian space.

"Wow, Major," Jake said. "Is that true? Did you really have a Bajoran spy station here?"

"We no more had a Bajoran spy station here than Dukat was on hand to protect *Deep Space Nine*, Jake," Kira said. "Rule number one of Cardassian diplomacy: whoever humiliates the other guy first wins."

Jake's eyes widened. "Remind me to stay on your good side, Major."

"Don't worry," she said. "After all you did today, you'll always be on my good side, Jake."

CHAPTER
27

THE LIGHTS WERE low in the infirmary. The crowd made Bashir nervous, but Commander Sisko had insisted upon having visitors. Bashir stated it was against his medical judgment to have so many people in the room—it might stress the Supreme Ruler at a time he didn't need stress—but Sisko said that the Supreme Ruler would want it this way.

When all the parties involved saw the ruler awaken without tricks, without the chance to substitute an imposter, then they would accept him. And even if the awakening was difficult in the beginning, the ruler would be grateful later.

Doctors Wasner and Silverstein stood behind the diagnostic chair and monitored the ruler's levels. Bashir stood beside him, clearly the pointman on this operation. Captains Higginbotham and Kiser also watched as Starfleet representatives. Captain Mouce remained on her ship to keep guard on the mercenary ships still arriving from far points in the galaxy.

The leader of the Jibetian Council, a thin nervous man who perspired more than anyone Bashir had ever seen, stood beside the bed. The Jibetian general, the leader of the fleet, stood beside him, almost like a guard. The advisors remained outside the room. Bashir judged their presence five too many.

The Supreme Ruler, the subject of all their scrutiny, no longer looked like a wasted survivor of a long journey. His cheeks glowed that odd mixture of red and white that Jibetians had when they were healthy. His organs were running well, and his brain scans were turning out fine.

Although no one knew if he would ever be able to think on his own again. Bashir believed he would, but Wasner was skeptical. He'd seen brain death on the cellular level too many times in cold-sleep chambers to believe that a man who lived this long under such adverse conditions would survive intact.

The vital signs had shown the ruler regaining consciousness for the last fifteen minutes. Soon, though, Bashir would call an end to this vigilance and have only a few of the observers remain. The ruler could remain in this half-waking, half-sleeping state for hours.

No sooner had that thought crossed Bashir's mind than the ruler moaned.

"What was that?" the Jibetian high councillor, Hibar Ribe, asked.

"Shh," Silverstein said.

The ruler stirred, moving a hand toward his head. Bashir felt like applauding. Instead, he leaned in to shield the ruler's eyes from any ambient light.

"Take it slowly," Bashir said.

The ruler opened his eyes. They were bright green and vibrant. Bashir resisted the urge to jump back. He had thought of this man as a patient for so long, it was startling to see the personality.

"Vital signs are normal," Wasner said, his voice rising in triumph.

"We're not on the ship," the ruler said. His voice was raspy. He coughed as if he were trying to clear his throat.

"Be gentle," Silverstein said. "You haven't spoken in a long time. It will take a while for you to feel normal again."

"Where are we?" the ruler asked. He gazed at the faces around the room, clearly recognizing none of them. Finally his gaze rested on the Jibetians. "And who are you? Did Bikon send you?"

Ribe started. The general nudged him.

"Welcome," Ribe said, his voice shaking. "I am Hibar Ribe, of the Ribe-Iber-Bikon family. We've been waiting a long time for this moment."

A frown creased the Supreme Ruler's forehead. He coughed again and struggled to sit up.

"Wait just a moment please," Bashir said. He put a firm, but friendly hand on the ruler's shoulder, holding the man in place. "You've seen him wake up. You may all leave now. We still have a long way to go here."

"Will he be all right?" the general asked.

"If you leave now," Bashir said.

Higginbotham and Kiser left immediately. Sisko waited until Ribe and the general left before nodding his approval at Bashir. Then Sisko exited.

Wasner continued to monitor the vital signs. Silverstein looked at the ruler's face and smiled.

The ruler ignored her. His bright eyes met Bashir's. "Something went wrong," he said.

Bashir nodded.

"You are not Jibetians."

"We're allies," Bashir said. "We assisted your people."

"My ship?" Despite Bashir's efforts to keep the man down, the ruler rose on one elbow. The movement clearly made him dizzy, but he did not lie back down.

"The *Nibix* is here."

"My family?"

Bashir took a deep breath. The doctors had agreed to answer the questions the ruler asked but only those questions. The rest, they decided, could wait until later. "They didn't make it," Bashir said.

The ruler closed his eyes. For the first time since he woke up, he looked vulnerable. He almost eased back down, then caught himself.

"The crew?" he asked.

"Your ship was sabotaged, sir," Silverstein said. "It's amazing you survived."

"Sabotaged?" the ruler asked. His eyes opened again filled not with the sadness that Bashir expected, but with a fury so powerful that it filled the room.

"Yes, sir," Bashir said. "Probably right after you left Jibet."

"His vital signs are traveling all over the map," Wasner said. "We have to end this little session."

"No!" the ruler said. "You can't leave it here. You have to tell me what happened."

The three doctors looked at each other.

"It's better for a patient to know," Silverstein said. And she was right. It had been shown in study after study that patients who knew what they were up against coped and eventually survived. But that didn't make this one any easier.

"After the sabotage, the *Nibix* drifted," Bashir said. "The wakeup systems were dismantled. When the ship got near its destination, no awakening sequence kicked in, and when the ship got into trouble, no one woke up either. We found you on an asteroid not far from here."

"How long did we drift?" The ruler didn't miss a thing. And his brain probably wasn't operating up to par yet. He must have been formidable when his mind was working at peak efficiency. Bashir would have to study Jibetian history. He didn't understand how a man like this was overthrown in a revolution.

Unless that revolution had help from the inside. The same help that sabotaged the ship.

"Eight hundred years," Bashir said.

The ruler shook his head. "That isn't possible."

"I'm afraid that yours was the only chamber to continue working," Bashir said.

The ruler rubbed a hand over his face. Then he nodded. "The staff? Where is it?"

"Beside you," Wasner said. He lightly touched the green rod as if it would break at the slightest movement.

The green of the glowing staff was the same color as the ruler's eyes.

"You need to sleep," Silverstein said.

"I have been asleep for a long time," the ruler said.

"Yes," Silverstein said, "but you need healthy recuperative sleep now."

The ruler tucked the staff beside him and eased back down on the diagnostic table. "One last thing then," he said, his voice breaking as he spoke. He was clearly exhausted. "Did my world survive? My people?"

Bashir nodded, glad he could say something positive to the young man. "Very much so. They now live on eighty worlds spread out through space."

The ruler looked puzzled for a moment, then smiled. A sad, hopeful smile. "Eighty worlds. We only hoped for one."

He closed his eyes, and after a moment he was sleeping.

A normal sleep.

Guards lined the Promenade, all trying to ignore the shouting coming from Quark's. Jake, Rom, and Nog were leaning over the railing on the Promenade's second story. The shouts carried well up here. Better than anywhere else in the Promenade.

"It is your duty as a Ferengi to report to me immediately," the nagus yelled. "You have failed me again, Quark!"

"I didn't fail, Nagus." Quark's voice quivered. "I was injured. I was even unconscious for a time. I—"

"Imagine my position when Cardassians, *mercenaries,* even Jepson himself learned about the *Nibix* before I did. And I have a man on the scene."

"I didn't mean to embarrass you," Quark said. "I was injured."

"I'll injure you again if you use that excuse with me, boy. I expect an apology. And compensation. I brought ships here expecting profit."

"I didn't send for them," Quark said.

"I know that!"

"Then why do you want compensation?"

"Because if I had known how difficult making a

profit would be, I wouldn't have come, Quark. You know that. You're supposed to protect me from all of this."

Jake looked at Nog. Nog shrugged. Rom was grinning.

"If you give the bar's profits for the next month, I might forget this little incident."

"The next month?" Quark said. "But I've been shut down for days. I need to make money to survive. How about half the profits?"

"All of the profits, Quark. And if you continue to complain, I will charge you two months."

"That's a lot of money," Rom whispered.

Jake leaned in to him. "Do you think Quark will understand now what you feel like when he yells at you?"

Rom shook his head. "The nagus has yelled at him before. It is our way, I guess."

"I guess," Jake said. He sighed. Then he looked at Nog, whose lower lip was jutting out.

"It won't be my way, Father," Nog said.

"I know, Son." Rom grinned. "You are a new breed of Ferengi. You make me proud."

"Me, too," Jake said. "I'm sorry about bashing your uncle on the head."

"It's okay," Nog said. "We decided on that plan together."

Beside them, Rom moaned.

"Father?"

"I forgot about my brother's injury. We had better find something to do for the next few days, Nog. Between the nagus and the injury, my brother will be insufferable."

"You mean he isn't already?" Jake asked.

"I'm serious," Rom said.

Jake was, too, but he decided not to say that. Instead, he said, "If you want to hide, I know the perfect place."

"I'm not going back in those tunnels, hu-man," Nog said.

Jake grinned. "Well," he said, "it was worth a try."

EPILOGUE

Two Weeks Later

As CEREMONIES WENT, this was a small one. But it was one that Benjamin Sisko would remember forever.

He and Jake stood outside docking bay three. Dax stood on his left, and Bashir on Jake's right. At the entrance to the docking bay, General Caybe stood a few steps behind Jibet's Supreme Ruler.

The ruler still looked too thin. He wore the same robes he had worn in cold sleep, only they had been cleaned and pressed. He clutched his staff at his side. His hair had grown in the last two weeks, and his stamina had improved. His eyes retained their brightness, but his face had a few new lines.

Sisko remembered the look. He had seen it on his own face after Jennifer's death. But, like the Supreme Ruler, people had counted on him. In Sisko's case, Jake had counted on him. And Sisko had gone on.

The Supreme Ruler would to.

Sisko had said as much to him during their long talks.

The ruler had nodded. It was only when Sisko had been about to leave that the ruler said, "Mortal beings know they must get used to the death of loved ones. But not many of us must also mourn the centuries. I am not sure how to do that, Commander."

And Sisko had no answers for him.

"Forgive my presumptiveness," the general said. "But I would feel better, milord, if you rode to Jibet in the flagship."

The Supreme Ruler smiled at him. Clearly this argument had gone on for a while. Sisko just hadn't been privy to it. "For now, General, the *Nibix* will be the flagship. I need to return home in the same ship I left on. It is important."

Extremely important. Each decision the Supreme Ruler made these days had importance. His decision to imprison Ribe had been one he agonized over. Finally, he took Ribe into custody for his acts against the Federation, not for the sins his ancestor committed centuries before.

"I must put the past behind me," the Supreme Ruler had said.

"This time though," Sisko said, "you will see the parts of space you passed through."

"And," Dax added, "what took eight hundred years will now take five days."

The Supreme Ruler laughed. "Yes, this modern world is wonderful in many ways."

He had been like a child in the infirmary. Each moment he was awake he asked questions. Sisko finally assigned him two around-the-clock ensigns just to answer the ruler's questions about the past. If anyone could catch up, the ruler could, although he had already expressed his wish for a Federation councillor and assistance in his homeland. He wasn't sure if his mind was modern enough to rule Jibet.

Sisko suspected his mind was modern enough for any age.

The ruler turned to Dr. Bashir. "Thank you for your fine work. I have been told that waking me is considered groundbreaking in your medical world."

Bashir smiled. "I'm just glad we succeeded."

"As am I, Doctor. Otherwise I would have never had a chance to see this wonderful future." Then the ruler turned to Dax and bowed slightly. "Thank you, lovely lady, for being the captain of my ship through its first and only battle."

"It was my honor," Dax said.

Then the Supreme Ruler turned to Sisko. As the ruler regained his health, his eyes had become an even more vibrant green. It was almost as if his life force flowed through them and touched everyone he met. Sisko felt the warmth now.

"You are a brave man, Commander Sisko. Thank you." He stuck out his hand and after only a moment of hesitation, Sisko took it and shook it. The ruler's hand was warm.

"You're welcome," Sisko said.

The Supreme Ruler smiled. "I have no doubt our two cultures will work well together in future years."

"I think you are right," Sisko said.

"Of course I am," the Supreme Ruler said. "You can't live over eight hundred years and not know a few things."

There was a stunned silence—everyone knew how much difficulty the ruler was having with his leap into the future—and then Sisko saw the corners of the Supreme Ruler's mouth twitch with suppressed mirth.

Sisko laughed, and so did the ruler.

"Come," the ruler said to the general. "We have a long trip back, and I'm getting cold out here. You know how I hate cold."

The Supreme Ruler winked at Bashir. Bashir shot him a startled look and then smiled and winked back.

The ruler laughed again. He waved his staff over all of them, an ancient, formal Jibetian thank-you, and then he led the general through the airlock. Sisko watched them enter the *Nibix,* the ship of dreams.

And nightmares.

But the long night was over now.

The day had begun.

STAR TREK®

Legends
never
die...

THE
RETURN

A NOVEL BY
WILLIAM SHATNER

William Shatner, bestselling author and creator of
the acclaimed TekWar novels and television series,
brings his unique blend of talents as actor, writer,
director, and producer to create a coda to STAR
TREK GENERATIONS—and reveal the awesome
secret of the return of James T. Kirk...

THE
RETURN
Coming soon in Hardcover from Pocket Books

POCKET
BOOKS